The Sibylline Oracle

The beginning of The Sibylline Trilogy

A Novel by Delia J. Colvin

www.TheSibyllineOracle.com

The Sibylline Oracle

ISBN-978-1478358954 Fiction

Fantasy/Suspense/Romance Novel

When self-proclaimed unextraordinary Valeria Mills' life is saved by the mysterious and charismatic Alex Morgan, Valeria's life takes on a thrilling and terrifying turn as she discovers his secret; Alex is an immortal and Valeria is the reincarnation of his beloved Cassandra. Together they must confront the dark forces of an ancient curse to restore her immortality in a desperate battle against time or both die in the attempt!

In this deeply romantic and suspenseful first novel of the trilogy, The Sibylline Oracle captures the struggle to overcome self-doubt and in that discover deep passion and abiding love.

For information address:

www.TheSibyllineOracle.com

To

Jen-my original Rory

My best friend and daughter-your unconditional love, wisdom and absolute faith in me have been an extraordinary gift in my life!

This story might not have been told except for your encouragement, editing and demand for more!

I love you kiddo!

∞

CONTENTS

There's this place in me where your fingerprints still rest,
your kisses still linger,
and your whispers softly echo.
It's the place where a part of you
will forever be a part of me.

Gretchen Kemp

CHAPTER 1

1186 B.C.

The sky was a perfect cornflower blue, deepening to almost black in the center with circles of white puffs that clung to the air, undisturbed. Alex loved this time of year, the coolness, the clearing of the summer heat and haze through the coastal mountains north of the Adriatic. Though all the leaves had fallen, the forest was still a dazzling emerald green. Perhaps some of his mood was that he knew that he was closer to *her* now than at any time of the year.

Over the raised roots of the tree, he saw the movement first. The size and pattern left little doubt that this was his target. Alex moved quickly to brush the dark blond bangs back out of his face, revealing his brilliant blue eyes and lifted the bow to position. His angled jaw, with the slight cleft, tensed with concentration, barely diminishing the deep dimpled lines in his cheeks. And although it had been hard won from years of slave labor, he was pleased with the strength his arms now possessed as he drew the bow back. The light caught the edge of the decorative carving just above the grip of the bow and, without looking, his thumb affectionately brushed it. Alex suddenly realized that at 34, he was probably older than his father had been when he had chiseled the design onto the bow.

Permitting himself a moment—and no more—of melancholy, Alex thought how much he missed his father, mother, and little sister; wondering if they had ever guessed that they would never see each other again. Alex had been only a young boy when his family had helplessly watched the soldiers carry him away, kicking and screaming. Still, he could feel the spirit of his family in these woods and sometimes if he listened carefully, he could almost hear his mother's joyful laugh in the house. If the gods smiled on him, he might someday be here with his own family...with *her*...his Cassandra.

The visions had been what had given him hope of more than the loneliness he had experienced most of his life. But the visions had also caused it—along with many hardships for him and for his family. Alex remembered hearing the story of his first vision; he had been only two years of age and was incapable of properly communicating what had happened. Although they never said it, Alex was certain that his family had feared for his sanity. Eventually they discovered that, when heeded, these visions seemed to reliably produce wealth; particularly in the form of crops, showing Alex what, when and where to plant. The visions had also protected them against invaders...well, most invaders. They had provided Alex a vision of his life as a man with Cassandra. Even as a young boy, he could feel the joy and fullness of that life. In fact, that was the only reason he was still here in these woods...and why he had been taken away.

Although this was his land, he had seen the squatters; the Trojans who looked weary from years of battle with Sparta. He wouldn't deny them. The ground was fertile and there was plenty to share...and one of them could be *her*.

Without removing his concentration from the boar, he drew an arrow from his pack and set it in place. The target moved into view—just a few more inches for a perfect shot. Alex strained the bow back expanding the triangular tattoo on his hand. Slowing his breathing, he focused as the boar moved out. Patiently, Alex sucked in his breath, awaiting the shot. Then he felt something on his neck. An insect? He attempted to ignore it. It hit his neck harder this time as the boar was about to move into range a few more seconds. The third time it hit his neck with enough force that his hand involuntarily dropped the bow and reached to the sting on his neck. He turned around to see an attractive redheaded woman taunting him with a pea shooter and a handful of pebbles. Alex rolled his eyes and returned his focus to the boar and then watched as a larger stone moved over his head and dropped a few feet behind the boar causing it to squeal and shy immediately back into the brush. Daphne's teasing laugh echoed through the woods.

"Daphne!" Alex said almost patiently.

With a seriously flirtatious glint in her eyes, that Alex didn't notice, Daphne took off running through the thickly covered forest, daring him to follow. Alex sighed. He had no real interest in her games. She could be a real annoyance sometimes! Still, a part of him would always be grateful to her. Alex rolled his eyes again and took off after her. She was fast and strong, he had to give her that! As he ran his sandaled feet sank deep into the decaying leaves and ferns. On his next leap, his foot caught a root and held him as he twisted and slammed into the hard earth. Alex breathed out heavily and moved a fern out of his face as he checked his smarting ankle. No sprain.

Then he noticed a sudden surreal shift of light as the sun moved to the edge of a cloud. The wind had picked up...and there was something in the air...an electricity? Something had changed. He pulled up on his elbows and began the task of critically analyzing his surroundings; he searched for the shaft of light between the boughs and the position of the early sun and found it to his left. Alex looked up and saw the single cloud placed almost perfectly between tree tops, just as it had been in the vision 16 years before. All the years of waiting and planning all came down to his actions now!

He pushed himself up with superhuman strength as his heart thundered with a mix of adrenalin, hope and a desperate need to remedy what he knew would be the outcome if he didn't arrive in time—he blocked the last thought from his mind as he ran down the heavily wooded hill with every ounce of strength he had.

"Daphne!" He called, knowing that she wouldn't answer. She wasn't in the vision.

As Alex pressed through the brush down the mountain, he recalled the first time he had seen this vision; he had been only 18 and working in Myrdd's candlelit cave when the kaleidoscope effect had begun at the outer edges of his range of vision. Recognizing the effect, he had slinked down to a crouch against the cool soil that formed the cave wall before he lost his balance. Myrdd noticed, but simply continued working on the tablets that had obsessed him since leaving Troy; tossing his long beard of white and darkest gray over his shoulder to blend with his uncut white hair. His ancient face and faded blue eyes focusing on the tablets.

The kaleidoscope effect broadened and blinded Alex to the present as it began to reveal the future. While most of his visions had been innocuous, this vision was different and had terrified him.

"Myrdd!" Hearing the tone of Alex's voice, Myrdd looked up and his eyes narrowed. "It's the girl!" Alex cried out.

Responding to the panic in Alex's voice, Myrdd walked to him and patiently kneeled, placing a hand on his shoulder. Alex was especially grateful for Myrdd's presence during that vision.

"Details, boy! Observe the details—time of year, smells, sounds and light. What do you see?" Myrdd's faded eyes encouraged.

"I...I don't know! I can't..." Alex's heart was racing so hard that he couldn't think.

"You do not have the extravagance of not knowing! You must observe!" Myrdd demanded. "How old is she?"

"I don't know..." Alex forced himself to take a breath. "She...she's a woman."

Myrdd's eyes narrowed—calculating and his voice softened. "How long ago did we leave her, boy?"

"I was...fourteen. We left Troy four years ago." Alex's nerves calmed slightly. "She was young then. I have time to reach her. I have time to change it!"

With the vision now finished, Myrdd retrieved a ladle of water to help Alex with the nausea that could accompany harsh visions.

"Myrdd?" Alex said, between thirsty gulps, *"Can I change it?"*

Over the past 16 years, since that vision, *that* had been the critical question. Through the years of trying to return to her, through his capture and enslavement and escape, never did Alex think of any other purpose. That was what had brought him back here to his home...waiting for the time when he would have the chance to save her from the fate that had been laid before him in that vision. His future depended on finding her in time—and discovering the answer to that question—*could he change the vision*?

Running down the mountain, Alex's heart raced as much from his speed as from the panic in him. The branches and thickets whipped against his body leaving deep scratches on his quest to the sea.

He reached the flat lands and kicked himself. He had gotten sloppy; as the years had passed he had allowed himself to be further away than he should have. His foot slid on unsteady soil and he crashed on an upturned stump, falling straight forward, splitting his lip on a boulder. He pushed himself off and at last reached the shoreline.

The waves crashed rhythmically against the gray-blue stones as the clouds now seemed to dart across the sky, momentarily casting long shadows over the beach and blackening the waves. Alex waded knee-deep into the sea, orienting himself to his exact location—a momentary delay—why did it have to be water? But it was what it was, Alex thought with frustration. His legs were already going numb from the cold. He searched for the tree that concealed the boat he had hidden three years prior. At last finding it, he shoved the boughs and branches away, giving it a strong shove off—trying to get the inertia to move the boat beyond the incoming waves.

Alex jumped in and grabbed the web-coated oars. The water roughly slapped against the boat, pushing him, momentarily back towards the shore. He paddled with everything he had for an hour—his arms and lungs aching. The sea slapped his body, burning with its cold; salt stinging the numerous scratches from his race through the woods, and finally dissipated into numbness. He stood up several times, wasting precious time, knowing it was too soon and he was too far away.

At last the position looked right and while still paddling madly, Alex permitted himself hard glances, frantically looking left and right. His heart beat so loudly in his ears that he heard nothing else; not the soft sobs of the woman with her gentle brown curls and bright blue eyes. Not the sound as she rolled the boulder tied to her ankle, into the gray sea—all hope gone, nor the sound as the boulder yanked her body off of the boat, capsizing it as she was swallowed by the sea.

Still paddling, Alex thought about the many years he had dreamed of her and only her. Myrdd had told Alex to never give up—as if he ever could! She was his heart—his life! And yet, he barely knew her—except for his visions that had given him something more of her than he could ever express. If only he could reach her before the time in the vision. Alex's heart sank at the memory and he worked to keep his hope alive.

How many times had he asked Myrdd if there was a possibility of changing the vision? If he couldn't, then the visions were simply a curse—despite the wealth that they brought.

It always seemed that Myrdd was avoiding the question. But the last time they parted ways, Myrdd had taken Alex's arm, "Boy, know this: I have always supposed that if a Being possessed the power of visions, he should also possess the power to change the outcome of his visions."

Carrying that piece of hope in his heart, Alex spotted something white between the waves and said a silent prayer to Apollo, begging for his intervention. He paddled harder until his boat crested a swell. Alex's heart sank as he saw the capsized boat tossing about aimlessly. Perhaps it had only been a few minutes, he prayed. He pulled the knife out of his belt and dove. He knew the sea would be cold enough to force an involuntary breath, but in his hurry, he dove and breathed in sea water anyway. He coughed it out and then dove hard towards the bottom.

Through the dark churning water, he saw only black. He felt the force of the current and worried that he would be moved off course, or that he would find her and not be able to return to the boat. Then he saw the rising bubbles that would lead him to her.

His lungs were about to burst and momentarily forced him to abandon the pursuit and rise to the surface. He quickly gasped air and dove back down. Too quickly he had to come back up for another breath. This time he dove and followed the bubbles until he saw the white flesh of her hand reaching for the surface, her hair delicately curling around it. He touched her fingers, giving him a new sense of hope. Her face stared into his in what looked like shock and then calmed as her fingers grasped at him and then he saw her pain as she choked in the seawater. Alex held onto her wrist as her body continued to be pulled down through the depths. His lungs were about to burst again and the boulder would pull them both down. He would gladly die with her if that was the only choice. But he had to believe she could still survive and he could do her no good if he were to drown.

He raced to the surface and forced himself to take three deep breaths before diving with all that was in him. Reaching her, Alex worked his knife on the cloth around her ankle, trying to ignore his pain from her blank stare, until at last she broke free. He kicked with all that was in him to reach the surface before he would require a breath—doubting he could make it. Just as his lungs reached their limits, his face broke the surface, and he gulped air along with the wave that threatened to smash both of them into the side of the boat. Alex protectively threw his body in front of hers—though his arms were beginning to lose sensation from the cold. He lost his grip on her momentarily as his skull hit hard on the edge of the boat, leaving it bruised and bloodied.

Pulling her back into his arms, coughing and vomiting sea water that burned his throat, Alex rolled them both into the boat and held her in his arms praying for a change of the fates.

Her body remained cold and blue. Alex looked at the face that he loved, willing life back to her—refusing to accept his failure. When his hope would no longer hold, he let out a long, anguished sob, rocking her body in his arms as a cold, hard rain began to fall.

CHAPTER 2

Present day

The Columbia classroom was packed, as it always was for Alex's lectures.

"All right, Mr. Staunton questions the reality of the Greek gods." Alex shrugged, "Anyone else want to contribute to this discussion?" No one responded. Alex's head cocked to the side with a crooked smile, "Come on!" His eyes danced, "A group of soon-to-be attorneys and no one is challenging this?"

Despite the fact that Louis Staunton was an irritating human being, Alex always enjoyed their discussions.

Tom Cunningham, Staunton's not-so-bright friend took the bait, "Professor, I don't understand, last week we discussed the fact that there *were* no contemporary historians of the Trojan War. All of them were writing from a viewpoint of at least 300 years after the fact. So, how can you now argue that the writings about the Greek gods are accurate?"

Alex nodded, pleased as his little finger tapped lightly on the podium, the sound from the built-in microphone echoing through the room, "You're right to a certain extent, Mr. Cunningham. The subject last week was whether Cassandra, the tragic prophetess of Troy, who foretold the Trojan horse, was insane. And I did argue that the historians of 300 hundred years later had a skewed perspective of a sibyl. The historian's sibyl presided at the Delphi or other temples by 800 BC. The belief was that communication with the gods was made possible by way of intoxicants and hallucinogens; such as ethylene vapors that probably emitted from those sites.

"Cassandra did not reside at the Delphi or other temples that were created hundreds of years later. Still, we know that her foretelling of the Trojan horse was not believed." Alex paused, "Imagine having the gift of vision but not being able to change those visions…quite a curse rather than a gift." Alex shook off the thought.

"History is full of examples where what was in vogue changed the writing of history! Remember that Apollo was alleged to have had numerous male and female lovers? Recall that we discussed the origin of those stories was not until the seventeenth century. So, we attribute it to seventeenth century imagination as opposed to probable truth." Cunningham nodded.

"My lecture last week was more concerned with the fact that there were several conflicting accounts of how Cassandra received her power and what happened to her. Not to argue her existence—as Mr. Staunton is attempting to do with the gods."

Staunton jumped back in, "Professor Morgan, Occam's Razor states that the simplest explanation is the most plausible."

"Well, okay." Alex sighed and looked up as in deep thought. "Mr. Staunton, are you really going to do something as pretentious as argue sixteenth century logic in a class called 'Ancient history'?" The class laughed. "We do have a *few* philosophers in Ancient History to choose from."

Staunton started to argue. He never could catch the subtleties of Alex's humor. Alex interrupted Staunton with a wink. "Go on Mr. Staunton—you're on a roll!"

"Well, Professor, the simplest explanation is that the gods were fictional—versus the idea of immortal deities or beings from where? Outer space? Or that these so-called gods actually possessed magic. That's just... ignorance!" Staunton held his head arrogantly waiting for the rebuttal.

Alex raised an eyebrow, "Ignorance? *So we are the enlightened ones*, are we?" He turned to the other students, "By the way, Occam's quote is 'entities (or ideas) must not be multiplied beyond necessity.' We could analyze each of the entities or ideas that you just suggested and see which is the most plausible." The corner of Alex's mouth turned up slightly in a mischievous grin, "Who knows, it may end up an assignment!" The class booed the idea. "But consider this; some of the greatest thinkers in history believed in beings from other planets, and immortal deities and…magic."

Staunton shrugged, "That doesn't mean I should!"

"Absolutely! Perhaps what makes those beliefs seem odd to you is that they challenge what you have learned all your life."

A woman in the front row raised her hand. Women tended to hit the front row of Alex's class. But he never seemed to notice them other than as students.

"Professor?" She fluttered her eyelashes and waved her hand. Alex nodded to her, "I follow your thinking. It's like the Swedish burying fish to rot and then eating it. We call it trash, they call it dinner!" Several students laughed.

"Exactly!" He said, while the girl garnered nods from her fellow female classmates.

Staunton had been silenced and sat in a near pout with his arms crossed. Alex continued, "Mr. Staunton invalidated the idea of immortal and powerful gods because those ideas are not within his reality or understanding.

"My only point is that once you accept the concept, if you do accept it, that the human spirit is immortal and came from another body or from the breath of God, how big of a leap is it really to think that maybe there are deities, or that 'we', as spiritual beings reincarnate? How big of a leap is it to believe that out there somewhere in the heavens are other life forms?

"Professor Morgan, while I understand your intent, if there had been immortals—what happened to them?" Staunton challenged.

"You haven't met one lately, have you?" Alex flashed a perfect smile of even white teeth, as his class laughed again. "Do you *know* that they disappeared? But, speaking of myths, were you aware that the giant panda was considered to be a myth until 1918? Haven't you heard reports of flying saucers or Sasquatch? There's a lot out there that we don't know about!"

The hour ended, Alex leaned against the podium and raised a hand, "Oh! Professor Dean will be taking over this class, beginning next week." There were grumblings from the class.

"I know you will be as respectful of Professor Dean as you have been of me! It's been a pleasure." Alex lifted a finger, "Well except for you, Mr. Staunton." Alex winked and the class laughed, even Staunton.

∞

From his office he glanced out appreciating the view. He liked Columbia but hoped that this was his last fall quarter here. Shrugging on his jacket over his maroon turtleneck Alex walked quickly across campus. He noticed the female students trailing him, but as usual after this class, there was no time for being social. Alex glanced at his watch; he had timed the light the past few days and guessed it to happen sometime between 9:45 and 10:15. He could make it there in 35 minutes. So he had plenty of time. He liked it when he could walk—it distracted him and he could watch for her.

Alex went over what he would say for the hundredth time. He'd had a long time to practice. He took in the smell of the city—he loved Manhattan—if he had to be in a city and away from home, this was it! It was faster to cross campus and walk down Amsterdam. But if he could get out of class on time, he loved walking down tree-lined Broadway. The leaves were turning and the air felt refreshing. He passed the coffee shop on the corner and the owner waved to Alex's nod.

As he entered the northwestern rim of Central Park, there were some suspicious thugs. No time to take chances. Alex cut down to the 110th street entrance. He knew she would be coming off the loop around the park and every day he tried another route to see if she might be there. He watched for her long brown hair. If today wasn't *the* day, perhaps she would be running by him or perhaps walking a dog, or in the camel hair coat—as he had seen in his vision. He watched all potential candidates, knowing her face so well that it would never be mistaken for another.

Arriving at the corner of 5th and East 76th, Alex glanced to the south. Juan wasn't at his booth. Alex would check with Rosendo in a few minutes. Glancing to the north, Alex saw the milky white of the sky. He drew in a deep breath—this could be it. He reminded himself that he had thought that dozens of times before. But still the temperature seemed right. The sky looked perfect. And if it was the day, he had a few minutes. He walked the few steps towards Juan's stand.

"Hey Amigo, where's Juan? Is he late?" He said causally to Juan's brother Rosendo, secretly hoping that, as in his vision, Juan was not simply late.

"Juan's daughter had her bambino." Rosendo responded, excitedly. Alex gave Rosendo's shoulder a congratulatory pat—though his joy was more for himself than Maria's little one. Alex found his breathing getting a little off with excitement. But he still had a few minutes.

Alex bit his lip, "Well, I probably won't be around much after this week. So, please tell Juan congratulations and please give him this for his grandchild." Alex pulled out his wallet. Rosendo first saw the triangular tattoo on Alex's hand and then saw the many bills in the wallet. Handing Rosendo five crisp one hundred dollar bills, he said, "For the bambino." Rosendo's mouth dropped.

Heading back to the intersection Alex evaluated the light. The sun was about where it should be. Today could be it, he thought again. He had to stay alert. Of course, it had been years of hoping. But today everything seemed to be where it should be; the diffused light showing through between buildings to the east was perfect, the bright orange, red and yellow of the remaining leaves, Juan was absent for the first time in years. The light wasn't quite right. But that could change in an instant in New York. Alex knew it would be as he'd seen it. She would be coming from the park. A cloud moved and suddenly he knew this was the moment. His eyes locked on the trail watching for her.

CHAPTER 3

Valeria was asleep on the floor between two books, *Money Magazines 50 Smartest things to do with your money* and *100 Best Vacations to Enrich Your Life*, with the book she was actually reading still on her lap, her finger subconsciously holding the page, when she was rudely awoken by the intercom buzzer. She struggled to open her eyes and then tried to focus her eyes at her watch; 7:30 am. What was anybody doing at her door and especially at this god-awful early hour of the morning? Although it was only this week that 7:30 seemed early to her.

Pulling herself off the floor with the overstuffed couch as leverage, she straightened her legs and dropped her book. Then pulling her long brown hair back into a ponytail holder, she padded across the wood floor to the intercom for her apartment. "Yes?"

A woman's voice came over the intercom, "Would you just fricken open up? It's cold out here!" It was her best friend Weege—who was really her only friend. Five years ago, Weege had been her first employee after she had developed several large floral contracts and could no longer handle all of the orders herself. Six months ago, Valeria had been offered more money than she thought she would see in her entire life for her little floral shop—without hesitation she had sold.

Valeria had never intended to grow her business. In fact, she had been happiest when she was creating all the designs herself and selling them on the street near Central Park. But all of that changed when her designs became popular. She had been forced to lease a shop. That was fine. But then the large hotel accounts began to come in. Valeria was at once out of room and required a delivery service, purchasing department and bookkeeper. For these duties she had hired Weege. But Valeria insisted on hand-selecting all of her own flowers and would never hire anyone else to design. Later, Valeria caved in, she needed help to keep up with the contracts—and her body seemed to require *some* sleep.

"Weege? What's going on? Everything all right?" Valeria answered, concerned. Only delivery men ever showed up at Valeria's apartment, and on occasion, and only briefly, when it was scheduled weeks in advance—David. Weege didn't answer Valeria. To her chagrin, Valeria heard Weege now hitting up one of her neighbors who was entering the apartment.

Weege's voice was thick with New York, "Hey...excuse me...sir? Sir?? Yeah, I mean you! *Is there another 'sir'* anywhere around here? Hey, I forgot my key. Help me out, huh?" Valeria rolled her eyes—praying that the neighbor didn't see Weege come to her door. Why didn't Weege just wait five seconds and Valeria would have hit the button to let her in, instead of lying. She hated lies! Valeria heard an irritated grunt from the neighbor, followed by the sound of the door opening. Weege whispered into the intercom as she went in, "Never mind. Coming up!"

Then, minutes later Valeria heard the pound on her door.

Too loud, she cringed. She opened the door and Weege stomped in without invitation or greetings.

"What the hell am I doing?" Weege breezed past Valeria into the living room and began pacing, eventually stopping to notice the books, a pizza with two missing slices, an open bottle of wine still two-thirds full and a half glass of wine sitting next to it. She glared critically at Valeria. "You aren't hung over with, what? One glass of wine?" Weege sighed and looked at the books, "Any answers?"

"I don't know. I mean, what do I want? What do I really need? I like my brownstone! I don't want to move just because of money. And I don't really want to travel alone."

As Valeria glanced around, she knew it would take something very special for her to consider ever giving up her home! She loved that the place wasn't set up to focus on a mind-numbing television but rather a built-in bookcase that took up the entire length of her living room. Her dining room was a simple table set up as you walked in the door. She loved the huge windows in the kitchen and bedroom. The colors were a subtle pastel that seemed to deepen as the sun rose and made it look larger than it was.

Glancing up at her nine foot ceilings Valeria crinkled her nose, "David's not really fun to travel with."

Eyeing the pizza, Weege slid onto the floor and shoved a slice of the cold pizza into her mouth, "He's a diplomat. He doesn't have to be fun or interesting." Valeria rolled her eyes at the paradox. Weege mumbled through her bite, "That's why you need to hire someone. Really, Val, I wish I had your problems. Now me: I have REAL problems." Weege looked at the bottle of wine and deciding it was a reasonable vintage drank from Valeria's glass as she shoved another bite of pizza in her mouth.

"Okay." Valeria waved her hand to signal that Weege should begin.

In mock contrition, Weege shook her head, "Nah. You don't really care how awful things are for me. Do you?"

Weege was mid-forties with short grey hair and a face so expressive that one glance and you knew what she would say—or rather what she wanted you to know. Still, Valeria smiled and didn't answer. Weege knew Valeria would solve the problem.

"Those assholes in big business think they know everything! I told them that the Waldorf expected crystal vases…not plastic! Crystal! But they tried to do it with—"

"No! They wouldn't!" Valeria covered her mouth in horror.

"Can you imagine cheap plastic vases going in that place?" Weege said between bites.

Feeling the outrage well up within her, Valeria cried, "They can't do that! I gave the Millennium and the Waldorf my word that nothing would change! Townsend *promised me* when they bought My Secret Garden that there would be no change in quality or service! I'm gone one week and…! What kind of person does that?"

"Lawyers and accountants!" Weege answered, taking another swig and emptying the glass of wine. "Ramsey at the Waldorf is, of course, threatening to pull his account. And, as you well know, there is only one person that can handle Ramsey when he's like this!" Weege tilted her head to the side, in a dramatic pause, "He still wants you to meet his son." She said enticingly.

Valeria plopped herself on the couch next to Weege, "The contracts at The Millennium and Waldorf state 'Glass or

Crystal'. You know it's my integrity on the line here, not theirs! And the hotels, well, they'll just get another vendor!"

"And then I'll be out of a job. I'll be known as the woman that lost all the key contracts; and all within one lousy week. Val, I don't even want to talk to Ramsey." Weege sighed.

Rolling her eyes, Valeria said, "I'm out of this Weege. I gave them six months and I've transitioned now. It's their company and you are the general manager for this branch. I know you can fix this."

"Oh no! Don't tell me that!" Weege crawled up on the couch next to Valeria, "Besides, you told me Ramsey reminded you of your poor old dad."

Shaking her head in disgust, Valeria challenged, "Are you REALLY pulling the, connect with your dad deal?" There was no use in playing the game. Valeria knew that Weege could manipulate her easily, especially when it came to the florist shop. It was her baby and now someone else owned it. It felt strange. Still, during the six month transition, Valeria had vowed that she would not hang onto the shop as hers and would let it be theirs. It was that point now.

Weege shrugged, "Kinda desperate."

"You know I wasn't very close to dad." That was an understatement.

"He was an asshole." Weege offered.

"I never said he was an asshole." Valeria countered.

Weege's mood changed to mild upset, "No! You never say anything—about anything! I tell you EVERYTHING! And you repay me by telling me NOTHING! I have to assume things—like even with David—HE told me you were engaged! You never told me!"

Valeria eked out a, "Sorry." She didn't really want to be that secretive about her life. She guessed she had just learned it was better to keep her life to herself. She ran her hand over her face in thought. "Weege, how did you make this determination about Dad?"

Cringing guiltily, "Now don't go nuts on me…" Weege hunched her shoulders, "I read your journal—and YES, he was an asshole! Did he even realize he was raising a daughter?"

Disbelief overran Valeria's embarrassment and more than minor irritation. The anger and outrage would come after she had thought about it more. Valeria put her hand on her hips, *"You read my journal?* When?"

Weege shrugged innocently, "Every day! What? You kept your whole epic tale back there in the accounting office! You expect me to sit back there and do the bookkeeping with NOTHING to keep me interested? Why do you think I kept the door closed? Because I, for one, respect your privacy…I didn't want any of those other jerks seeing your private journals!"

Valeria's jaw dropped and she felt the heat in her face—all her fears and concerns and desires laid out there for someone to read. She took a deep breath. She would deal with this later; nothing could be changed now. Valeria jumped up and grabbed her journal off the coffee table with its black cover, stomping into the bedroom she tossed it into her bedside table and shut the drawer loud enough for Weege to hear. Then taking another deep breath she walked calmly back to the living room. Valeria had left her journals at the office because they were under lock and key. And although Weege had the key Valeria never imagined that Weege would violate her privacy to that degree.

"I thought it was really sweet when you called your diary 'Dear Kitty'." Weege said, grinding salt into the fresh wound.

Further embarrassed, Valeria defended, "I was a kid then! That was my Anne Frank stage."

"If your dad didn't love you, he was an asshole!" Weege justified. Valeria also knew that Weege meant it. But it hit a chord and Valeria didn't like discussing it with anyone—not Weege and not the endless stream of social workers who had always wanted to know how she 'felt' about things—her dad and his death in particular.

Coffee…she needed coffee! Valeria walked to the kitchen and before grinding the beans said, "I think he was just heartbroken." She defended for Weege's benefit. Valeria poured the purified water in the pot. "By the way, I went to his plot yesterday and do you know all of the flowers I planted last month were dead!"

Weege popped up, "What do you pay those people for? When I'm dead, just cremate me!" She looked around, "Can I sit on your hearth, in one of our fancy urns when I'm dead?"

"No!" Valeria had to laugh.

Throwing herself dramatically back on the sofa, Weege felt something under her; she reached down and pulled out the copy of *Sense and Sensibility* that Valeria had been reading. Weege's face filled with utter consternation as she marched to the kitchen with the book and the box of pizza just as Valeria started getting the first drips of coffee. Weege waved the book as her evidence. "So, you were reading *this*, instead of the books that I brought you?"

"It's like an old friend." Valeria grabbed the book and sighed—busted.

"You need to just face up to the responsibility of your wealth and take me with you on the best vacations."

Turning to lean on the kitchen counter, Valeria looked up.

There was something odd about the whole business of selling her company and no longer needing to fight for a living. How could she possibly explain it to anyone without feeling…ungrateful? It was like now that she didn't have the shop she felt empty. Interestingly, the money didn't seem to fill that void. "Weege, you know, you think it will all feel great. I expected to feel great. And it did when we were signing the sales contracts—I guess. But I keep thinking 'what's next'? How long can I vacation. And making more money from good investments just isn't very interesting to me."

"You need a hobby." Weege picked up another piece of pizza. "Can I have a coffee?"

Valeria poured herself a coffee and then glanced over at the framed and matted oversized picture of David on the wall—not a loving picture of the two of them, but a corporate portrait; with David's short brown hair smartly parted and combed back neatly, his brown eyes and strong chin, just a tad arrogant. His crisp white shirt and Windsor knot looking overly formal for a man of thirty-five. It was an 8x10 and much too big to have in her small home. She mumbled to herself, "I need a life."

"Weege?" Valeria said quietly.

"Yeah."

"Do you know, only a couple of his old pub buddies even came to Dad's funeral? He deserved more."

"So did you. Now, are you going to meet with Ramsey?"

Valeria shrugged a yes.

CHAPTER 4

Savoring the last drop of the coffee in her cup, Valeria grabbed the pot to pour her final cup of the day and frowned as only a thin stream dribbled into her cup and ended abruptly. She held tightly to her two-cup rule—knowing she could drink coffee all day and all that caffeine wouldn't do her any good at all! Valeria sighed, puzzled, and then saw Weege's empty cup in the sink. *Weege drank the second cup.* Valeria's eyes lit in an impish smile—she still had one more cup coming to her today!

Then she remembered Weege's confession about reading the journals. Valeria wondered why it was that she felt so compelled to always keep journals. But she had found that writing her troubles down seemed to diminish them and left her feeling hopeful about the future. Though she hadn't had many troubles of any significance in recent years—at least not troubles that others wouldn't wish were their own.

She pulled her brown riding boots from the upper shelf in her closet. The weather had turned cool enough to justify wearing them. She pulled them on and enjoyed their fit and feel. Fall was such a wonderful season!

Writing in her journals during the foster care years had been interesting! Valeria learned to keep them hidden and locked. And still at that, frequently found someone reading her most private thoughts. Her biggest fear was that they—the courts, the counselors, the social workers or foster parents—would decide she was nuts and needed to be on some combination of drugs that seemed to cause more harm than good and/or required regular appointments with a psychiatrist. Valeria felt that "feelings" were overrated! You had things you had to do and you just do them. She didn't need to discuss that she was alone in the world. That was just the way it was!

So, Valeria had learned early to say the right words to all of the enquiring minds. A casual, "I'm good" worked well—though it was typically far from the truth.

She had shared rooms with girls that were mostly scary and stole her possessions, rarely slept, broke most of what they touched and were overly interested in sex…any kind of sex. When Valeria was fortunate enough to have a room to herself—and rarely with a lock—she learned to always balance a book on her door knob to awaken her should someone come to visit during the night.

Taking her make-up bag to the mirror above the small desk in the entry, Valeria's eye caught the blinking of her answering machine. Why was it that David always left "bad news" calls on her house phone? He knew she never answered it—in fact she had turned the ringer off since last Friday; her last day at My Secret Garden. Besides, calls on the house phone were typically solicitors. She thought about having the house phone disconnected as she hit the message button. She appraised her face in the mirror. "Valeria, it's David." His chalky, smooth voice relayed.

"I know you're cancelling again." Valeria said aloud, as

she smoothed her dark curls back from her face. She wasn't half-bad sometimes, she thought. She dabbed some light blush on her high cheekbones—those she got from her mother, as were most of her looks. Her eyes were long and almond-shaped. With a bit of mascara they looked all right. At least she had a good complexion!

David's message went on, "Sorry dear—I'm afraid I'm flying out today. I was invited to attend a conference in Hamburg tomorrow that looks interesting. Then I'll be heading back to Prague."

Valeria nodded in slight irritation, "Of course you are!"

The message went on, "So, obviously dinner is off…but you could join me?" The voice said, hesitantly.

"No thanks!" Valeria said, as if David could hear her. Why would she choose to sit in a hotel room waiting for him—as David was not 'comfortable' with her wandering streets of foreign countries without going on formal tours, or being accompanied by him. Then, David would insist that they join all of his new friends—who rarely spoke English.

David's voice continued, "I know it isn't really your thing…Oh—don't we have something on the calendar for next week? Hmmm? Oh well…it'll have to wait."

Valeria stared at the answering machine for an instant of almost disappointment, "Yes…my birthday! We were supposed to go away for a week for my birthday."

"See you next trip. Love you." David's voice finished.

It was amazing to Valeria how David managed to find every international conference with so much ease, never, ever missed a business dinner—and never failed to forget her birthday. Still, she wasn't too disappointed. She smiled a half-smile, more of a grimace and saw her dimples coming out—another gift from her mother.

David did seem pleased with the way Valeria presented herself to his crowd; she had nice table manners—one thing she did learn from her dad, and she knew how to dress appropriately—though that had taken some learning; especially the pantyhose, which for the life of her she could not keep from running! Her previous wardrobe had consisted of jeans and sweats. And lastly, David was most pleased because she didn't make a spectacle of herself by over-indulging in wine, even when pushed on her.

Her life was so much better than what most of the kids that had come from her background would fare. David was a good man, with good intentions. He cared about her. He was kind and handsome and smart and interesting. David liked good food and an occasional show. So what if he wasn't the most romantic person in the world, or if he occasionally forgot her birthday—the man had to have *some* faults! Besides, love worked better when you didn't expect too much, she thought. Valeria glanced at her copy of *Pride and Prejudice*. Passion was a fleeting emotion and she was just too common sense to have that kind of love.

She pulled her camel hair coat from the hook near the door, wrapped a burgundy scarf around her neck, pulled on her brown leather gloves and cinched the belt around her waist. She was all ready to sweet-talk Ramsey at the Waldorf into giving her former company another try. But if he bucked it was Townsend's fault. She had done her best to keep the accounts for them.

Valeria decided to walk since it was so beautiful. It was a long walk, but she would take a cab back if she got tired. Staring out from the steps of her brownstone, her tree-lined street never failed to thrill her. She had come a long way in ten years!

Remembering her childhood, Valeria again searched for the moments of light in that sea of darkness. The light overtook the darkness in her life, when at sixteen she had become emancipated and was able to move into her own apartment. Well, apartment was a bit of an overstatement. It was more of a hotel room where she could pay her rent weekly. That worked so she could sell her floral designs on the weekend and pay rent the next day. There was a wonderful feeling of freedom living on her own.

The drab studio didn't have a kitchen sink or a stove. So she would cook up hamburger helper in an electric skillet and wash dishes in her bathroom sink. Valeria loved it! It had been her own home and no one invaded her privacy. Well, not usually. Still she had learned many years before to invest in a baseball bat—though she had never had to use it, it occasionally came in handy to ward off potential trouble. Like the time the biker had decided to hide from the police in her apartment. Valeria had let him stay until the police left, keeping the bat in hand all the while—and then walked him to the door, in a friendly sort of way. The biker took the hint.

Walking down her street Valeria plunged her hands into her pockets and smiled. It was a dream come true to be on the street she had picked out all those years ago. The street was bounded by a few blocks on either side by the Hudson River Greenway and Central Park. Most of the windows had flower boxes and it was always clean. Rarely did you hear someone raise their voice. During the summer all the local restaurants would set up outside.

Valeria liked watching the people in the restaurants as friends or families would meet and hug and chatter bright-eyed for hours, with rarely a lull in their conversations. For some reason Valeria never had those kinds of relationships—not even with Weege—or David, for that matter.

Sometimes it would cause her to analyze what was wrong with her. She didn't really know how to have that kind of deep friendship or trust—though she didn't for an instant indulge in self-pity—only a distracted curiosity, combined with the knowledge that she was different from others.

Walking along the crowded street, Valeria thought about what she would say to Ramsey. When she first started dealing with him, he had been difficult. But in little time at all, he had become one of her favorite clients. He, of course, wasn't like her father at all. But there was something in the look of the man that reminded Valeria of her father.

Crossing into Central Park, Valeria admired the change of colors of the leaves. She cut over to the Reservoir and enjoyed the view of the buildings above the lush trees and the calm water. She decided to weave her way through the park to the East Side, and then walk down Park Avenue.

The sun set the colors of the leaves ablaze in brilliant red and gold. She had to resist collecting them. Her favorite was the Gingko leaves—there was something magical about Gingko leaves, she thought. Valeria decided that because she wouldn't be too far off, she could enjoy her last cup of coffee of the day at Via Quadronno, one of the best coffee bars in Manhattan. Valeria wondered why she had agreed to taking on Mr. Ramsey's rage. But then the answer was immediately there—for Weege...and for the honor of her own word.

Valeria was almost to the East side of Central Park when her phone rang, it was Weege.

"Hey! Did you already talk to Ramsey?" Weege inquired.

Glancing at her watch, it was ten o'clock and Weege had

only left her place a little over an hour ago. "No. I'm just heading over there now. Why?"

"Evidently everything is fine. Of course, we have to correct the error. But he's not pulling the account. So, I'm saving your help for the next time I need it!" Weege commanded.

Valeria rolled her eyes. She suspected it would be an easy fix this time. She started to turn around to walk back home and then decided to continue over to Via Quadronno for her coffee.

CHAPTER 5

Alex kept his watchful eye on the trail and his heart stopped and then rose into his throat as he saw the camel hair coat wrapped at the waist, her brown riding boots that matched her long, brown curls. From the distance he could even see her blue-green eyes. Alex forced himself to start breathing again. She was talking on the phone and laughing. He noticed her graceful, easy gait.

He had been momentarily mesmerized and distracted by her and realized the crosswalk flashed green to walk and she had started across 5th avenue. Then he heard Rosendo's wolf whistle that would distract her from the danger. Alex's heart jumped as his feet moved on the pavement, dread creeping in that he was a moment too late. Suddenly, the Red Mustang flew around the corner towards her. Valeria saw the Mustang and knew it was over for her—but faced it without regret.

The next thing she knew, she heard what sounded like the crunching of bones and tearing of cloth or flesh and then she was airborne. Valeria found it interesting that she didn't hurt. She thought this must be what it feels like to be in shock. She found herself on the ground but she had landed on something soft. Her knee had hit the sidewalk. Actually, not even hit it—more, her knee lightly scraped the sidewalk. She didn't feel hurt, but she definitely felt confused!

Rosendo came over, "Miss, are you all right?" As she reached for his hand, she realized someone was underneath her and was holding her with an iron grip. She tried to stand but his arms were still around her. Finally his grip released and she rolled off from him, seeing the scrape on her knee—thank god she wasn't wearing hose! Valeria looked to the red mustang. A young boy sat behind the wheel with his eyes as big as saucers—a slight dent on his hood and the paint on the fender looked muffed. Valeria stared with amazement at the man still lying on the sidewalk, his body was trembling slightly.

"Are you all right?" She knelt, setting her hand on his shoulder. Alex was the one in shock—he had helped her evade death—he had even held her in his arms for a moment. He wondered how badly she was injured from his delay. He tried to gracefully roll to his feet but failed due to pain in his rib and knee. He looked her over, she didn't seem injured. He saw a slight tear in his leather jacket. The driver of the Mustang continued to stare at them. Alex nodded and waved the boy on. And the boy, obviously relieved, obliged.

Alex tried to rise as if he hadn't just thrown his whole body into a car and then into the cement sidewalk. And he attempted to ignore what he was certain was a bruised knee and elbow and possibly a broken rib from caroming off the bumper and hood. If he relaxed a moment the knee would be alright.

"Yes. I'm fine." His eyes narrowed. "Big question is—how are you?" He asked, suddenly aware that he was staring into her eyes for too long.

"I think I'm okay—thanks to you!" Valeria replied, pulling

Rosendo's arm off from hers, while trying to be kind. Then she offered her hand to Alex. He smiled seeing her beautiful gloved hand and took it, but didn't use it to pull himself up. Alex winced as he stood, knowing that if he had followed his own plan he wouldn't be standing here like a wounded boy, moaning over his injuries and his clothes would still be in good order.

Rosendo, seeing he was no longer needed or wanted, instead saw opportunity from the gathering onlookers and worked to tempt them to his paintings.

Valeria brushed off her coat and smiled as Alex pulled a leaf off his shoulder. "Well…thank you again. I think you saved my life." She looked into his face and saw something…not quite familiar.

"No big deal." Alex smiled.

Valeria stared for a moment at his dark blonde hair, his strong jaw and full lips. She noticed the build of an athlete—perhaps a runner? And then the sun hit his eyes—the most amazing shade or actually *shades* of blue, she had ever seen. She took a deep breath and looked away as she realized she was staring into his eyes. What was wrong with her? She must have hit her head. Subconsciously, Valeria ran her hand over her head and satisfied, laughed. Alex noticed a moment when she seemed to be appraising him and looked down before his eyes betrayed him.

She felt torn. Valeria wanted to stare into those eyes for just a moment longer. But *she couldn't do that!* She turned away from him, glancing over her shoulder—in an attempt at being casual. Valeria started heading down 5th, totally oblivious as to where she was now going.

"Well…I…I guess I need to…" She swallowed, as Alex

finished the sentence.

"—go to breakfast with me." Alex enticed.

Stopping, Valeria smiled to herself, noticing an uncomfortable feeling in her chest—or was it a glorious feeling? She couldn't quite decide. It was rude to keep her back to him—he did just save her life.

Alex sensed Valeria's confusion and stepped in front of her, looking into her eyes—there he saw the connection again. "Come to breakfast with me!" He said, over anxiously.

Valeria thought for a moment, she couldn't possibly sit next to him over breakfast without practically being mesmerized. She realized her head was shaking 'no' while the flutter in her heart was pushing her outside of her comfort zone, in an unquestionable 'yes'.

A slight breeze moved by them, giving a welcome distraction. Then Alex, noticing her reluctance, shook his head, speaking out loud to himself, "Okay too much! Cool down." Alex forced himself to take a deep breath and ran his hands through his tousled blond hair. His brilliant, blue eyes met hers again and she realized she couldn't look away if she wanted to.

"I'm sorry. I came on too strong." His face lit in an extraordinarily charming way with a hint of mischief. "But I know somewhere inside, you're thinking, 'I should go have breakfast with him'…" Alex paused, looked down at his knee and pretended an increased value of the injury, "Of course, not because I was just injured in the line of duty—but because…"

She smiled, still uncertain, then found herself laughing, "Are you really going to use *guilt*?" He shrugged innocently. "So, I'm waiting to hear the '*because*'?" She challenged.

Alex found himself at a loss of the easy wit that he so often used with his students. He moved in towards her. His closeness made the flutter in her heart turn into a lurch. She wasn't certain she liked it, but she didn't want it to stop. "*Because*...there's something about me that you just—," He moved even closer so she could feel his breath and spoke softly. "—you *just like*."

Cringing, Alex thought his words sounded arrogant. But he felt certain it was true. He could see that she felt their connection. Alex continued, "You don't want to walk away, and I don't want you to." He took her gloved hand. "Have breakfast with me."

Valeria had to take a deep breath to calm her pounding heart—wondering if he could hear it. She was certain her face was flushed. But she could easily excuse that from the near-death experience. She nodded softly, afraid to speak.

Then he turned on his most charming smile, "I'm Alex Morgan. I'm a History Professor at Columbia and I assure you, I do not make a practice of throwing myself into moving vehicles in order to pick-up women!"

"I'm Valeria Mills." The corners of her mouth turned up in a wicked smile, "Well Alex Morgan, that is a shame! Because it appears you may have wasted your efforts on education when you are so successful with your Clark Kent/Superman imitation!"

Alex held out his arm for her and she grasped it and they strolled across 5th. As they passed Rosendo, he rolled his eyes, "Man, you got them moves down!"

∞

Sitting in a cozy booth in Sarabeth's, Valeria drank in his

features from beneath her lashes. She was so distracted that she broke her two-cup rule and was sipping her third cup of coffee while she picked at the remains of her frittata. Alex gazed into her eyes, lapping up every word as if it were the most interesting thing he had ever heard.

"My mother was a rodeo rider from Oklahoma who *somehow* made the decision to marry my dad, who by all accounts was a nerdy accountant that liked his beer a bit too much!"

"How old were you when she died?"

Valeria looked at Alex critically, "How did you know—"

Alex kicked himself internally. He had relaxed his guard. Being with her—talking to her, was throwing him off. "I'm sorry. I assumed the way you spoke of her that you hadn't spent a lot of time with her."

"My mother died giving birth to me; leaving dad a very unlikely and undesiring recipient of a baby girl." She offered a faded laugh, and looked away, noticing a father affectionately listening to his young daughter prattle on about something.

"It must have been hard on your father to lose someone he cared about."

She shrugged, nonchalantly, "Dad cared about his beer—and telling stories to his pub buddies." Valeria swallowed, "He died when I was thirteen, a few weeks before Thanksgiving." She said with little emotion. She hated that most people got so emotional over the whole thing. Perhaps, Valeria thought, it brought to light that there was something wrong with her that she didn't get upset about it. Still, she wasn't ready for this charming stranger to realize it.

"I'm sorry to hear that. Who raised you?" Alex asked.

"I went to a number of different foster homes." Valeria sipped her coffee wondering why she was telling Alex all these details of her life. But she couldn't seem to stop herself. She wondered if she really was in shock—or if his eyes had somehow hypnotized her. Whatever it was, Valeria thought how much she enjoyed actually sharing details of her life with him. She avoided looking at the clock—fearing their time might be drawing to a close.

"I changed schools a few times a year. I guess that was alright though." She sighed, "I spent most of my time outside in the woods and parks anyway. As it turns out, that was where I found my gift."

"Gift?" Alex seemed surprised at her words, but then buried his surprise in his coffee.

Flushing, Valeria said, embarrassed, "Yes; seeing the beauty in nature." Alex looked up and smiled without missing a beat. She went on, "I started making homes in the woods, places where I could be and read in private."

Alex's brows drew together, "Aren't the woods considered a bit dangerous for a young girl?"

There was a moment when Valeria's pupils flashed and then she tilted her head. "Sometimes it was safer there."

Seeing that she had broken Alex's light mood, she returned to the lightness of her magical woods. "I had books hidden in every knoll outside. I started decorating my…outdoor homes with moss, stones and flowers that I found." Valeria played with a strawberry on her plate.

"One of my teachers encouraged us all to enter a local art contest." She shook her head and rolled her eyes, "I don't know how I ever got the nerve, except my passing grade relied on it. I created a terrarium with things I found in the woods."

She smiled humbly, her face flushing again as she glanced down. "Believe it or not, I won." She tore off a bit of her English muffin and put it in her mouth.

"Sounds like a scholarship to me." Alex said as he leaned his chin on his hand.

Her eyes narrowed and she shook her head, "School really wasn't my thing. Besides, before that was ever an option, I was making enough money to support myself. I was emancipated at sixteen and I loved what I was doing. So I didn't really see any point."

Alex was again mesmerized. "I don't mean to change subject, but your eyes are beautiful! What color are they?"

Valeria blushed. *He* was commenting on her rather ordinary eyes, "Thanks. Uh, well, kind of blue-green, I guess."

"Yes, but they have some gold that makes them very interesting." Alex commented.

"Oh thanks." She thought he had the most beautiful eyes she'd ever seen. But she really couldn't say that. She looked at his plate. "Didn't you like your food?"

"It was good." Alex glanced down and realized he hadn't taken a single bite of his Eggs Benedict. "Well, it's always good here." He covered and then laughed.

Alex looked at her calculatingly, "Let's see—my guess is that you are about 24?"

"I'm 27."

A bolt of surprise seemed to hit him and then she continued. "Well, not 27 yet, next week. I haven't even thought about what I might do." Valeria noticed that Alex seemed suddenly frozen. She felt the deep flush move over her face and neck. "Not that I have to *do* anything. I mean, I *do* things by myself all the time." She prattled on, feeling totally ridiculous.

Alex looked down with barely missed anxiety. "When is your 27th birthday, exactly?" Sound casual, he warned himself—don't scare her.

"Monday."

His breath caught, "This coming Monday? Five days from now?"

The change in his tone didn't escape Valeria's notice. Of all the times she had decided to talk about herself! Certainly he was bored to tears—though he didn't look it. Valeria wished she had left a smidge of mystery to herself. But it was too late for that!

She felt the heat in her face, "Yes...I'm sorry. That sounded like I expected you to ask me out." Realizing what she just said, she stopped, feeling mortified that she had actually said it out loud. She lowered her face to her hands as she felt the flush move over her neck and shoulders.

Relax, Alex thought, as he forced a smile on his face. "I would love to! It's just that you don't look more than 24." He looked around trying to collect his thoughts—trying to even his breath.

Looking anywhere, but in his face, Valeria went on trying to ease her embarrassment of his response, "I don't usually even celebrate my birthday. Well, because my mother died when I was born, you know. But, uh, well, my boyfriend, David...well, I guess we're engaged now," Valeria cringed, why had she felt the need to fill the silence with talk about David? She glanced up to see how Alex had responded to this bit of information. To her disappointment, he didn't seem to notice at all. In fact, he was in deep thought. Why did she have to bring up David?

Finally, Alex looked at her with a half smile, his eyes narrowing, "Excuse me a moment, I need to make a quick call." Valeria's face dropped, Alex added, "Don't go anywhere, beautiful!" He winked at her again and then she saw him outside the restaurant, engaged in an intense phone conversation for a few minutes. Alex returned to the table seeming more relaxed than moments before.

"Is everything all right?" Valeria queried.

Alex put on his most charming smile, "Absolutely! I just realized I was supposed to meet a friend."

"Oh." Valeria swallowed, "Well I guess you need…to leave." She tried to hide her disappointment.

Alex furrowed his brow. "No! I don't need to leave! I was hoping—,"

Interrupting him, Valeria said, "Well, I mean, if you had a date and you needed to run and meet her." Valeria was stunned that she said what she was thinking…again!

"It's not a date. It's a friend of mine, a doctor."

"Are you sick?"

He chuckled, "No, although some of my students might disagree."

Valeria snickered nervously at herself. What was wrong with her that she was jumping to all of these conclusions? She picked at the last of her fruit. "I can't believe I haven't eaten here before…" Valeria was pleased that she had successfully changed the subject. She looked up to notice Alex looking at her with an inquisitive expression. "What?" Valeria asked.

The waitress came to refill both of their coffees and Valeria noticed that again, the waitress smiled at Alex a bit too long. Realizing that this would be her fourth cup, though these mugs were smaller than what she considered to be a full-sized coffee, Valeria decided to cut herself off and covered the mug with her hand—she was jumpy enough as it was.

"No...thank you!"

Waiting for the waitress to leave, Alex leaned forward and in a knowing voice said, "You do love your coffee, don't you?"

Valeria shrugged with a smile, "Yes, I do! You...," she paused, a bit embarrassed to continue.

"What?" Alex said with a laugh.

"You seem to notice everything about me! I mean...not that...I mean, you are probably just a very observant person." Valeria covered.

Alex winced, and with his most charming smile said, "I'm sorry. I'm probably a little too intense. I'll work on that." He winked and then tightened up. "Listen, I have been enjoying the pure pleasure of your company. But there is something—well someone, I need you to meet."

"Somebody *I* need to meet?"

Alex leaned towards her. "Yes. Well," he glanced out onto Park Avenue. "Here he is!"

A giant of a man walked by the window. Valeria noticed that he was thin, immaculately dressed with very short, dark grey hair and brilliant, blue eyes, like Alex's. She guessed that they must be related—two unrelated people could never have *that* eye color! The man entered the restaurant and headed straight towards them.

"Valeria, I'd like you to meet my friend Dr. Immanuel Castro. Mani is the friend that I told you about. I hope you don't mind but I invited him here to meet you. Mani is a top researcher from Johns Hopkins."

Taking her hand, Mani graciously held it and almost bowed. "It's very nice to meet you, Valeria."

"Mani, your accent—what nationality are you?"

"Most of my time has been around Portugal, the Azores and Italy, of course." He responded kindly.

Alex cut in a bit nervously. "So, Doc has a kind of communication for you."

Mani winked at Valeria. "Excuse my friend. He's a bit impatient when it comes to you."

"We just met." Valeria corrected.

"Yes. I know."

"So, beautiful, I want you to just relax." Alex indicated letting his shoulders move down. Valeria wondered what was going on with this.

"Alex is correct. It will be easier if you relax." Mani pulled off his gloves.

The waitress came by and glanced at Mani, "Menu, honey?" The waitress touched Alex's shoulder while speaking to Mani—annoying Valeria to her core!

Completely ignoring the waitress's mild flirtation, Alex answered for Mani. "No, thank you. He can't stay." Mani didn't seem to pay any attention; his focus was on Valeria. Alex continued, as an afterthought to the waitress, "Oh, and the check, please, when you get a chance."

Hearing Alex ask for the check would have disappointed Valeria, if not for the fact that she was getting nervous about what was going on with Mani—though he seemed friendly enough. "I don't understand what's going on."

Mani smiled at her kindly. "You will, very shortly. Alex thought this might be an easier gradient for you." Mani faced Valeria and took her hands in his. Somehow she felt safe. She glanced at Alex, who looked tense.

"Valeria, look at me." Mani said in his soothing voice.

Looking into his eyes, she noticed that although they were identical to Alex's, she could actually analyze the color without getting lost in them. She noticed that they were an almost translucent blue, bejeweled with streaks of various shades of deeper blue, and occasionally, almost a deep purple. Valeria thought it was like you could see into his soul—just like Alex's. She felt her body relax slightly.

Suddenly she was struck with a force; at least it felt like a force. It continued for several seconds. Something like a filmstrip running too fast went off in Valeria's head; so fast that she couldn't quite take it all in. Yet something seemed so…familiar about what she saw. As suddenly as it started, it ended. Mani was still looking at her with his kind eyes. Alex's look was intense. Satisfied with something, Alex patted Mani on the back.

"Okay, Doc. Thanks buddy."

Rising from the table, Mani lifted a long finger at her. "Valeria, I want to see you in my lab. Okay?"

She wanted to protest or at very least question what had happened but found that she didn't quite have the strength—or desire. Alex came around and helped her stand.

"What's going on?" She decided that she really was in shock from the accident. It had just been a delayed reaction.

"Well, we can talk about it, while I walk you back to your place." Alex said as he paid the check. Valeria felt too disoriented to argue or question him. She took Alex's arm and started to walk back towards Central Park. As they got to the park, Alex stopped and turned towards her. Valeria looked at him totally baffled as to why they were stopping.

His eyes softened with a playful glint. "Despite all appearances, I don't know where you live. I just assumed you were on the upper west side, since that's where you came from."

"Oh, this path is good. I'm at 95th & Columbus, just on the other side of the park."

As they entered Central Park, Alex waived to Rosendo, with his attention focused solely on Valeria. "Let's talk about what happened with Mani." Alex said, as if he were teaching one of his classes. "So, what did you see?"

"I'm…I'm just not sure." Valeria responded.

Alex nodded several times, knowingly. "Well, all right." He seemed to be considering for a moment. "So, what *did* you see?"

"It was like a—…" She paused, trying to put it together.

"Yes?" Alex nodded encouraging her to continue. They turned onto the trail around the reservoir. Valeria noticed how much more she enjoyed the trail with Alex's company.

"It was like a filmstrip." She looked at him for confirmation. He nodded slightly for her to continue. "Except there were smells, tastes…everything."

"So, you saw pictures with perceptions. And what was in the pictures?" Alex asked, as if he already knew the answer.

"I saw…I saw a little girl, sitting on a man's lap, on like a…a big chair?"

"Focus on her face. What does she look like?"

"Well...she has brown curls and she has...blue eyes like yours!" Suddenly, she turned to Alex, "Did Mani hypnotize me?"

An amused smile lit the corners of Alex's mouth when he suddenly became completely distracted by a stray curl blowing lightly across her face. Unable to control himself, he reached over and tucked it behind her ear—brushing his finger along her cheek as he did so.

For Valeria it felt as if time had suddenly stopped, she felt an electrical energy with a thousand volts moving through her body, bringing new life to her cheek. She forced herself to breathe, still feeling his touch on her face. Alex noticed her response. His voice went soft and she noted a hint of something else in his voice. "No beautiful. No, he did not hypnotize you."

Her heart was racing, and she was certain he had noticed her flush. She liked that he called her "beautiful".

As they began walking again, they passed a legless man that had a sign that said "Veteran—please help!"

"Hey Hector!" Alex waved.

"Alex—hey man!" The legless man replied. Valeria had seen the man and his sign several times but had always avoided his eyes.

Glancing at her, Alex said, "Excuse me for just a moment, will you?" Alex waited for Valeria to nod approval.

Reaching into his coat pocket, he pulled out his wallet and removed a hundred dollar bill. Hector eyed the bill, hungrily. Alex pulled a pen and started writing on the bill. After numerous lines, he recapped the pen and placed it back in his breast pocket. "Hector, do me a favor?"

"Me do *you* a favor? Sure man." Hector was waiting for

the pay-off.

"You play the horses don't you?" Alex said, evaluating what he had written on the bill.

"I don't know man—I can't get in anymore trouble." Hectors voice was wary, and his eyes narrowed, considering what Alex had in his hand. "You got some inside dope?"

"No…no trouble." Alex pulled several more crisp bills from his wallet. "I just need you to place a few bets for me at the track." He kneeled and handed Hector the bill with the bets written on them. "These are for Saturday's races. Then I need you to take the winnings to this gentleman." He took a card out of his pocket and handed it to Hector. It was Dan Frankl, one of the best investment bankers that Alex knew. "Dan will give you further instructions."

A slight breeze picked up as Hector stared at the card and the large bills, "Holy sh—!" He caught himself and then tried to play it cool.

"Buddy, I'm going to be out of town. I need you to place these bets for me."

Hector's eyes narrowed, "What's my take if I do?" He knew there was always a catch!

"You're doing the work…so; I'll take twenty percent of the winnings. Just put my share in a savings account. Dan will help you with all of that."

Though he had no interest in any of the winnings, Alex knew that Hector would drink it or smoke it if he thought Alex wouldn't know. But he also knew that Hector would have the integrity to ensure Alex received his share of the money. That's how he would get Hector the help he needed. Dan had specific instructions. Money wasn't Hector's biggest problem!

With a knowing look, Alex added, "Hector—buddy, don't waste this money." His voice softened, "You do exactly as I say and you won't *ever* worry about money again." Alex's eyes narrowed in intensity. Hector caught the subtlety and nodded.

"Okay man. I'll do it." Hector promised. Alex smiled and rejoined Valeria.

"I'm sorry, Val. Something I promised myself I would handle." Alex took a deep breath, "So, back to what happened with Mani." Alex placed his hand on Valeria's back returning to their previous pace. "So there are certain people," he appeared to be searching for words—though, in fact he had rehearsed this scene a thousand times. "These people are connected in a sort of way that allows them to share pictures or memories in a more simple way than perhaps others might be able to." It wasn't deception. Alex had simply found that it worked better if it didn't appear that he knew his lines too well. It wouldn't be long before she would know everything.

"He was sharing his memories?" Valeria queried. "I don't understand how. But I guess I'm wondering why didn't he—or you just tell me."

"I guess it seems easier that way. So, let's get back to the pictures. Tell me what you saw."

"There were maybe thirty or forty people standing there around the little girl and the man. There were some men with...swords?! This is ridiculous." Valeria felt silly and stopped.

"Go on." Alex encouraged.

"The little girl is making some decision. She's looking from person to person and occasionally smiling."

"Yes?"

"Well, this sounds crazy, but there's something familiar about it." Valeria turned to Alex.

"The little girl is familiar to you?" Alex prodded.

"No." She responded. Alex made a barely perceptible frown—it would be more difficult than he thought.

Valeria continued, "But the situation seems to be…well I don't know." She shrugged. "It's probably nothing." She continued, "The little girl pointed at a very strange looking woman." She suddenly remembered, "And there's a man in a long robe standing by the little girl and he seems to be directing things. There's something kind of creepy about him. You know what I mean?"

"I understand. Go on."

Valeria stopped hard enough to spin Alex around. "I don't understand this Alex! I feel like this is my memory. Will you tell me what's going on?"

They had reached the other side of the park. "Val, I know it's different. But you don't need me to tell you what happened. You can figure this out!"

Alex's confidence in her was encouraging, "That picture is so real. I think it must have been real. It seems like that little girl is being careful about something. There are several strange women that are pleading to be chosen. But I think the people that should be chosen don't want to be. Does that even make sense?" She sighed in frustration, feeling like if she were bright at all, she would be able to figure it out. And right now, with Alex she wanted to be bright!

As they approached the steps of her brownstone, she asked, "Did this all really happen? I mean, did Mani's memories transfer to me by his touch?"

His eyes narrowed, "What do you think?"

"I think it really did happen." Alex shrugged it off. Valeria reached hesitantly for Alex's hand. She was certain she saw something in his eyes. "Why did you need Mani?" She watched Alex, aware of his scrutiny. He seemed to be pulled in because of her touch. "You have memories you don't want me to see." Alex's eyes dropped a degree.

He put his other hand on her's, a deep sadness coming to his beautiful blue eyes, "Yes." Then he started them both up the stairs to her door. "But you'll need to see them anyway."

As they entered her home, she suddenly realized how odd it was that she should let this stranger in. But she couldn't even conceive of him leaving.

"Your birthday is in five days?" He asked. Valeria nodded, surprised how his nearness took her breath away. Alex continued, "Then you'll need to pack a bag." He pressed and then his lips turned up in a gentle smile. Alex held his breath. He didn't want to reveal more than he already had.

Cocking her head to the side, Valeria's mind felt completely scrambled! She couldn't just meet someone and run off like this. This wasn't like her—she was stable girl. She didn't fall for men she just met. In fact she didn't *fall* for men...well except for David. Valeria thought for a moment—really her relationship with David had been carefully planned *by* David. She guessed that despite the fact that she, of course, loved David, that their relationship had happened more calmly—probably more the way things should go! And then without permitting herself to evaluate the situation, Valeria said, "Okay."

She pulled out her suitcase from under her bed while Alex meandered around her apartment. "Is this you?"

Valeria glanced out from the bedroom and saw Alex holding the only personal picture she owned. "Yes. That's me and my father." She shook her head, "I don't know why I keep it." It was the only picture she had of her childhood; her and her dad at Christmas the year before he died. It was her dad's last stand playing Santa. He loved playing Santa. It was as close to a father as he ever got.

Noticing Alex's pleased expression, Valeria asked, "What should I bring?" She wondered again why on earth she was letting this man with the beautiful blue eyes into her brownstone—let alone packing to go away with him.

"Comfortable...casual—really, whatever you would like." He replied. "So...where are the rest of your pictures?" Alex carried the small picture frame with him as he brushed his hand over the injured rib.

"Uhmm. Well, that's really about it."

Coming into the kitchen area, he winced at the formal portrait of David. *This must be the boyfriend,* Alex thought. He didn't like the guy—he looked arrogant. Alex thought it was a good sign that there were no romantic pictures of the two of them. "No school pictures?" He asked as he brushed his fingers through his hair.

"Oh..." Valeria's voice came from the bedroom, "No. I didn't really see any reason. Pictures are for other people and I didn't want to pay for them."

"Hmm." Alex responded and then removed the picture of Valeria and her father from the frame, placing it in his coat pocket. He might need it later.

Valeria went to her closet. "Comfortable" would be sweats or jeans and a tee shirt or sweater. She grabbed a token pair of sweats and a single tee shirt and then finished with a few pairs of nice slacks and jeans. Then she went to her closet and pulled out two of her favorite cotton dresses that appeared casual while enhancing her figure—so she had heard. She wondered how many days she was packing for, but didn't want to ask any questions.

"Val, mind if I look at your music collection?" Alex asked, raising his voice so she could hear.

Peeking her head out of her bedroom, she said, "Go ahead."

Sorting through her lingerie drawer, Valeria realized with disgust that she had nothing but cotton—nothing even remotely sexy. She bit her lip and then felt completely irritated with herself for searching for sexy underwear. *What was wrong with her*? Had she suddenly become like those girls that she abhorred? Valeria finished packing and came out of her bedroom with her suitcase in hand, still wondering what she was possibly thinking going away with him.

She found Alex still scanning her music shelf. She bit her lip and sighed. Alex sensed her presence and turned. "Tim McGraw to Jason Mraz, from Bach to Boney James, I see you are a Puccini fan; you are eclectic aren't you!" His eyes shined with admiration causing Valeria to flush again.

"I just like what I like…I guess."

Alex grabbed her suitcase from her. Valeria thought she noticed a frozen moment as their hands touched but decided it was her imagination. "Where are we going?"

"Italy—got your passport?"

Even as Valeria grabbed her passport and her purse, she wondered what the hell she was doing. But then Alex looked at her with his dazzling blue eyes that seemed to bewitch her. And although she thought, if she were wise she would say something else, all she could do was say, "Alright," as she turned off the light and locked the door.

CHAPTER 6

The car wove along the rolling hills of Northern Italy with Alex and Valeria relaxed and enjoying the view. Valeria thought how odd—she couldn't recall feeling this at ease with anyone in all of her life. She allowed herself a glance at Alex and couldn't imagine what someone like him, so perfectly...perfect, saw in her. No one else saw anything in her that remotely equated to special. In fact, if anything, the responses she had received most of her life were more closely likened to quite the opposite. As Alex sensed her gaze, he turned towards her slightly and the corners of his mouth turned up in the most delightful way that caused a charge in her heart.

Valeria continued to mull over the images that Mani had given her and was still trying to make some sense of them. She knew she should be trying to make sense of her loss of sensibility: to meet a man and hours later get on an international flight with him. She just didn't *do* that kind of thing. Yet here she was, in Europe, with a man she had met less than 24 hours before. Maybe the near-death experience had transformed her. Valeria nearly laughed out loud at that thought.

The previous afternoon Alex had secured them first class tickets for a flight from JFK to Milan, Italy. During the flight, Alex asked Valeria numerous questions about her least favorite subject—her. While answering the questions and trying to discover more about him, she noticed that the flight attendant referred to Alex as if they were lifelong friends after only a few minutes, but remained coolly professional with Valeria. Perhaps that was Alex's gift. She had certainly warmed up to him quickly! What was particularly disconcerting was that he didn't seem to be aware of his effect on women! He just seemed terribly interested…mostly in her! In fact, every time Valeria would try to discover his story, Alex would give her a quick answer, and then would turn the subject back to her. She didn't sense that he was avoiding talking about himself. More, that he seemed to be absolutely delighted by every aspect of her life; regardless of how uninteresting it seemed to her.

When Valeria would notice Alex looking away for a moment, she would wonder if he was laughing at her little life, so devoid of…life. But then he would gaze at her with that look in his eyes of absolute delight and she would scold herself for doubting him.

She told him about building her florists shop out of her own tiny apartment. After several years, her creativity had won her the florist contracts at Waldorf Astoria and several other posh New York hotels. She told Alex she had been absolutely stunned to receive the staggering buy-out offer months ago. She would have turned it down, except that she had never wanted to manage others. Really, she had preferred her small business—except for the part where she worried about paying her rent and eating! Alex wasn't like the rest, who had questioned her sanity when she suggested she preferred her small life before she went corporate.

"What's next for you?" Alex asked.

"I don't know. I've been asking myself that same question!"

Time and location all seemed to blur together while Valeria was with him. She tried to analyze why that was. So much about Alex, and her response to him, was foreign to her. They had been talking almost all night without either showing the least sign of tiring, when the subject of books came up and Alex's face lit with a new excitement.

"So what's your favorite?" Alex eyes narrowed inquisitively.

"Why is it that people think you have to have only *one* favorite?" Valeria teased. "Okay, favoritest...I'd have to say *To Kill a Mockingbird*. I love how she conveys the concepts of prejudice and ignorance. I think it's a story that changed how people thought about the mentally ill and race." She paused and cocked her head to the side, "Such a beautifully told story! If I could write, I'd want to write like her."

Alex tapped his little finger lightly on the armrest of the first class seat in agreement, "I love that story myself. I enjoy reading *Walden*. It sits so close to my heart: 'For what are the classics but the noblest recorded thoughts of man.' Fantastic! And by the way, I definitely agree that one can never have too many favorites.

"Favorite author?" Alex asked.

"Hands down, Jane Austen." Valeria said. "Harper Lee would have been…"

Alex smiled and added with Valeria in unison, "…if she had written more than the one novel." They both laughed.

"But Jane Austen seems to be writing about women from

an enlightened viewpoint in a time when women weren't really appreciated as anything more than ornaments or domestic help. Did you know that she had to publish *Sense and Sensibility* anonymously? In those years, authors were warned against challenging the status quo."

Alex narrowed his eyes in thought, "Let's see, wasn't that about the same time as the Thomas Paine trial?"

Valeria nodded, as she became mesmerized by his eyes. "I...I believe so." She would have to look away to talk intelligently. She shook her head, "Did I say, 'I believe so?'" She laughed nervously, "I'm sorry—actually I don't know anything about Thomas Paine." She confessed as a flush overtook her face.

Swallowing her embarrassment, she continued. "What were we talking about?" She asked. "Oh. Jane Austen's characters...they seemed to know their own value even if no one else did. And despite her feminism, her books are filled with just the most delicious romance!" Valeria made the mistake of meeting his eyes—and she was lost again.

Longing to reach over and take her face in his hands, Alex clasped his hands to keep him from moving too fast. Now was not the time! As he might with a skittish fawn, he would wait for her to come to him. "I'll have to read more of her work!" He sighed, "I'm a fan of Aristotle and Dickens, Homer, Hawthorne; Too many authors."

"You're an Ancient History Professor and yet no Plato?"

Alex shrugged, "I love *The Cave*. But I disagree with Plato that forms exist beyond and outside the ordinary range of human understanding. I believe the human mind is capable of amazing feats! But enough about me." Valeria noticed Alex perform his now typical turnabout to her interests...again.

As they exited baggage claims, a valet pulled up with an ocean blue Porsche Panamera. The valet almost clicked his heels as he nearly ran to open Valeria's door. She slipped into the tan leather seat. It was the most comfortable car seat she'd ever sat on. The valet loaded the luggage into the trunk and she noticed that Alex tipped him well before slipping into the driver's seat.

One thing she knew was that he didn't skimp on tips! Valeria hated that David would assess the perfect percentage; never adjusting it based on quality of service, and then round down. Her father had been worse! He used to toss a dollar or some coins down on the table regardless of the check. Or worse, ask her if she had any change!

Before pulling out from the airport, Alex turned to Valeria and brushed his hand over her hair. She felt electrified by his touch and was too tired and weak to turn away. They sat for a long moment just staring—the electricity getting so heavy that Valeria again wondered what was wrong with her. Alex smiled softly, "You look tired."

She smiled sleepily in response. Valeria was surprised how easily her face rolled into his hand. Alex winked at her, "No worries." He took a short breath, "I want you to be able to enjoy the drive. I thought we would stop so you could get some sleep and clean up." He brushed his beautiful jaw line. "I know I could use a shower and shave."

"Okay." Valeria whispered, drawing in a deep breath.

Alex pulled expertly into the lane and drove only a few miles before signaling into a beautiful country estate turned hotel. She wished that she were more awake to appreciate it. As they pulled around the circular drive, stopping in front of the hotel her door was opened by a uniformed doorman and Valeria suddenly felt shy. She felt grungy from the road and too sleepy to make any decisions about her and Alex.

She knew other women jumped in bed with men far less entrancing than Alex. But she wasn't other women! And if this was a romantic trip—and Valeria had her doubts—she would need time to think about it and to get to know him better. And right now she felt so exhausted and felt like she needed a shower and rest. Her anxiety built and she was almost in tears, until she saw the clerk hand Alex two keys and saw their luggage held by two separate bellmen. Valeria watched nervously while Alex walked with her to the elevator. Then he leaned over and his lips momentarily brushed her cheek—creating again, that now familiar electricity, before he stepped back off the elevator.

Alex smiled as if he saw her thoughts, "I'll be in my room. Sleep until you're done and give me a ring when you're ready. It's another three hours to Morgana. Don't sleep too long." He winked, "I'd like for you to be able to see the drive."

As the elevator door closed, suddenly Valeria's emotions flipped and she was surprised that she was now feeling disappointed that Alex hadn't wanted her or at least hadn't even tried to stay with her. She found herself pouting all the way to the elegant room. The bellman unloaded her luggage and she was about to tip him but he was gone before she could think that fast. She sat on the edge of the bed as her world began buzzing around her in her exhaustion. She laid back and closed her eyes for a moment. When she opened them the light from the window changed and Valeria realized it must be afternoon.

She picked up the phone and tried to recall Alex's last name. But the operator didn't seem to require any information and connected her to Signore Morgan's room. Alex Morgan was his name. What a nice name, she thought.

Answering his phone on the first ring, Alex said he would see her downstairs when she was ready. There was a knock at her door and it was room service with fresh fruit, warm brioche and cheese. Valeria ate a strawberry and found she was famished. She ate every bite before jumping in the shower. She dried her hair and realized that this was the first time she had dressed for a date with Alex. She pulled out her favorite cotton dress. Not wanting to take too much time, she pulled her hair into a ponytail and brushed on some blush, mascara and lip gloss before heading downstairs.

Alex had showered and changed, wearing a greenish gray V-neck shirt, blue jeans and a sports jacket. Valeria was careful not to comment on how much she enjoyed his wonderful scent or how incredibly handsome he looked.

They drove through the countryside and Valeria felt a thrill as she saw the sign, "Verona! I've always wanted to go there!"

Alex smiled, "Home of Romeo and Juliet."

She beamed as Alex touched her shoulder, "I thought we would have an early dinner here, if that's all right with you, before heading on up the hill."

"Up the hill? I guess I should ask: where are we going?"

"I'm sorry. I thought I'd bring you to meet my family at our home near Trento called Morgana."

"Morgana?" Valeria drew her eyebrows together. "As in Morgan? The estate must have been named after your family."

Alex winked a smile, "Other way around! The name came from the estate before there were last names. Morgana was the wife of the original owner. When she passed away, their son named it for her."

"Your family is Italian? You don't have a hint of an accent."

Alex smiled, as he easily parallel parked on a cobblestone street. "I've spent much of my life traveling. I guess I've developed the ability to pick up subtleties in languages and dialects."

"So...I'm going to meet your family?" One thing Valeria was absolutely certain of was how she felt about meeting Alex's family—mortified! She hadn't even met David's family yet! She was particularly concerned with what they would think of her. Especially if that family had any concept of whom Alex was.

"Well, we aren't related, that way. We are related by common experience. But we are closer than family. They are looking forward to officially meeting you."

Somehow she knew there was some kind of business that had to take place. She had gotten that idea from what had happened with Mani. But what it was exactly she hadn't bothered to find out.

The breeze was a teasing shimmer on the air, calming Valeria. It smelled rich with grapes and Italian cookery. They sat in a beautiful courtyard with Italian music playing softly and drank wine and ate Caprese con mozzarella and warm bread with olive oil. Alex offered his arm to her as they strolled the narrow cobblestone streets of the ancient town, barely surviving a swarm of brightly colored Vespa motorscooters with women in business suits and helmets.

"Would you like to see where Juliet lived?" Alex queried, mischievously.

"Juliet was fictional." Valeria smiled.

"Maybe. But she has a home and a museum here. Would

you like to see it?" Valeria nodded.

It was a romantic tour, Valeria thought, as an opera singer sang from Juliet's balcony. Then they wandered, wonderfully and without purpose until Alex guided Valeria into a small antique shop where the shopkeeper greeted Alex by name. Eyeing the extravagances casually, Valeria saw a beautiful Limoges box with forget-me-nots painted on all sides. Alex nodded to the clerk, who took the box and placed it in a bag with several lengths of fragrant dried flowers. Valeria looked to Alex in surprise. He winked and smiled to thank the shopkeeper. Valeria saw the exchange of looks and caught herself wondering how many women Alex Morgan had brought to Verona. But jealousy was an unknown feeling for her.

Back in the car, Alex loaded a carefully chosen selection of romantic songs by Jason Mraz. His romantic guitar and beautiful vocals filled the air as they drove into the foothill of the Alps.

The fall colors were particularly spectacular as they gained elevation. It was early evening as Alex, driving like a professional racecar driver through the sharp mountain curves, finally turned off the highway onto a private tree-lined road. He pulled the car to the front of a beautiful stone and wood cottage that was lit by what appeared to be firelight, as if someone were there.

Alex jumped out and opened Valeria's door. They walked past a mass of hydrangeas that seemed to surround the house and up the stone steps, onto the cedar deck with a porch swing and flowerboxes. Valeria noticed the details of the door, it was a double cedar door hand carved with iron loops and an intricate design that looked like two large C's facing each other. Alex took a deep breath and swung open the door.

Valeria's eyes got even larger as her mouth fell open with a sigh.

"Alex! This is…" She turned to him. "I don't even know how to describe it—breathtaking doesn't seem to be enough."

Leaning on the door frame, Alex glowed, as he watched Valeria with what she thought might be nervousness. She looked up with awe at the wood beams high above her and the wrought iron candelabra's on each wall. Wandering across the great room, she brushed her hand over the massive library full of leather bound classics. Valeria noticed at eye-level *Sense and Sensibility* and *Walden*. The other wall was home to a stack stone fireplace that was already ablaze and encircled by a deep brown, leather couch, a loveseat and two leather chairs. The floors were dark and spotted with colorful rugs.

Arriving at the marble kitchen island, she moved her hands over the hanging pots and pans and noticed the state of the art steel appliances. Not that they would do her much good. She had never been much of a cook. She also noted the door-less arch to the bedroom. Carrying the remainder of their bags, Alex dropped his by the door and continued with Valeria's suitcase towards the bedroom.

Suddenly feeling awkward, she wondered if Alex understood what a big step it was for her, just going away with him. The expectation might be that she was ready for intimacy but for some reason, she didn't feel that was the case. Valeria knew Weege would call her naïve. Especially if Weege could see this extraordinary cottage, with this extraordinary man, who certainly had never been told 'no' before!

She followed him into the bedroom, nervously and watched as Alex sat her suitcase on a bench at the foot of the four-poster feather bed. "Here's your room." He said uncomfortably. "There's the bath and there's the closet." He indicated a walk-in and abruptly exited back into the great room.

"I hope you don't mind but tonight I'll be sleeping on the couch." Alex brushed his hand through his hair, obviously ill-at-ease. "Sorry, I didn't have a chance to make other arrangements."

Feeling unexpectedly let down again, Valeria realized that suddenly the feeling of intimacy was gone and this romantic setting seemed wasted. She followed him back to the great room and into the kitchen area.

"The others are up the hill at the main house. Lars thought it might be good to give you a night to yourself. So, I thought I would pour you a glass of wine while I meet with them. You can bathe or sit on the porch." Alex anxiously sucked in a deep breath and hesitated before exhaling. "But don't worry; we'll be keeping an eye out to make sure your safe." He said as he pulled the bottle out from under the marble counter.

"You're leaving? Won't you join me for a glass of wine?"

"No." Alex said absentmindedly, as his hands fumbled with a task that was typically simple, and finally released the cork with a pop. "I need to stay sharp."

Valeria could barely hide her disappointment. "I guess I'm surprised you are leaving. You drink wine don't you? Yes. You drank today."

"Yes and I really shouldn't have. I guess I got caught up in the..." Alex's voice faded as he took a wine glass from a cupboard. "I drink occasionally. I like Scotch. I'd join you, but as I said, I really need to stay sharp."

"Why?"

"You'll understand later."

The pinging of the wine on the glass told Valeria that this was very fine crystal–not that she knew much about fine crystal. But she knew she hadn't heard that sound before. Alex came around the counter to where Valeria was standing by the fireplace. He passed the glass to her, being careful not to make contact with her hand. Then he immediately went to stir the fire averting his eyes from hers.

"It's just for a few hours. But I'll be keeping an eye out. So you don't need to worry about anything." Alex put his hands in his pockets for something to do with them. "Just make yourself at home."

Valeria felt the sting of disappointment as Alex went out the door. Why had he left? He brought her to this beautiful place and then deserts her? What was going on and why was she here? Her head spun in answerless circles. And that comment about someone keeping an eye on her? She didn't need anyone keeping an eye on her! She had done quite well for most of her life keeping an eye on herself. Granted, she would have been squashed yesterday if not for him. But that didn't mean she was an imbecile or incapable of defending herself!

The irritation seceded as she took her first sip of the wine. It was very good! Valeria opened her suitcase and took out her toiletries and journal. She knew she should hang up her clothes but instead, she laid back on the bed, setting her wine down on the table and stared into the fire.

She wrote in her journal, "I met a man." And then her eyes closed for a moment and she was out.

She dreamed of *him*—she dreamed of him holding her in this bed.

Somewhere during the night Valeria felt a blanket cover

her. Later her eyes opened to see Alex there. But her mind drifted back to sleep, determining that she had dreamed the past twenty-four hours. In her near dream state, Valeria thought she saw a beautiful, redheaded woman sitting with Alex drinking a glass of wine. Her arm touched his as if there was an intimacy between them. Valeria caught some of the conversation but was too tired to process any of it and rapidly drifted back off to a deep slumber.

She woke several times through the night and again thought she saw Alex watching her.

CHAPTER 7

"Good morning." Alex said a bit roughly. "I'm sorry to wake you, but the family is waiting for us."

"What?" Valeria, startled, threw open her eyes and bolted straight up in bed. She had a moment when she wondered where she was, and then with some embarrassment, realized that she was in Alex's bed. Her next thoughts had to do with her appearance; she cringed as she realized her ponytail had fallen, with stray hairs all around her face and probably smudged mascara under her eyes. She quickly tried to pull her hair out of the ponytail and then realized she was fully dressed. She noticed Alex looking awkwardly at her. He was already showered and dressed but carried a hint of stress in his eyes.

"I'm sorry. I didn't mean to barge in on you like this." He let out a nervous sigh, "I really should have put in a door here." Alex seemed to be internally kicking himself. "If you're up to it, the family is up the hill at the main house waiting for us."

There was an odd mood stirring in her. One she wasn't familiar with. To Valeria's surprise, she realized that she was upset with him. Though she knew it was ridiculous—she could not think of a reasonable reason for her mood. Pressing her lips together in thought, she wondered if this was what people meant when they spoke of waking up on the wrong side of the bed. She always woke feeling at least somewhat pleasant, so there must be a reasonable explanation!

Then it hit her! The redheaded woman! And now Valeria's upset became anger. Did Alex really ditch her here—at this beautifully romantic cottage to go meet another woman? Then just as suddenly, the content of the words the redhead had said began to take shape.

"Alex, you must know she is expecting more from you!" The redhead had said.

Valeria thought, how does this woman know ANYTHING about me? Valeria tried to recall Alex's response—why hadn't she paid more attention?

Then the redhead had laughed in a condescending manner, "Just look at her! She's in your bed for Christ's sakes! What do you think she expects?"

Now Valeria was not only angry, but mortified that she was in fact in this man's bed!

Despite her outrage and humiliation, deep down she knew that it all made more sense; this was a platonic relationship and Alex had left to make love to the beautiful redhead. She was probably his wife and was wondering why a strange woman was sleeping in her bed! And now, Valeria needed to get a grip on the fact that although there seemed to be something more—Alex was just a friend. Maybe he had brought her here—all the way from New York—to fix her up with a friend, who knows! Although, Italy didn't seem to have ANY shortage of beautiful women for set-up's.

Besides, Valeria was reminding herself with irritation, she was engaged! What the hell was she doing running off with another man? And why had it NEVER occurred to her to ask Alex where exactly they were going or why? Valeria felt beyond ridiculous!

Then Alex made the perfectly marvelous amend that improved her disposition, slightly. He swallowed and stepped into the bedroom, "I'm sorry for intruding but…well…here." He handed her a cup of coffee, in a perfectly sized mug.

Valeria saw the blanket over her and realized Alex had covered her. She pushed it off, grabbing the cup and Alex quickly turned. She glanced down and saw that her dress had pulled up in her sleep, revealing most of her thigh. She quickly pulled the blanket up and her dress down—feeling her face flush deep purple. A look at Alex told her that he most definitely had noticed and had covered her to save her embarrassment.

Wow, Valeria thought, she was not one for black moods, but one certainly had bit her this morning. She attempted a smile. But Alex had retreated from the room and seemed to be cooking in the kitchen. It smelled wonderful but coffee was one thing, enjoying ANYTHING else he prepared was simply condoning this whole, awful situation!

Sipping the dark brew, Valeria appreciated the perfect ratio of cream to coffee and then it hit her—this was the absolute perfect cup of coffee! She took a deep breath and her eyes rolled into her head in bliss. "Thank you!" She said apologetically, loud enough for Alex to hear it.

She heard Alex, sounding distracted say, "Sure."

Alex's wife must be upset that she had fallen asleep—or that Alex had volunteered their bed. Valeria glanced at the clock on the side of the table and saw it was after ten o'clock in the morning. They had arrived at seven the previous evening and she was asleep within the hour. That was a record amount of sleep for her.

Fighting the urge to throw on a pair of sweats and a wrinkled tee shirt, Valeria grabbed a white blouse and jeans from her suitcase and showered and changed. She didn't need to be that nervous now. Alex was most certainly sloughing her off on some ne'er do well friend or brother. She would thank Alex and explain that she was engaged to a diplomat and really wasn't so desperate that she needed to fly half way around the damn world—escorted at that—to find a man!

Pulling her wet hair into a ponytail, Valeria resisted the hair dryer. She was aware that it was only a desperate attempt to prove that she didn't really care how she looked. Still vanity forced her to add a touch of make-up. She sighed, wanting to disappear from this picture. It was one thing to look awful; another altogether to look like you didn't care how you looked.

When Valeria stepped out of the bedroom, having made the bed and folded the blanket, Alex had an extraordinary breakfast set out for her with fresh squeezed orange juice, a half grapefruit, frittata and all kinds of pastries. Their smells wafted into Valeria's head and she could feel the pangs in her stomach. But she wouldn't for the life of her let Alex believe for an instant that this incredibly luscious display of food would change anything.

So what if he was this *incredibly* nice looking…incredibly caring guy that she could *so* easily fall for. Valeria watched as Alex turned to get jam from the refrigerator. She realized that Alex wasn't just nice looking, he really was *beautiful*! Even now, it was work to avoid a swoon. But with his obvious game-playing and girlfriend or wife or whatever the redhead was,

Valeria decided to play it cool. Besides, she thought, even if there was a competition—which their wasn't—the redhead was far more beautiful than Valeria's simple looks. She saw the empty bottle of wine on the counter and the empty glass that confirmed that the redhead was real.

"I'll just have the coffee. But I'd like a refill." Valeria said, grabbing a croissant, not wanting Alex to know that she enjoyed any of it. He took her coffee and dumped it into a metal cup, filled it to the top and screwed on the cover, handing it back to her. She thanked him and walked towards the door letting him know she was finished.

As he nodded hesitantly, Alex placed the juice back in the refrigerator, and then followed Valeria to the door and helped her on with her light coat as they stepped onto the deck. The air was a pleasant fall crisp—not as cool as New York. The sun fettered down through the golden, red and green trees, in a lacy pattern, with the music of birds happily chirping. Valeria took a deep breath and the air smelled so fresh and felt so delightful that somehow, instantly, her mood improved.

Stepping down from the deck onto the rich ground in front of the cottage, Valeria continued to take in her surroundings noticing the heavy woods of evergreens juxtaposed with brightly colored deciduous trees. Alex led her around the corner of the house and Valeria's jaw dropped.

"What is it?" She said, wishing she could hide her enthusiasm. And then she answered her own question, "Gingko?" She glanced to Alex and then ran to the tree. It was a giant, with beautiful even branches all covered, like a fairy tale, with red, yellow and green triangular leaves erupting from every portion of the branch, as opposed to just the ends of the branches, like most trees. Valeria was certain it was the most beautiful tree she had seen in all of her life!

In an instant, Valeria started to feel sad; she would have loved to see this incredible tree in these breathtaking woods in spring and summer—and even in winter. The amazing cottage that was everything that she would want…and the man… No! She wouldn't think about the man, not now.

With just a hint of a tear, Valeria sighed and swallowed back her overwhelm at the achingly beautiful location—and the man. They walked through the woods in silence as she followed Alex onto a trail that wound around giant Beech and Chestnut trees, with the density of trees darkening the woods. Valeria noticed lights along the edges of the trail and hoped she would have the opportunity to wander the trail at night.

Within minutes, the sunlight was obscured by the wooded canopy and then they stepped to the end of the trail and Valeria saw the 'main house', which looked more like a ski resort than a house with its river stone and redwood. It was breathtaking. There was a giant deck in front where a magnificent arched entry displayed equally magnificent doors.

Alex led her up the stairs and onto the deck and through the front door. She stepped onto the golden travertine floors noticing the large woven area rugs in hues of red, blue and gold with American Indian designs. She stared up at the thirty foot cathedral ceilings and caught the log staircase that wrapped around the edge of the living area, with black wrought iron accents that appeared to lead to bedrooms in the back of the house. Valeria glanced at the enormous river stone fireplace, with mission-style rocking chairs, and two long leather sofas extending from the fireplace, with a leather ottoman serving as the coffee table.

She noticed the cushions and blankets that perfectly matched the colors of the rugs. Valeria moved to the full wall of windows in the front of the living area. On the other side of the door, across from the living area she saw a long dark wood table. Stepping to it, Valeria ran her hand along it and noticed the upholstered chairs in the matching shade of red with thin, light blue stripes. From the dining room Valeria could get a peek at the kitchen from the pass-through window. And as in the living area, the front wall was all windows looking out on the woods. Valeria thought she could almost see part of the cottage from the window.

A dark-haired boy of about 12 came in from the kitchen, smiling brightly. "Hi! I'm Caleb." He walked towards Valeria, extending his hand, with a mischievous smile. Valeria heard both Alex and a woman's voice anxiously, admonish the boy, "Caleb!"

Caleb tucked his hands into his pockets before bounding off to one the rocking chairs by the fireplace, "I wasn't really going to do it! I just wanted to see what you guys would do!" Caleb pushed the chair to force it to rock.

Before Valeria could respond, a tall, beautiful black woman with long, straight hair and bright blue, cupie doll eyes entered, "Good Morning! I'm Camille".

"Nice to meet you both, I'm—," Valeria started and was immediately interrupted by the redhead with her overly bored, British accent.

"We got the message. You're Valeria." The comment was a blow-off.

The redhead was even more beautiful than Valeria had remembered, with brilliant green eyes and a creamy complexion. The redhead went directly to Alex and leaned her elbow on his shoulder, possessively. She seemed to be ensuring that Valeria was watching. But other than that, the redhead avoided Valeria.

Camille rolled her eyes at the redhead and continued pleasantly, "Valeria it's very nice to finally meet you!"

The redhead added, "Again," and Valeria noticed both Alex and Camille glaring at the redhead in unspoken words. The redhead responded with an irritated expression as if they had actually spoken to her and moved to take a seat on the couch.

"Oh and that's Daphne." Camille added pointing at the redhead.

The redhead now had a name.

Noting Daphne's 'again', Valeria decided that Daphne was talking about the previous evening when Valeria had fallen asleep in Alex's bed. She decided that she would get her courage up and apologize to Daphne when they had a moment alone. Valeria had the urge to also defend herself that Alex had said it was where she should sleep, but decided that would only cause more problems. She decided that she would take responsibility for falling asleep there—though Valeria didn't expect a good response. Daphne seemed like the kind of woman that would hold a grudge. It was difficult to imagine such a kind man as Alex married to a woman like that. With a side glance, Valeria found herself observing their hands and neither wore a ring.

A boyishly handsome man, with blond curls, a light, freckled complexion and the frame of a football player entered with an air of confidence that struck Valeria as the leader.

"Valeria, I'm Lars." His eyes sparkled with vibrance, as he offered his hand, "And we are all very pleased to meet you officially."

Loud footsteps could be heard coming down the stairs. She turned to see a tall bearded man with dark gray hair and an irritated expression. He came in and leaned against the fireplace mantel. Valeria thought with a grimace, so that's the one that can't get a date. Alex pointed to him, "That's Tavish."

Tavish grumbled a hello.

Caleb laughed, "Tavish is upset because Camille told him he couldn't wear his kilt." Valeria thought, no wonder Alex had to bring her all the way from New York. Poor Tavish's disposition would run off most women.

"It is my traditional dress!" Tavish snorted.

"Yes, but it is inappropriate for this informal setting. We don't want to scare poor Valeria too badly." Camille said.

Lifting himself up, Caleb said, "Yeah, but you have to admit it is fun when a breeze comes up and..." Caleb indicated the kilt rising up on Tavish and mimicked him trying to pull it down. Tavish rolled his eyes in irritation with a sarcastic laugh escaping the side of his mouth.

Camille gave Caleb a look that silenced him and then she gestured to Valeria, "Please Valeria, have a seat!" Camille pointed to the loveseat near Alex. Valeria went to sit down and noticed that Alex made sure that he didn't sit by her.

Lars began, "Valeria, I guess we need to fill you in on why we are all here. I guess you have heard some of it. I understand you met Mani." Alex's attention was locked on Lars. "So, I'm just going to jump into it." Lars continued, as he sat on the leather ottoman in front of Valeria, "Obviously we have a purpose and you are principal to that purpose. But for you to understand what must be done and why we are here, I believe it's important for you to first understand the history of the situation." Lars drew a deep breath. "I want to warn you that this is not going to be easy. It's going to require that you open your mind to other realities." Lars waited for Valeria's nod. "Let's suffice it to say that we have a common enemy and if we all work together we can eliminate the threat."

"I don't understand, is it some disease? Are you looking for money? I can probably help." Valeria offered.

"No." Lars attempted to hide his mild amusement before continuing, "It's a man."

Oh God! Valeria thought—they really are trying to fix me up with some man! Glancing at Tavish, his eyes met hers and his face appeared to be in battle with all side of his face shaking and shimmying until at last the right side of his mouth popped up, followed by the left side in what appeared to be a smile...or a sneer. She quickly looked away, trying to hide her horror.

She tried not to look Alex in the eye. Lars continued, "Valeria, we all owe you a great deal of gratitude for what you did for us." He looked to Alex, "Lexi, does she remember?"

Valeria thought, GREAT—Lars is starting with gratitude! She decided that she would make certain they ALL knew she was happily engaged...and to a handsome diplomat! She didn't need their pitiful attempts at setting her up with anyone!

"She's had a familiarization with Mani but we've had no significant discussion as of yet."

"Familiarization? Is that what you call it?" Valeria queried Lars. She tried to think of something in the vision that would indicate who Alex was setting her up with—feeling absolutely ridiculous. Valeria worked, somewhat unsuccessfully on her poker face, which she had been told by Weege that she did not possess.

Lars nodded, "Yes. Let's talk about what you saw. Do you remember the situation? Does any of it seem familiar to you?"

Valeria drew her eye brows together and looked up, trying to recall the entire scene, "You know, some of the people seem somewhat familiar."

"You wouldn't forget me!" Caleb said, his smile taking up most of his face.

"I didn't see you in the vision." Valeria said, conversationally. Then seeing Caleb frown, Valeria added, "But I'm certain I wouldn't forget you."

Caleb let out a joyous laugh of vindication, "SWEET! Told ya!" He pulled his arm down in a fist of victory.

Daphne piped up, "Caleb, you weren't even there!" Caleb ignored her.

After thinking about the vision, Valeria said, "There was a little boy in Mani's vision, the boy was maybe five, with blond curls. I guess he looks a bit like you, Lars?" Lars nodded. "And you." Valeria pointed to Daphne. "You were there. But you look about the same age."

Laughing coolly, Daphne refused to speak directly to Valeria, "I'm ageless. That's why." Daphne aimed the comment at Camille, who gave her a disapproving look.

"I guess that's all." Valeria said

Lars nodded and then looked to Alex, "Lexi?"

Valeria noticed a hint of disappointment cross Alex's face. He stroked his fingers through his hair and then nodded. "In that case…let's just…" He took a deep breath, "Let's jump into a history lesson." He narrowed his eyes, "Val, how familiar are you with Pre-classical antiquity? That's the period of Greek history prior to Homer." Alex said being careful not to gaze at her directly for more than a moment.

"Prior to Homer? Well, I read the Odyssey in high school.

But I don't remember much about it." Valeria answered.

"Well, all right. Let's begin with Apollo and the gods." Alex said as if he were beginning a class.

Valeria wrinkled her nose and looked to Lars, who she could actually make eye contact with, as opposed to Alex, whose glances sent her off to another world. "Gods? Are we talking fiction?" She was trying to follow where this was going. Who was this guy they were going to spring on her, *a history buff—or just ancient*? Valeria looked up to see Tavish's smile/sneer again. *This was going to be a long meeting!* Then Alex seemed to shift closer to Valeria.

"Back 3000 years ago, we *all* had more power. We were newer. We didn't expect that we couldn't do things. We expected magic to be all around us and available."

"Alex, I'm not certain what this is about, but why do I get the feeling you aren't speaking in generalities?"

Alex and Lars looked at each other. Alex raised an eyebrow and then gave a slight chuckle, "Sorry Val, I guess we didn't expect a comment like that so quickly." Alex winked.

The wink from Alex energized Valeria and she smiled; momentarily catching her breath.

"So you were talking about magic?" Valeria took a quick breath to recover. She wondered if her face flushed in that moment and if Daphne had noticed it. Of course, Daphne must be used to women being drawn to Alex.

"Yes. Magic!" Alex turned away from her for a moment and took a deep breath as well. When he turned back his game face had returned, "There were those who had tremendous power. Because of their strength they were the rulers of the land. But, strength and magic alone was not enough to make someone a god." Alex paused for effect. "It had to be written in the stars. So, if you were a very clever ruler, you found someone who could 'locate' you in the stars."

Caleb added with a laugh, "Celestial dot-to-dot! Want to see my drawing?"

"Not just yet, Caleb. Maybe you can show Val later." Alex instinctively sat on the ottoman in front of Valeria, "If you were written in the stars, you were a god!"

"That's interesting!" Valeria smiled. Alex found himself smiling back at Valeria, as he would any student, and then realized he had looked too long and quickly looked away.

"So the god, Apollo found this beautiful child, a princess of Troy, named Cassandra who had the gift of vision. In fact, her gift was more powerful than Apollo's oracle Myrdd and far more powerful than Apollo's priest, Aegemon."

"Are you telling me what I read, or what you teach, or is this something else?" Valeria asked.

Lars and Alex looked at each other, uncertain what to say again, when Camille jumped in.

"Valeria, it will all make more sense as you get the big picture. So I suggest for now, you just accept the facts as Alex presents them."

Valeria glanced a thanks to Camille. Lars nodded for Alex to continue. "Are you familiar with an oracle?"

"Isn't that a prophet? I remember in art class we studied the Sistine Chapel. Wasn't there an oracle and a sybil on the Sistine Chapel?"

Alex nodded, "Yes, on both accounts. An oracle was typically a prophet but could also be used to describe a prophetess. A sibyl was a prophetess or could be called a sibylline oracle. Their visions were considered divine. And in fact, there are actually 5 sibyls on the Sistine Chapel.

"Those names, oracle and sibyl, were also assigned to their prophesies. The Last Oracle, also sometimes called a Sibylline Oracle was the most powerful of all the oracles. She was also the author of the original *Sibylline Oracle* document, which disappeared not long after it was created.

"There are documents referred to as *The Sibylline Oracles*, that are considered to be original utterances from the sibyls. Those documents were created much later by other sibyls and have since been edited by various religious sects over the centuries."

Alex stopped to give Valeria a chance to absorb the information. "At first there was only one oracle, Myrdd, who was a very wise wizard. Apollo gifted Myrdd with the powers of vision." Alex smiled, momentarily entranced by Valeria's smile. "Apollo liked the effect that he created and so he blew into the stars—spreading 50 oracles around the world. Then he blew again and split those stars in half, creating perfect mates for his immortal oracles."

"But Apollo's priest, Aegemon was angry. Apollo had granted this gift to so many others and not to Aegemon, who had served Apollo so faithfully as a prophet. So, Apollo gifted Aegemon with immortality."

"Aegemon?" Valeria interrupted.

Lars nodded, "Our enemy."

"The robed man in the vision." Alex added. Valeria frowned, wondering how Lars and Daphne had aged so differently. They certainly were not twenty-five years apart now, as they were in the vision. But she had told Camille she would take it all in first. She was certain Alex would clarify her confusion.

"For Aegemon, having the gift wasn't good enough. He became enraged by the thought that others possessed powers that at one time had been only his. Aegemon used tarots to foretell the future. If Aegemon was wrong, he would blame the stars, or the general's for having changed their own fate.

"One day Aegemon had just delivered the message from the cards. At four years old, the little girl from Mani's vision, Cassandra, innocently re-read the cards with a different fate. Aegemon denied the child's accuracy, but as it came to pass, she was correct."

Alex rose and walked to the fireplace, "Aegemon realized that Cassandra had far more power of prophesy than he had.

"A few years later, Aegemon overheard Cassandra ask Apollo when the others like her would be arriving. Aegemon had seen a vision and was aware of a handful of true oracles that would cause him trouble. He ordered all the existing oracles to be brought to the court of Apollo and given the 'opportunity' to serve the court.

"All of the potential oracles from across Europe and Africa were brought to Apollo..." Alex walked back to Valeria, returning to his position on the ottoman and looked intensely into her eyes, "including a few of us." Alex paused to allow Valeria a chance to take in what he had just said.

She bit her lip, "You mean your ancestors, right? I know that's how European's talk; they say 'we' and they mean 10 generations before. That's what you mean. Right?" Valeria looked around the room.

She thought for a moment, "The vision I saw...was that what was happening? Was that Cassandra and Apollo?"

No one responded. Valeria started to laugh and again saw no one else laughing.

"That couldn't be true!"

Alex nervously held his breath.

The silence was deafening as Valeria took in this new reality. "Alex, did I misunderstand you? If I'm hearing you right...you are...I mean...that would mean that...what? You are over 3000 years old?"

Alex seemed to be carefully evaluating her response. Valeria narrowed her eyes and did some of her own evaluation; Lars, Alex and Camille seemed to be frozen, awaiting her reaction. Daphne stared at the fire. Caleb sat smiling, excited with the tension. Valeria had no idea what Tavish's expression meant; it appeared to be a cross between boredom and irritation.

Instinctively, Alex pulled Valeria's hands into his—giving her another flash of heat from the thrill of his touch. The move had been intended to calm her but it had quite the opposite effect. Alex took a deep breath and gazed gently into her eyes, "Yes, beautiful, we are."

Valeria knew she should be pondering the absurdity of what she just heard but despite her heart rate, she felt an almost tranquil haven; lost in Alex's beautiful blue eyes that seemed to bar her from rational thought and actions.

With all the force she could muster she turned away from his eyes to re-evaluate...well, as soon as she could force herself to breathe again.

Deliberating over the ludicrous concept that these people sitting in a room with her were over 3000 years old, made Valeria feel ridiculous. That can't be right! Still, she thought, these people didn't look like the kind of people to con her. She had first-hand knowledge of that kind of crowd. These people, even Tavish, seemed like they would be truthful. Valeria didn't want to pull her hands from Alex but she knew that until she did, her thinking would be colored by his touch. He released them, but she sensed, almost unwillingly.

With a clearer head she decided, these people weren't like anyone she had ever met—and she felt she could trust them implicitly. She decided to see where this was all heading and to reserve her judgment until later. She had the opportunity to look into Alex's eyes to respond. She was half afraid that she would get lost in them again and forget to answer with everyone—including Daphne— watching. But risking it, she grabbed the opportunity. They were the most remarkable blue—opening up the world where she could lose herself.

Smiling dreamily, Valeria sighed, "Alright." Then she swallowed and looked away.

Rising from her to collect his own thoughts, Alex turned and walked towards the fireplace. The critical data had been conveyed and she hadn't yet run from him, as he was certain she would. Alex had hoped that the transference would help to give her a new reality. And although Valeria hadn't realized the main purpose of the transference, she seemed willing to accept the concept of immortality.

Alex heard Lars say in his head, "Don't stop now—you're on a roll."

But Alex needed another few seconds to collect himself. He had needed to touch her—if only for the fear that it would be his last opportunity before she left. Alex had looked into her eyes and imagined what it would be like to touch her face and hold her in his arms. But that was a luxury he couldn't enjoy just now.

"Lexi, do you need me to take over?" Lars asked.

Valeria watched as Alex remained turned from her. As

she wrestled with calming her own heart—for the first time, she wondered if Alex was doing the same. She noticed as he gave a slight shake of his head, before continuing.

She noticed Alex's voice was a bit hoarse, "Aegemon, so concerned with his own power and Apollo's trust in him, sent troops out to kidnap the oracles from their homes.

"Camille and a few others saw them coming. Most of us didn't. Some hid, but were betrayed by friends and neighbors.

"The first step was to have us identified by Cassandra as the true oracles. And then Aegemon had a predicament..." Alex cocked his head to the side and narrowed his eyes, "How do you maintain your power with more powerful beings?"

Valeria shrugged.

Camille jumped in, "The same way they do it today—you enslave them."

"You make them slaves or you simply...drug them." Lars added.

Alex nodded, "Even as a young child, Cassandra recognized Aegemon's intentions and protected us—selecting only those beings that were insane or already prone to rantings and would surely be put to death if not selected."

Lars jumped in, "Valeria, one thing to understand is that in ancient Greece it was believed that divine communication only occurred through drug-induced meditation.

"Mani suspects that it is the differences in our physical make-up that makes our reactions to mind-altering or psychotropic drugs more...devastating. For us, these drugs take on a whole new dimension creating what appears to be permanent damage."

Alex nodded, taking a moment to enjoy Valeria's face,

"Aegemon recognized this and used various methods to drug the other oracles so that their visions were transformed into gibberish. One of Aegemon's drugs was Ergot-infected grains. Ergot is a fungus that causes hallucinations and insanity.

"Later, it was discovered that cracks in the earth's crust in particular locations released Ethylene gasses, which created similar effects. Aegemon used these locations as holy sites and home to the various so-called oracles."

"Those women, who became known as the sibyls were mad or driven further into insanity from Aegemon's Ergot infested wines or from the Ethylene gasses, or both.

"Thanks to Cassandra the rest of us survived—at least *that* attempted purge."

Valeria turned her head to the side, "Alex, now that I think of it, were you there? There was a teen-aged boy that Cassandra seemed to be smiling at quite a lot." Valeria's eyes narrowed, "It's as if you share a secret." She thought for a moment, noticing Alex's chin and straight nose, "Yes, I think that was you."

Alex's eyes sparkled for an instant, "Yes. I was there." He turned again, feeling his heart begin to beat faster with hope.

Despite the fact that this was a little girl and Alex had been a little boy, Valeria found a tightening in her chest that she didn't understand and wondered if it was jealousy.

Alex heard Lars' voice again in his head, "She hasn't put it together. I think we should tell her."

"No. She can figure this out. We just need to give her some more time." Alex said silently to Lars.

"What are you afraid of?" Lars thoughts came to Alex.

The answer of course was everything! He had waited an

eternity for this moment. His gut told him that if he didn't give her the space to figure this out that she would doubt it all. Still he hadn't counted on the fact that she had invalidated her own beingness to the degree that she couldn't see the truth.

"Lexi, we only have days. We need to get to the point."

Alex shook his head, "Lars, I know she senses that there is something between her and I—she came with me! Let me try one more thing."

Daphne's thoughts interrupted, "Oh dear god! Alex, this is painful! The girl doesn't have the sense of—,"

"Daph, please! You aren't helping! Alex needs to go at his own pace!" Camille added to the non-verbal conversation.

Lars eyes narrowed as he looked at Alex and then stood, "Valeria, if you would forgive us, I think it might be helpful to give you a bit of time to process all this before continuing."

"Alright." Valeria could sense that there was a private discussion going on. She stood. "I guess that means that you want me to leave?"

"That might be best." Alex said, still not facing her. Valeria hadn't expected Alex to desert her again.

"Do you need someone to walk you back to the cottage?" Lars asked.

Valeria stared at Alex's back for a moment before he turned to face her. "I'll walk her back."

"I can find my way." Valeria walked out.

Ignoring her comment, he stepped out the door with her. The family discussion was upsetting him. But he would respond when he returned. As the door closed, Valeria noticed that the room erupted in heated conversation. Alex followed Valeria down the trail, placing his hand on the small of her back, giving her a brief hopeful moment when she thought perhaps Alex would join her.

He stopped on the trail near the cottage. "I'm sorry Val. This all *will* make more sense later." Alex said as he turned to go back up the path. "Help yourself to the books, or anything else you care for."

CHAPTER 8

"Some birthday week." Valeria muttered in complaint as soon as Alex was out of earshot. Then she immediately felt bad. She was in a spectacular place, with a spectacular guy—even if he did belong to someone else. She loved his company—no *appreciated*. Appreciating his company was safer.

Now, not only was this guy that she "appreciated" incredible, beyond words—now he was also supposedly *immortal*! Valeria rolled her eyes in disgust; the disparity between their attributes just continued to grow! She wondered why it was that she even considered this a possibility. She decided she would think about that later.

Valeria realized that the romantic feel to the previous days had given her hopes of much more—rather than Alex's actual words or actions. Well, except, he had asked her to go away with him...then deserted her, she reminded herself. She looked up to see the magnificent Gingko tree and felt slightly better.

Stepping inside the door of the cottage she discovered that the breakfast had been picked up. Valeria pulled the container of fruit out of the refrigerator. Her empty stomach had started complaining an hour before. She reached into the cupboard and pulled out a small bowl. The look and feel of it was far more extraordinary than her simple dinnerware. She noticed that the design matched the box that Alex had purchased for her in Verona. Valeria loaded some fruit into the bowl and then poured herself a glass of the orange juice. The strawberries and mango were fresh and flavorful. She tasted something in the mix of fruit…was it cinnamon? Valeria leaned against the counter while she ate.

What was it that she was supposed to comprehend from the discussion, Valeria wondered. She felt certain that Alex was waiting for her "aha moment" and she hated to disappoint him, but he was used to very bright college students. She had barely survived high school! Valeria thought about the image—there was something she felt that she should know, but her brain just didn't seem to be capable of putting it together.

She finished her bowl of fruit and washed and put away the dishes. Then took the glass of orange juice and went outside to sit on the porch swing. The temperature had warmed pleasantly.

An old man and woman appeared off the trail from the south with flower baskets. They smiled and spoke to each other in what Valeria thought to be Italian or Greek. They seemed to be saying something about her.

She wondered what Alex's purpose really was in bringing her here. And then there was the discussion about Greek gods…what was all that about? Valeria thought about the fact that they claimed to be over 3000 years old. She didn't think she could buy that. But she would continue to listen and take in what they had to say. She wasn't one to end a discussion because she was uncertain about a piece of it. Granted, *it was not a small detail*! Still, she tended to take in data, rarely reacting to alarming information until later when she processed it as a cohesive chunk. Her mind was slower than most, she thought. Most people could see a situation and react immediately—not that she couldn't when she needed to. There had been plenty of times when her quick actions had kept her from harm or saved an account. David had told her that her ability to take in all data first was a winning business and diplomatic trait.

David! Valeria realized, David would have eventually recalled her birthday. Perhaps he had even cancelled his event...what was she thinking? David cancelling anything that had to do with his work? Never! Still, he had probably called and she wouldn't have gotten his message up here in the mountains. Valeria thought with disgust; here she was with another man—another man who didn't even seem interested in her. Things would be over between her and David and all for what? *For the chance with Alex,* she thought with a deep sigh. She shook her head. This just wasn't the way that she did things. It felt dishonest. But it had happened so fast that she...just got caught up in it.

Then Valeria realized that there wasn't really anything wrong with all of this! Alex was with another woman. So, it really wasn't *that* way. Still, she knew that her attraction to Alex was why she was here. She had felt an immediate and strong bond with him that made her defy her own rules and logic. Valeria pushed thoughts of Alex away and dialed David's number. Before it rang through, she hung up and dialed Weege instead.

"What happened to you, girlfriend?" Weege sounded concerned.

"I'm in Italy. I met a man—,"

Weege interrupted, "You...you what? You ran off with someone! When did this all happen? You know David called me! Can you imagine? A diplomat called me! How did he even have my number? Well, I guess they have their ways."

"Weege, you gave David your number when we went out to dinner last month." Valeria laughed.

"Oh. Well, anyway, a diplomat has been desperately trying to reach you and has only been able to get your voice mail. It could be important. You know?" Weege took a breath.

"Was there an emergency?" Valeria asked, concerned.

"Well, how would I know?! He's a diplomat. He doesn't have to tell me anything. I mean, I don't have any kind of...immunity."

Valeria started laughing. "Weege, I'm sure he just dialed you because my phone didn't appear to be working."

"So, are you sleeping with him?"

Rolling her eyes, Valeria said, "Alex? No! It...well, it's a bit complicated." *She* didn't even understand it, how would she explain it to Weege.

"Well, girl, this guy he didn't sleep with you? What's wrong with him? I mean, he isn't gay is he?"

Valeria made an attempt to laugh again, "No, it's not like that. I think he's just being respectful...or something. But you're right. What am I doing here when David is a day's drive away? I am kind of engaged to him, I guess."

"David did say you two needed to take the next step, right? And he told me you were engaged." Weege went on, "Of course, you are talking to a girl that took 'babe let's move in together' as a proposal from Jimmy." Weege responded. "But it really isn't like you to be so inconsiderate. So this guy *must* be really hot!"

Weege's words stung. Valeria wondered, did she really just ditch a perfectly nice guy to run away with someone because he was...hot? What kind of person would do that? There was probably some kind of karma kicking in and that's why she was sitting on the porch by herself. David was a good guy. And although he had never officially proposed...and she had never really accepted, there was kind of an *understanding*, she guessed. What was wrong with her?

"Weege, you are right; I need to call David. I'll do that now. I'll talk to you later."

Hanging up, Valeria started dialing, suddenly a few voice messages popped up from David.

"Hello Sweetheart. Just thinking of you. Great conference! I'll try to call tomorrow night."

Valeria hit "call back" and she got the international response that the lines were tied up. She started to re-dial when suddenly Caleb appeared on the deck. "Wanna see a trick?"

With his hands behind his back, Caleb walked towards her. The Italian couple seeing Caleb swore at him in Italian which made him laugh even more. The couple left hurriedly as he held a light bulb by the glass.

"Okay." Then he put his finger on the end of the bulb and it sparked and then lit up causing him to break into a boisterous laugh.

"How did you do that?"

"It's just one of my many abilities!" He sat the light bulb down on the railing. "I'm supposed to keep you company."

Valeria frowned, irritated. "Why? You're one of them. You should be there. I don't need a babysitter!" She was immediately upset with herself for taking her anger out on Caleb.

"Well, I'm actually *not* like them. At least we don't think so." Caleb said as he took a seat next to her.

He held out his hand as if to shake hers. Valeria wondered what it was all about, but reached up and took his hand. Immediately she was zapped. "OUCH!" She pulled her hand back quickly.

"Sorry!" He laughed, unapologetically, "They wouldn't let me do that this morning."

"You mean that happens all the time?" She asked, as she rubbed her stinging hand.

"Yeah. You're lucky I discharged on the light bulb, otherwise it can be a little…electrifying."

"I don't understand. You aren't an oracle?"

"I found Alex a little over 2300 years ago. I was supposed to find him. I don't remember why." Caleb got thoughtful. "Tavish helped me so I don't electrocute anyone…well most of the time." He scratched his head. "It's not as bad now. But not a lot of people like that."

Reaching under the table Caleb pulled out a small leather case and suggested that they play Backgammon.

"Caleb, are you from the states? You don't talk like you're Italian."

"I'm on the web a lot…and I watch a lot of American movies." He finished setting up his pieces. "We travel a lot. You start picking up things like language pretty easily."

They sat on the porch for hours and played. Valeria found Caleb's joyful playfulness a welcomed distraction.

"Caleb, are any of the family married?" She was interested in only one person in particular.

"I think Lars and Camille have something going." Caleb said matter-of-factly, concentrating on the backgammon board for his next move.

"Lars and Camille, really? What about Daphne?" She asked in her most innocent voice.

Caleb laughed like there was an inside joke, "*Oh yeah*! Daphne and Alex are friends!"

Trying to smile, as if there was humor in any of that statement, Valeria smiled. "Are they…friends…or are they…"

"Don't worry about Daphne!" Her next move cost her two chips. He laughed and put his arms up in the air, "Sweet!"

Valeria re-grouped, "Alex and Daphne seem like they have a special relationship."

"Yep." He made another move and bounced another two chips and blocked her route out.

"Oh. They want us to go up there now." Caleb said suddenly looking up towards the main house.

"Caleb? How do you talk to each other like that?" She asked, moving the pieces back into the tray.

"Like what?"

"Well, how did you know they were ready for us?"

He looked up. "I don't know. I never thought about it. I just heard Lars telling me to go up to the house. And Alex is *constantly* asking me if you are alright."

"What did you tell him?" Valeria asked defensively.

Caleb shrugged, "Oh…you know…that you aren't very

good at backgammon."

"Oh."

"I guess we have just been together for so long that we don't need to talk if we don't want to—well as long as we aren't too far apart."

"What's too far?"

Scratching his head, Caleb said, "I guess a mile is too far." He turned up towards the main house and yelled, "ALRIGHT! WE'RE COMING!" He rolled his eyes. "But sometimes voices work better." He laughed.

Suddenly Caleb frowned, "Oh-oh! Guess I'm in trouble for saying too much!"

Off from the trail, Valeria noticed Camille bounding down the trail and up the steps onto the deck. She smiled at Caleb, "Why don't you go finish your chores!"

"See what I mean!" Caleb pouted off.

Camille smiled warmly at Valeria. "They aren't quite decided on how they want to proceed. Alex doesn't want you involved in that discussion. He doesn't want to worry you."

"Camille, what does all of this have to do with me?"

"Let's walk." Camille said, "Alex wants the opportunity to explain it all to you—and I need to respect that." She gave a side glance to Valeria as they stepped off the deck, "Caleb told me that you wondered about our relationships."

Valeria blushed. "I would guess that you are very much like a family. And that everyone else is…kind of an outsider. I would guess that your relationships would be with insi—," Valeria realized she had headed down a conversation she didn't want to finish.

Camille laughed softly, "First off, I don't have any idea what Caleb was telling you about Lars and me. Lars is married to Ava. I think she is supposed to be here tomorrow. She's wonderful! My closest friend! And I can totally see us—you, me and Ava being the three musketeers!" Valeria flushed at being part of a friendship.

Continuing, Camille said. "Alex is a bit concerned. He's afraid you will be overwhelmed by all of this…information and want to leave." She rolled her eyes, "We have all been telling him that you don't seem that fragile."

"I'm not fragile." Valeria said defensively.

"That's what we've been telling him. Lars is feeling a time pressure to jump into the real business." Camille looked up at the house. "Looks like Alex won the debate for now. Let's head back up." They continued on up the trail.

Then Valeria stopped. "Camille, my guess is that this is a pretty closed group."

Analyzing the question before responding, Camille said, "Yes, we are. When you are the only ones together for thousands of years, you become very close. And we trust each other. We disagree a lot but we do trust each other. And not to invalidate your reality but mortal relationships of 50 years are considered short term for us.

"You can live with someone for 20 to 50 years and put up with all of their idiosyncrasies. But when you are around for what looks like probably an eternity, you had better figure out how to communicate and how to respect each other. We are all we have. So, we are close!"

Feeling defeated, Valeria nodded as Camille continued, "But, I'll just say this; you are here. You know our secret. Val, you aren't an outsider!" She looked at Valeria and in her animated voice continued, "If I say more than that, he is gonna be upset with me!"

Valeria gulped and pushed on, "And Alex and Daphne?"

"They are close. Daphne saved Alex's life. And I think their relationship has kept him from being so lonely." Camille stopped again. "But Alex brought *you* here."

"Camille, *why* did he bring me here?" Valeria risked.

"I'm getting crap for talking to you about this. Come on, let's go." Camille picked up her step and Valeria knew there was no more information to be had today on that subject.

Entering the main house, Valeria noticed a painting leaning against the sideboard in the dining room that hadn't been there before. Camille steered Valeria back to her seat in the living room.

Looking around at the expectant faces, Valeria realized that her brain had finally engaged and was now prepared to ask a few questions. She glanced at Alex, "Is it okay—I have some questions." Alex nodded, pleased to see her engaging in the conversation. She tilted her head, "You are all true oracles?"

"Yes. It appears that we are the only remaining oracles." The rest seemed locked in unresponsiveness.

"And all of the true oracles are …immortal?" Valeria asked, incredulously.

Alex gave the others a quick look before proceeding. "Well, true oracles are mostly immortal." Valeria noticed that he failed to meet her glance.

"What do you mean 'mostly'? Are there exceptions? I mean *really*, have you all been alive for thousands of years?" It had finally hit Valeria and she didn't know if she could believe it. There was dead silence in the room.

"Val, I want you to know that every one of us in this room went through a period of adjustment when we came to understand the secrets of our own mortality—or rather immortality. Most of us didn't have anyone to discuss it with. So, if you have doubts, there is no one in this room that wouldn't understand."

Lars jumped in, "This isn't a comfortable topic for us to discuss with someone…"

With a sardonic laugh Daphne added, "Lars is being nice. He means we don't discuss this with outsiders." She said glaring at Alex, as if he had broken their agreement.

"Well, if that's all true then why doesn't anyone else know?" Valeria asked.

Lars spoke, "Valeria, we choose for other's not to know."

"Why hasn't anyone recognized you? I mean, why is it such a secret?" She continued to challenge.

Daphne and Tavish looked at each other sneered and nodded.

Lars went on, "Great questions! We spoke of the purges earlier. After we lost many of our own kind, it became clear that we needed to stick together and that it was better if we stayed undercover."

Daphne spoke up again, "Which is why Alex's little obsession with you has been such a pain in the—".

"Daph!" Camille admonished.

The comment took Valeria by surprise. *Alex was obsessed with her?* Certainly if Daphne believed that, it would explain her behavior towards Valeria. She noticed Alex was glaring at Daphne in more than irritation—more like anger.

Tavish spoke up, "Camille, whether you and the rest like

it or not, Daphne has a valid point." He pointed towards Valeria, "*Her* arrival here and letting her in on this puts us all in danger!"

Valeria didn't like the way Tavish said "*her*".

Lifting her arm to calm the situation, Camille soothed, "Look, we've discussed this and Valeria is *already* a part of this! We all decided that this was the best way to handle this situation."

There seemed to be an unspoken discussion occurring. Valeria noticed what appeared to be flashes of anger between Tavish, Daphne and Alex. Camille and Lars seemed to be attempting to calm things. Caleb seemed to enjoy what was occurring.

Daphne stomped across the room, "Well, some of us agreed—and some of us were ignored."

Approaching Daphne and then turning towards his family Alex pleaded, "Please give me a chance to do as we agreed! Let me give Valeria some history. I think we can resolve all of this!"

There seemed to be some agreement. Alex took Valeria by the arm, "Beautiful, I'd like to show you something." They walked to the large painting in the dining room that Valeria had noticed when she entered.

She studied it; it was a picture of a young girl with brown curls, her face lit up as she looked into the face of a boy. The colors were vibrant, with a deep blue sky in the background that matched some of the prisms in the children's eyes. Their hands came together and there seemed to be an energy between their hands. The painting had a joyful feeling to it—perhaps it was the expression on the face of the children. Valeria looked at the boy and then again at Alex.

"That's you!" She said. Alex nodded in expectation. She looked at the little girl. She wanted to get it. She wanted to be bright! Suddenly the realization hit her, "Oh! That's…what did you say her name was? Cassandra?"

Alex's eyes narrowed, "Take your time…anything else?" Valeria took a deep breath. There was something nagging at her that she just couldn't quite put together.

"I don't know Alex. What is it you want me to see?"

He glanced downward in barely missed disappointment. Valeria feared that he was about to discover that she was not as bright as others. He shook it off. "Nothing, Val. It was just a…"

Studying the painting again Valeria realized, "That is interesting that there is a painting of the people from the vision in my head."

Lars spoke up, "Val, take another look…anything else familiar to you?"

Alex shot Lars a glance and said silently. "Lars, drop it. She doesn't see it. But I feel like she is so close to getting it! I want to try one more thing. And then I think we should break for the night and let her put things together in her own time. She will, you know!"

Lars shrugged and said silently to Alex, "This is your show. We are here to help. But Alex, we are running out of time! We need to be spending our time solving the problem—not helping her to identify it."

Without missing a beat Alex responded to Valeria. "Beautiful, that's fine. I just thought you would like to see that the picture in your head was …not just in your head."

He would have to take the steps he had hoped to avoid.

But it was the only link that he had to her and the only way that he could think of to move things along. Still, he felt that it was a bit of a risk—he could see that she was starting to feel the connection between the two of them. Alex didn't want to abuse those emotions as leverage to get her agreement. This was such a dangerous game and she needed to understand the risks and make decisions because it was the right thing to do. But Alex was torn, even if Valeria agreed to do what was needed only for him, wouldn't the results be the same?

No, Alex decided, she needed to make the decisions intelligently, not because of her feelings for him. He would push the envelope only far enough to help her understand their connection—but no further. He hoped that his heart didn't betray more than he intended.

Valeria felt Alex's frustration. "Alex, while I appreciate seeing the painting—it really is beautiful! I don't understand what I have to do with any of this. I'm not an oracle. I don't have any powers. I'm just a…" *Say it*; Valeria thought, he may as well know what he is already thinking, "Alex, I'm just a very ordinary girl."

He looked at her and flinched, "Well, first off, there is *nothing* ordinary about you!" He swallowed and looked away. "Secondly, this has actually quite a lot to do with you. Primarily, your role with Aegemon; he has a great deal of interest in you."

Valeria laughed it off and then looked back to Alex, "Me? Why?"

"Well, for one reason, and there are several, Aegemon knows you will lead him to us." Alex said gently.

"I still don't understand—is there something you haven't told me?" Valeria challenged.

Alex looked to Lars and then Camille and said, "There seems to be some…conditions of immortality. Some of them, we are still trying to understand. We'll talk more about that later. But right now, let's resume where we left off this morning."

Gathering his wits about him, Alex led her back to the loveseat. "We were talking about Cassandra." He drew a deep breath and let it out slowly. "Aegemon saw that even at Cassandra's young age, there was no question that she would be a great beauty. Cassandra was the daughter of King Priam of Troy and if Cassandra and Apollo wed, Aegemon's services would no longer be required. Aegemon went to the King and told him in secret that the cards said that Cassandra's visions would save Troy in a great war—as long as she remained a virgin.

"Most of the gods were prone to fits of rage—with devastating effects! However, despite what was written by historians, Apollo did not care to interfere in the lives of mortals. Apollo also knew that Cassandra, being a princess would have an arranged marriage before she was 12." Alex's eyes flashed over to meet Valeria's. He moved towards her and sat on the ottoman in front of her. He needed closeness—despite his pounding heart.

"Apollo also knew that Cassandra's Symbolon would be searching for her—and he would find her…eventually. *He would never give up!*"

Valeria raised her eyebrows, "Symbolon?"

His face softened into an expression she had not seen on him. She attempted to read the expression as he leaned in towards her and said in a low voice that caused Valeria's heart to flutter, "Her soul mate.

"In Greek it means... two halves of a whole—neither half feeling fulfilled until they are reunited." Alex's eyes locked onto Valeria's eyes with a wistful smile that played on the edge of his lips that was so incredibly beautiful that she could only stare at him drunkenly.

Leaning in even closer, he took her hands. She could feel his breath as he softly murmured a phrase in Italian, leaving her frozen—as the rest of the room spiraled into a blur and it was only the two of them. Alex moved even closer to her, Valeria was aware that her pulse was racing at an indecent speed, as her heart leapt into her throat and she was cognizant enough to know that everyone in the room, including Alex would be able to tell. But she couldn't seem to turn away. She felt the weight of his stare and had a most irrational desire to touch his face. She found herself leaning in towards him.

"Oh my god! Mind if I just vomit here?" Daphne chirped as she got up from her seat; although Valeria barely noticed, unable to take her eyes from Alex's face.

Abruptly, the front door flew open and an athletic woman with short, spiky, blond hair made an entrance. "I'm here!" She announced, ready to be cheered and adored. The family responded appropriately and rushed to her, except Daphne, Valeria and Alex.

"I've missed you, baby!" Lars smiled. Ava slinked her Columbia jacket off, revealing lean, muscled arms. She had a deeply tanned face that accentuated her eyes and teeth, as both seemed to take up most of her impish face. Lars grabbed her around the waist and swung her around, planting a kiss square on her mouth.

Alex's eyes were still focused on Valeria, until Daphne walked by and wacked his arm with her magazine. "Knock it off, will you?" He shrugged repentantly at Daphne and took a deep breath. Then he winked at Valeria and rose and held out his arms to hug Ava.

Taking Alex's arms, Ava pushed him back as her head tilted and her eyes narrowed for a full assessment under her critical eye. She noticed the look in his eyes and the slight flush to his face. She glanced briefly towards Valeria and then back to Alex with a hint of mischief. "A bit heated up, are we?"

Only Ava could embarrass him! "Just uh…" He shook his head at Ava's lack of a filter. But it was also one of the things that he loved about her. And it was good that she was here. He shook off the embarrassment and gave her a hug. "Ava, come and meet Val."

"Val, this is Ava."

"Nice to finally meet you!" Ava smiled and then handed a package to Tavish, "Tav, here's Mani's package." She pulled a sealed package from her backpack.

"So, I can see a request from Mani has more pull than a request from your husband!" Lars joked, "But if that's what it takes to see my wife, I'll be employing it more often!"

"Ava, I've missed you!" Camille said, as she hugged Ava.

"I've missed you, too."

"Any luck on this trip?" Camille asked hopefully.

"Not this one, hon. But I know we're getting closer!" She gave Camille a confident wink. Valeria noticed that Camille seemed more subdued.

Pulling his wife into him, Lars gave Ava a kiss appropriate for a homecoming. That was the last straw for Daphne! She threw down her magazine, "Ava, I am happy to see you but I have had about enough of all of this!" Then she stomped up the stairs. Alex barely noticed the door slam.

Looking up the stairs in amusement, Ava glanced back to Alex. "Evidently, Daphne's not taking this well." She laughed as she shot a glance towards Valeria. Alex shrugged as if he wasn't going to answer the question. Then Ava began looking around with concern, "So…uhh," She looked at Lars, troubled, "… No fatted calf?"

Lars affectionately retorted, "There would have been, if someone had given us a better ETA!" With an accusatory glare, Lars touched Ava's foreheads with his own. She kissed him lightly and turned around.

"Tavish, you usually do a better job on my ETA." Ava said in mock irritation. Tavish grumbled something that sounded like an insult. Ava laughed loudly and hugged him around the neck, which Tavish almost seemed to tolerate. Then she stepped back and scoffed as she rolled her eyes, "Well, you have my ETA now! Where's the barbecue?"

Tavish's eyes narrowed at Ava, "The usual?" Valeria noticed Tavish's attempt again at a smile.

Camille smiled at Valeria who seemed a bit lost, "Would you like to come with me? I'm going to fix a couple of salads for lunch. Camille glanced up the staircase as if she was trying to find Daphne, "Daphne will want to be part of this." She said.

A door flew open upstairs, "No! Thank you!" Then the door slammed again.

Camille smiled to Valeria, "Alex and the rest of them will be tied up in business until dinner. Come keep me company!" Although Valeria was glad for the distraction she wasn't ready for the moment with Alex to end. Despite the fact that she knew it would be best if she kept her mind occupied. She knew that without distraction she would replay that moment numerous times and convince herself that Alex meant more than he actually did. And that would be an unwise assessment for her to make; it would only cause her heartbreak and dissatisfaction with David, and most important, it could create problems for Alex.

CHAPTER 9

The afternoon light filtered into the enormous country kitchen, as Valeria sat on a stool slicing her fourth zucchini on the tiled island. She wasn't much for zucchini, but at this point, she was more than a little hungry.

"You don't usually like zucchini, do you?" Camille said over the tomatoes she was slicing and layering with mozzarella. Valeria shrugged a no, her darn lack of a poker face!

"Well, I'll bet you'll like this!" Camille winked and then put attention on the living room.

"Caleb! I mean now!"

"Just one more minute! I'm almost done!" Valeria heard Caleb's distracted voice.

Camille leaned her head to the side, "As I was saying...if I can ever get Caleb out there to start the barbecue, I think you will like this."

"You do all the cooking here?" Valeria asked, as she took

in the lovely French flavor of the kitchen design; the tiny etched vines on the knobs of the cerulean cabinets, displaying brightly painted bowls and casseroles.

"No! I'm not going to be the cook for this brood on a regular basis!" Camille laughed, and then turned and glanced towards the living room with a look of irritation. Valeria heard a sound in the living room and assumed it was Caleb. Then Camille smiled pleasantly, as she returned her focus to Valeria. "Still, I enjoy it now and again. Tavish does an amazing barbecue. And Lars's makes a mean Sauerbraten." Leaning her head to the side with a quiet wince, Camille added, "We don't *let* Ava cook.

"Poor Caleb wants to help. But he ends up running errands and cleaning." Camille raised her delicate eyebrows and leaned on the kitchen counter, "Do you want to know who the real gourmet is?" She teased.

"Daphne?" Valeria responded.

"Lord no!" Camille let out a sweet giggle, like that of a child, it was contagious.

Daphne's voice bellowed down from the stairs, "I DID hear that, Camille!"

Leaning her head apologetically to the side, Camille said, "Oops!" She said, releasing another one of her delightful giggles. "No, I was referring to Alex. He is truly a renaissance man! There isn't much he doesn't do well." Valeria was already battling her thoughts about Alex. She really didn't want more fuel for her imagination—yet she was hungry for information about him.

Pulling out another oversized, ornately decorated platter, Camille began layering tomatoes and mozzarella. Then she went to the window with a bowl and began artistically plucking leaves from one of the many fresh herbs growing there. Valeria had finished off the zucchini and Camille pushed the finished plate of tomatoes and mozzarella in front of her. "Can you place a basil leaf on each slice of mozzarella?"

"Sure." Valeria was glad for something to do. She tiptoed back around to the subject, "So…Daphne and Alex?"

"Yes…well…sorry about that! Daphne doesn't always behave the way she should when it comes to Alex. She's always a bit jealous of him; especially when new women join the family. It was many years before Daph decided I wasn't a threat with Alex." Lightly smiling, Camille continued, "It's just her way…but believe it or not, after a while she kind of grows on you."

There was no way that Valeria was going to give Daphne a chance to grow on her! Daphne, who had the heart of the man that Valeria…No! She abruptly stopped herself from that thought.

Valeria reminded herself again that she was engaged to a good man! But thoughts of David were definitely eclipsed by Alex. She wondered why. Both were attractive men. Though there was something in her physical response to Alex that she couldn't explain. He was easily the most beautiful man she had ever met. But physical beauty had never been a prerequisite for Valeria. There was something about Alex that made her feel like she had never felt before. Not that any of that seemed to matter. He was with someone else…and so was she.

Running in from the side door to the kitchen, Caleb announced, "Okay! Tavish says he's almost ready for the zucchini."

Liberally pouring olive oil over the slices of zucchini, Camille then grinded the salt and pepper and tossed it with her hands. Valeria grabbed the bowl to take it to Caleb and saw Camille give Caleb a non-verbal warning. He carefully grasped the side of the bowl—avoiding a shock.

After rinsing a mix of fresh berries in the colander, Camille poured them into another brightly covered bowl.

"Val, the temperature is pretty nice—probably our last few warm days. I think we'll eat out back. Can you grab the tablecloth and napkins from that drawer?"

Valeria opened a drawer next to where she had been sitting. Camille grabbed a pitcher of what looked like iced tea and a bottle of balsamic vinegar.

Within minutes Alex appeared at the kitchen door. Valeria noticed the turn of a smile on the corner of his lips. Her heart fluttered and she begged for something to distract her and immediately got her wish as she heard stomping on the staircase in the living room; Daphne was on her way.

Alex grabbed two serving forks and placed them on the plates with tomato and mozzarella. Noticing that Valeria was watching him, his eyes narrowed and then he winked, "Everything alright?"

Valeria couldn't stop her face from lighting up, "Of course!" She attempted to answer simply, as Daphne entered.

"What do you want me to do?" Daphne said in irritation and then looked over the food, "Where's the wine?"

Camille shook her head, "We have too much to do to be enjoying wine."

Daphne glared at Valeria before grabbing the bowl of berries and stomping outside. Alex's face was apologetic.

"Sorry about Daphne. She really does have a good heart if you can look beyond the tantrums!" He said while grabbing the two platters. "Ready?" He asked Camille and Valeria.

The backyard was extraordinary. The enormous lawn was surrounded by trees. Directly ahead, Valeria saw an outdoor stone fireplace. The dining table was long with woven chairs with the branch to a tree providing shade. Tavish was removing barbecued chicken from a built-in grill that sat next to the fireplace.

Alex grabbed the other end of the tablecloth from Valeria and helped her place it on the table. Camille took glasses, plates and dinnerware from a cabinet next to the built-in grill.

The breeze so gently kissed Valeria and she smiled at Alex—though not for too long. He stepped to her and while maintaining eye contact, grabbed half of the napkins from her stack and set them on the plates.

Camille began setting the table. Alex moved a vase filled with bright yellow flowers onto the table.

Lying on the lounger, while the others worked, Daphne lowered her sunglasses over her eyes. With everything loaded on the table, Lars and Ava exited the kitchen and headed for the table walking hand-in-hand. Caleb came running from behind. Alex sat next to Valeria and held the platter of tomatoes and Mozzarella for her as she carefully placed one onto her plate. Alex took a couple for himself and passed it on to Caleb. Tavish sat on the other side of Valeria with a platter of grilled zucchini slices. Valeria took one slice of zucchini and passed it on.

Helping herself to the grilled chicken, Camille noticed Valeria's selection. "Alex, she's never had the grilled zucchini. Give her a few more. You know with this brood there won't be any left by the time it makes a round."

As he placed a few more zucchini on Valeria's plate he

said, "Don't worry—you don't have to clean your plate here!"

The food was delicious and Valeria attempted to hide how hungry she was. She glanced around the table; she couldn't think of a time she had ever sat at a table like this and really felt a part of things. There was an odd feeling of comfort; yet a nervousness that she was feeling too comfortable. She thought of how wonderful it would be to belong to this family. Alex helped himself to a large serving of grilled zucchini and passed them on.

Daphne continued to glare at Valeria throughout the dinner. In fact, she noticed Daphne take a bite of her chicken as if she were ripping off a head. Attempting to ease the tension, Valeria moved just a bit away from Alex and then she realized, closer to Tavish, who offered her a smile/sneer for her gesture. Alex glanced at Valeria for a moment with a question in his eyes and then shook his head at Daphne in slight irritation.

"So Val, where is your family from?" Ava spoke up over her third piece of chicken.

Oh, questions about her life, Valeria cringed. "I…well, we lived in Youngstown, Ohio until I was 12. Then Dad took a job in Hoboken, New Jersey; a suburb of New York City."

"Tell me about yourself." Ava continued.

Dread filled Valeria. She decided to turn the tables on this discussion, "My life isn't really very interesting. Tell me about you? Where are you from Ava?"

Ava looked at Lars, taking a bite of chicken and laughed loudly, "Well, that is an interesting question! Yes…it is! Isn't it Larsi?" Lars and several others laughed.

"Here and there." She said, as she grabbed the remainder of the zucchini, "I guess we've moved around so much. But this is the closest to home any of us has had in..."

Ava's eyes sparked for a moment. Valeria noticed Camille and Alex giving Ava a look, as if she had said enough. "What?!" Ava glared at Alex, "I was going to say, *in some time*! That's all!" Ava's eyes danced with humor. "*Besides,* you said she already knew...about us!" She enjoyed the game. Valeria wondered why it was such a mystery.

With Ava now ending that discussion, Valeria knew it would return to her own life. She quickly asked, "How long have you been gone?"

Ava's eyes narrowed as the sun moved behind the house. She looked down the table, "How long has it been, Camille? This time I think it was about three years." Camille thought for a moment and then nodded.

"You've been gone from your husband for three years? Where were you?"

Camille dabbed her mouth with her napkin, "Valeria, you might as well know that Ava has been on a long term project to find my husband, Jonah."

"What happened to your husband, Camille?" Valeria said as she took a bite of zucchini and realized that it was really very good.

First glancing to Alex, Camille responded, "He was...murdered. At least that's what we think happened. There are indications that the murder occurred in the Caribbean. So, that's where Ava has been." Camille glanced at Alex. Valeria noted a gentle nod from Alex to Camille.

"But there is a project that has come up. So, Ava had several...details to handle. Otherwise she would have been here this morning." Something in Camille's tone and the exchange of glances made Valeria suspect that the "project" had something to do with her.

Still anxious to keep the focus off from her, Valeria asked, "Was Jonah an immortal? I mean, if he is immortal then I guess he couldn't be murdered...right? You must think he's alive." Her brow furrowed. "Oh. But then I guess you wouldn't believe he was murdered. Ava, are you searching for the murderer...or searching for information? Tell me about it!"

A burst of laughter erupted from Ava, "Wow! That's...well...that is just a lot of questions you have!" She shook her head in amusement, taking another bite of chicken.

Valeria noticed the amused expression on almost everyone at the table. She suspected that they had caught onto her game of diverting attention. Valeria murmured, "Okay...I guess that was the a bit much." She saw Alex's mouth dance in mild amusement as he winked at her.

Ava seemed to be watching the interplay between Alex and Valeria with some interest. She was about to ask a question and then glanced at Camille. Valeria noticed a slight shake of Camille's head. Ava glanced at Alex. Even from the peripheral view Valeria noticed Alex's pupils constricted as in irritation or nervousness. Ava leaned her head to the side as she stretched out her arms and leaned back in her chair. Her face took on an amused curiosity. "So, what's going on here with you and Alex?"

The table got incredibly quiet. Forks that had been just previously loaded with food were now held in suspense, awaiting the answer. Valeria wondered about the purpose of the question. Was it to cause Valeria to admit that she was after Daphne's man? Was it to shove Valeria towards the waiting arms of Tavish? Valeria wondered how she should properly answer the question—especially with Daphne listening so closely.

While certain that her face was flaming red, Valeria

decided this was the perfect opportunity to end ANY idea that she would be set-up with anyone by stating that she was happily engaged. But somehow she couldn't bring herself to say the words in front of Alex—despite the fact that Daphne was right there and it was the right thing to do in order to squelch the rumors.

"Why? Have I done something inappropriate?" Valeria raised a delicate eyebrow at Ava and then with more intensity at Daphne.

Seeing Daphne's response, Valeria thought, o*h god, there is going to be a war*! She saw that Ava was working hard to withhold a laugh. In fact, everyone around the table except Caleb—who had pulled out a computer game—seemed to be on the verge of hysterical tears with nearly silenced snickers filling the air. Even Alex was pursing his lips, withholding the laughter.

Daphne stood, "I don't know about the rest of you—but frankly, I have heard ENOUGH about what is going on here with this...this..." Daphne gestured towards Alex and Valeria, "*situation*!"

Yes, Valeria thought, the situation did seem slightly inappropriate. But, she thought, she couldn't really seem to stop her reactions towards Alex. He was sitting next to her...and across from Daphne. But he would have been sitting next to her or across from her—there weren't *that* many options! Valeria vowed to work harder to remember that Alex was taken.

"Daphne, I'm sorry! I promise to work harder to make you feel more...comfortable," was all Valeria could think of to say. However, her words seemed to have a completely opposite effect. Daphne's pale complexion turned purple as she glared at Alex momentarily before stomping off.

The entire table went from light snickers to rolling laughter. Alex's arm went around Valeria in affection, as he let out an enchanting laugh that she thought was the most beautiful sound she had ever heard. She worked hard to breathe easily. And then she decided that appreciating his assets was only natural. Though in the back of her mind, she knew that her attention to his assets was only going to make it difficult to be the friend that she obviously was.

Wiping a tear of laughter from her eye, Ava, was at last able to talk, she said to Alex and Valeria "I am so sorry—well…kind of sorry." She laughed again, "The tension was just getting too thick here!"

The subtleties of the joke did not escape Valeria. The question was not designed for Valeria but rather to dig at Daphne. Leaning her arm on the table and pointing to Valeria, Ava said, "I like this lady! She has chutzpah!"

While Valeria appreciated the compliment, she wasn't certain what she had said that caused the responses.

Lars with his arm around Ava patted her waist. "I'll tell you what, let's all reconvene in about three hours."

Camille piped in, "Don't worry about picking up." The comment was unnecessary; Lars and Ava were halfway back to the house.

Glancing at his watch, Alex then patted Valeria's back, "I need to go handle some details with Tavish. Don't worry about the dishes, it's Caleb's chore today."

Immediately, Camille started stacking dishes and Valeria joined in. From the feast, there was not a single bite of food remaining. Valeria learned that she loved the grilled zucchini. They carried the dishes to the kitchen. Camille filled both sinks with water, one with soapy water and the other with clear water. She took a pair of yellow latex gloves out and set them on the side of the sink.

They walked back out for another load of dishes. Camille placed her hands on her hips as Caleb played his computer game, "I'll tell you what Caleb, I'll dry and put away if you come in right now."

He smiled a mischievous smile, "I wondered if you'd ever offer!" He sat his game down. "So, what was all of that with Daph?"

Letting out a deep sigh, Camille responded, "Oh…you know Daph! Ava was playing with Daphne's temper." Camille stacked the remainder of the dishes. Valeria grabbed the linens. "But if you don't want them to get your goat—don't tell them where it's tied!"

After the dishes were done, Caleb asked Valeria if she played badminton. She decided she would go change and attempt the game. She found herself nearly running through the woods, excited for the game and enjoying the air and the friendships.

Approaching the cottage during the day, she found her mood was now one of near joy. Seeing the beautiful Gingko tree, Valeria hoped she would have the opportunity to sit under the tree and read…perhaps *Walden*.

She changed to a tee shirt and sweats and then surveyed Alex's bookcase. She brushed her hand over the copy of *Sense and Sensibility* and then pulled out *Walden*, hoping she wasn't overstepping the bounds of their friendship.

Back up at the main house, Caleb had the net set up and Valeria decided she would read and watch Caleb and Camille to get the idea of the game. Valeria opened the book and saw on the inside cover, beautiful hand script that read,

"However mean your life is, meet it and live it; do not shun it and call it hard names."

The sky became a deeper shade of fall blue as Valeria relaxed on the lounge watching Caleb and Camille bat the birdie back and forth—often laughing— especially when Caleb won. He would let out a joyful whoop and holler that made Valeria smile. She found that her face was lit with the hint of a smile for the rest of the hour.

She noticed a shadow on her book and glanced up to see Alex in front of her, "Ah! *Walden*! Are you enjoying it?"

"Very much!" Valeria smiled. "While I'm not certain I agree with Thoreau completely, the reading is soothing."

Alex nodded, "My feelings exactly. *Walden* is an old friend that I have turned to during times of great hardship. It seems to soothe me." He sat on the edge of her lounge chair. "I hope you don't mind that I've deserted you."

"No." Valeria responded too quickly, wishing for more time with him. "I'm enjoying my time here."

"Lars, Tavish and I are going to be tied up most of the evening, I'm sorry to say. I hope you'll forgive me."

Disappointed, Valeria forced a smile on her face, "Of course."

"But don't think for a minute that I'm leaving you alone!" Daphne must have won out and now he felt he needed to avoid her. Obviously they weren't shoving her into Tavish's arms right away.

"I haven't needed a babysitter for some time." Valeria said, her intention stern but her voice was light. Somehow talking to Alex did that to her.

He patted her leg affectionately, "Just the same…" Alex

rose. "Lars wants to reconvene here in about an hour and a half. So, if you are going to take on Caleb—you had better do it now!"

With that, Alex disappeared into the house—taking with him a piece of the world's brightness. Valeria jumped up from the lounger and grabbed the extra racquet, making it Camille and Valeria against Caleb, who was winning by a long margin.

Chapter 10

Playing badminton, the three of them, Caleb, Camille and Valeria, had laughed and relaxed. Several times Camille and Valeria had just barely missed hitting each other. They were certain that they had given Caleb a run for his money. Although, Valeria and Camille had lost—by a long margin—Valeria had truly enjoyed herself.

Camille tapped Valeria on the shoulder, "Lars is going to want to start back up in about forty-five minutes. But the weather's so nice I suspect we'll stay outside."

Wanting to ensure that she was showered before she saw Alex again, sweaty from playing badminton, Valeria hurried back down to the cottage. It was early evening and she found it almost magical to stroll along the wooded path now aglow with trail lights.

Back at Alex's cottage, she showered and took the time to dry her hair. She actually touched it up with a curling iron and put on a tad more make-up than in the morning. Valeria decided to put on another cotton dress. She headed back up the path—grateful to be able to wear a dress without the prerequisite panty hose that David required.

As Valeria returned, Alex greeted her with a smile that made her glad she had taken the extra time to fix her hair and put on the dress. If she could permit herself to be honest, she knew she was overly excited to see him again.

"Tavish says we only have a few more warm days. So, we decided to enjoy it!" Alex reported as he guided her to the blazing outdoor fireplace.

The rest of the family, including Daphne, sat waiting for her. Daphne seemed to be somewhat under control.

Almost looking at Valeria, Daphne said, "I hear I owe you an apology for my…" She huffed an evil eye at Alex, "tenue…I hope you will excuse…what you may have perceived as poor behavior."

Valeria had no idea what tenue meant—but she got the gist of the apology. Although she felt some sympathy for Daphne; Valeria thought, if *Alex were my lover…* Instantly, she regretted that thought, as she felt the blood rushing to her face, followed by the most extraordinary sensation of heat running through her entire body down to her toes. Valeria forced herself to remember that the relevance of the previous thought was that *Alex belonged to someone else.* She carefully rephrased her thoughts, if she were in Daphne's shoes, she was not certain she could conduct herself so well.

"No problem." Valeria said to Daphne, offering a reprieve to the tension between the two of them.

Lars and Ava arrived, again, walking hand-in-hand. Valeria shivered from the coolness as Alex ushered her to a seat near the fire. "Do you want me to get you a sweater?"

Camille offered, "I'll get her a jacket." Alex followed

Camille inside for a moment.

To Valeria's disappointment Tavish sat next to her—his eyebrow raised with evaluation. With no one else talking, Tavish squirmed and then looked at her.

"Ya a duffer?" He asked Valeria with his broad smile/sneer.

"I..uh..." Valeria thought, *oh god, the set-up has begun—Tavish is making his move.* "I'm sorry...what?"

Alex returned, wrapping a jacket around Valeria's shoulders. His fingers brushed her shoulder causing a wonderful quiver in her. *Why did his touch affect her so much?*

"Tavish is asking if you golf... Tav, she just might be a very good golfer." Alex cocked his head to the side in a challenge.

Tavish tucked his head in extreme doubt, "fo a gull?" He said, "Cudna be." He huffed an arrogant laugh. Valeria had no idea what he said.

"What about Babe Zaharias?" Alex's face lifted in amusement.

Tavish waved his arm in dismissal, "The lass carried luck."

Alex laughed, "Forty-one pro tour wins and she survived the thirty-six-hole cut in three out of four PGA tours against men." Alex winked to Valeria, "Tav is an avid golfer."

"Well Tavish...I don't think I even qualify as a...what did you call it? A duffer?" Valeria admitted.

This seemed to upset Tavish, "*A bloody hacker?* I'll be damned!"

Valeria understood that phrase—she had heard David's

associates insulting each other with the phrase "hackers". It was her only time on a golf course; out of boredom she had begun walking the edge of the fairways. David and the course management seemed terribly upset by her actions. The golf course management suggested to David that Valeria should not return. David, of course, found it all very serious. Valeria thought it pretty funny.

Seeing that this might be just the angle she needed to get out of Tavish's possible interest, Valeria added, "Yes—and it's been recommended that I give it up permanently!"

Alex broke into his marvelous laughter, as Lars called the group together.

"Where were we?" Lars asked.

"We were talking about Cassandra's Symbolon." Alex said, his eyes meeting her with a luminous intensity and caused her heart to stir.

Lars sighed, overly relaxed, "Go ahead Lexi."

Alex sat on the small table, doubling as a stool in front of Valeria. The glow of the fire shimmered over Alex and gave her heart a pleasantly painful little lurch. *Get a grip*, Valeria thought! As she briefly wondered what the heck was wrong with her.

"Apollo knew that Cassandra's Symbolon would come for her and if she were married, it would lead to tragedy. If Aegemon was able to keep Cassandra from marrying by a secret agreement with the king, eventually Cassandra would find her way to her Symbolon. So Cassandra was pronounced a virgin priestess." Alex lifted an eyebrow, "Disappointing more than one perspective lover, I might add!" He leaned forward, "Incidentally, Cassandra, as far as I have researched, was the original virgin priestess."

"Really?"

"Val, earlier you asked if all oracles were immortal. Lars is going to expound on that subject. Are you familiar with the term 'Achilles' heel'?"

"A weakness?" Valeria noticed the expression on Alex's face. Evidently this was the discussion that Alex had objected to.

Lars stood, "So, the story goes that Achilles' mother gained access to the River Styx when he was an infant. The River Styx is the river that runs into the underworld and carries the dead to their proper location.

"She held the baby Achilles by his heel and dipped him in the river, making him immortal, everywhere except his heel. And of course, an arrow to his heel was how he was killed during the Trojan War."

Valeria shrugged, "Okay."

Lars continued, "I don't really know if that story is factual or not. But it does apply to us. We are immortal. However we can die. Our first death, is called our 'Prima Mortis'. The method in which we die in our Prima Mortis is our Achilles' heel. If we die in that method again, we die like anyone. At least, that is what appears to be true."

Lowering her brows, Valeria said, "I've noticed that your age differences are not the same as they are in the vision. In the vision, Alex was about ten years older than you Lars but now you seem close to the same age."

Valeria did her best to ignore Alex so that she could concentrate. "So, you must stop aging when you have your first death. Your...what did you call it? Prima Mortis?"

"Yes." Lars turned towards Alex, "Alex we agreed. It's

time she heard it."

With a sigh Alex nodded and Lars continued, "When Apollo faded, Aegemon went after the oracles. As we said earlier, we didn't know the rules of immortality and I don't believe Aegemon did either. He captured those of us that he could, bound us with rope and threw us into the sea."

"Most of you were drowned?" Valeria shook off a chill.

Lars nodded, "I was able to evade Aegemon's troops until I was thirty."

"Camille, you said that Ava is searching for your husband. What does that involve?" Valeria asked.

With her face steeled, Camille said, "In the sea, there are several possible elements, primarily hypothermia and drowning. There's a chance that Jonah recovered. But there is some evidence that we don't recover from amnesia, which is one of the concerns." Camille's voice softened. "Jonah could be wandering alone having forgotten me." Valeria noticed the pain in Camille's voice.

"Ava didn't drown, so she can search the sea. The rest of us mostly stay clear of the water."

"Alex," Valeria could see that this was a difficult discussion for him, "did Aegemon drown you?"

"In a manner of speaking." Alex responded keeping his face down.

Lars spoke up, "Well, that's probably enough information for tonight."

Camille grabbed Valeria's arm, "Come on! It's girl's night!" Ava and Camille escorted Valeria a few steps before she turned around to look at Alex, who was in a deep discussion with Lars and Tavish.

Walking the lit trail to the cottage, Valeria had a touch of excitement. She would have loved to have spent more time with Alex—and really felt awful that she was keeping Ava from time with Lars. But Camille had convinced Valeria that Ava did whatever she wanted to do. Also, Camille was quite certain that when Lars and Alex finished up—probably in the wee hours of the morning—that Ava would sneak off.

Camille added, "But don't worry the other's will be keeping an eye on us!"
Valeria still wondered what was up with that. But frankly, she had never had a real girls night with women her age...and as far as Valeria was concerned these were two very extraordinary women!

Chapter 11

They arrived at the cottage and Ava walked in as if she owned the place. Taking a deep breath her eyes enlarged as she turned excitedly, "Let's see if I remember where Alex hides his *really* good wines!" She disappeared for a few minutes and then reappeared with a couple of dust covered bottles. She wiped them off and poured three glasses while Camille continued to explain that they really shouldn't be drinking wine.

The fire in the fireplace was already ablaze as Camille, Ava and Valeria grabbed their glasses. Valeria sipped the wine and couldn't believe how good it tasted. Ava raised a toast, "To friends!"

Valeria felt a tear well in her eye, but swallowed back the emotion with the extraordinary wine. "Ava, I don't want to keep you from Lars tonight—especially when you've been away so long."

"Don't worry about us! Lars is going to be tied up most of the night with Alex and Tavish." Ava looked to Camille and

Valeria with a smile, "Besides, I'm here to get the scoop!"

They clinked glasses and drank again. Glancing through her glass, Ava took a long look at Valeria and then took on a conspiratorial expression, "So…now—without Daph here to influence your response; tell me exactly about how it happened with you and Alex."

Valeria noticed Camille roll her eyes at Ava. "How what happened? Do you mean how I met him?"

Ava leaned back, "Yeah…tell me everything." Seeing Valeria's concern, she added, "Don't worry—I won't repeat a word of it." Then, Ava settled back on the floor next to the sofa.

"Well…" Valeria started, "Alex saved me from being crushed by a car." Ava nodded as if she didn't care about that part. Valeria went on, "I…well, I decided to go to lunch…or was it breakfast with him." She thought about it and was embarrassed and then her face lit; remembering the time in Sarabeth's, and on the flight, and in Verona...

Ava leaned forward, "That's the part I want to hear about! What caused *that* smile?"

"Really, we just talked." Valeria said innocently, "Actually, I guess, I mostly talked." She paused, "Well, we both talked about books and how much Alex liked *Walden* and—".

Ava picked up the copy of *Walden* that Valeria had dropped on the table, "Exhibit A!" Ava said waving her hand, "Yeah, yeah, yeah! *And then*?"

"Well…" Valeria took another sip of wine. "Well, and then we…uh…let's see…well, oh yes, Mani came and gave me a transference. And then Alex walked me back to my apartment and told me I needed to pack." Valeria thought, "Or something like that."

"Okay!" Ava's eye's got big with irritation, "I'm looking for *details*! You know...*when did he make his move?*"

Shaking her head with pretended irritation, Camille knew there was no silencing Ava. Valeria was taken back, "Make his move? I don't know what you mean...Alex wouldn't do that! He's way too much of a gentleman!"

Ava's jaw dropped as she moved forward and glared at Camille, "What is wrong with kids today!" Ava's eyes narrowed in disbelief, "*You mean he hasn't made a move?*"

Embarrassed by the question, Valeria wondered what caused that question. She suspected that her feelings for Alex must be obvious. Maybe in this culture running around on your spouse was acceptable—but it wasn't in her world. And Valeria couldn't believe it would be all right in Alex's world either. Obviously, Ava hadn't gotten the whole story. "No. Why would he?"

Again, Ava turned and looked at Camille with absolute disgust. Valeria realized she needed to jump in, "Tell me about you and Lars. How did you meet?"

Snuggling into the back of the sofa, Ava began, "Well, we both had been having fun with a number of...well I guess you don't need to know that." Ava looked up with energy, "Oh! I know, so I had seen Lars on the beach in Paxos."

"Paxos?"

"An island off the western shore of Greece." Camille added, while Ava gave her a look that said Camille was interrupting her flow.

"We were both doing the bathing beauty thing. You know, not actually getting in the water. Finally, I said, 'are you chicken or are you actually going to get in the water with me?' Of course, I didn't know he was an oracle at the time." Ava dropped her head to the side, her face lighting in memory. "After a little…well…fun, we saw each other at the Council meeting. Ours was a love born out of …well great sex! Fortunately, we enjoyed everything else too!"

Ava gestured at Valeria, "So, your turn!"

Realizing it was time to halt the discussion of her and Alex, Valeria began, "Actually, I'm engaged to a diplomat named David Wiley."

"No!" Ava contested, looking as if she doubted the information, while Camille silently sipped her wine.

"Yep." Valeria nodded attempting to convince Ava. "Three years now."

Ava looked skeptical, "I don't see a ring."

"Well…that's because David and I have decided that there is no need to rush into things. People like to rush into things! No. David and I are taking our time." Valeria said, feeling very relaxed about her presentation.

Ava refilled their glasses as there was a knock on the door. "Food!" Ava ran to the door and returned with several bags. Valeria and Camille followed her to the kitchen and dished out what Valeria recognized as American-style pizza. Emptying the other bag, Ava held up a giant bag of popcorn.

"You *bought* popcorn?" Valeria asked.

"Ava doesn't cook…as I said earlier." Camille laughed.

They ate as the fire roared and Ava poured the wine freely. "So, tell us more about this…this diplomat…what's his name? Oh yeah, David!" Ava tossed a couple of kernels of popcorn in the air and caught them in her mouth. Valeria thought popcorn and wine was an odd combination.

"Well...I met him at the hotel across from the U.N. where I have—I mean *had* a floral account. He saw me and sent his assistant over to ask me to join him. And...I guess that's about all." She said, her mouth already feeling a bit loose from the several glasses of wine and the friendship.

"I want the juicy stuff!" Ava's eyes lit up as she tossed a few more kernels of popcorn in the air again catching them with great accuracy.

"*Juicy stuff?*" Valeria asked, feeling a bit more relaxed.

"Tell us how he proposed?" Ava said, as Camille leaned forward to listen.

Valeria thought for a minute, "You know...I don't...I don't really remember...hmmm." She glanced up thinking, "I guess it was just decided."

Ava rolled her eyes, "So, how did he sweep you off your feet? Tell us about the seduction?"

"*Seduction?* Oh no! I'm not going to talk about that!" Valeria wondered in horror, *is that what girls talked about?*

Ava opened another bottle of wine and refilled their glasses. "Camille, tell me about Jonah!" Valeria sipped the wine and it was even better than the last bottle.

Camille's eyes softened with the memories, "All right. Well, Jonah and I found each other because of our eye color. Let's face it; there aren't many of us—especially of our skin color—with our shade of blue eyes!"

Valeria suddenly realized that Ava and Camille had the same eye color as Alex and Mani. "What is the deal with your eye color?" She asked, feeling the effects of the wine.

"I don't really know. But all true oracles have the same

eye color." Camille said, sipping her wine.

"Except Daphne. Her eyes are green." Valeria said.

"Yeah, she likes to be different—thanks to Bausch and Lomb!" Ava offered and then signaled for Camille to continue while refilling all of the glasses.

"Jonah and I had both been courting others. But even in those days there was SO much drama and trauma with these other people.

"Finally one day I said, 'you know Jonah? I think the reason nothing ever works with anyone else is because we belong together.' Do you know how when you try to mix friendship with love, it doesn't always work—well with us it was just…" Camille sighed, "…wonderful!" She nodded as if finished with her rendition of how she met her husband.

An hour later, having more wine than she should have had, while listening to great stories of Camille and Jonah and Ava and Lars—and hearing them both talk about previous lovers, Valeria's courage came up.

"You know David was my first. He really isn't the romantic type! Not like…well, not like Alex. David's more…thinking and planning…about everything—and I do mean EVERYTHING!"

Ava's eyes jumped, "Yeah?" As she poured more wine into Valeria's glass.

"David decided we would take our relationship to the next stage—that's what he called it…oh I guess that's how he proposed! He said it was about time to take our relationship to the next stage!"

Ava tilted Valeria's glass, "Drink up, sister!" She obliged.

"So…where was I? Oh yeah…so, after the fourth

date…well you know." Valeria thought for a moment about what she really wanted or would say. She never believed she would have this type of discussion with anyone…let alone her new best friends!

"Okay, so what happened? Did he take you to a romantic B&B? How did he sweep you off your feet?" Ava demanded.

Thinking about it for an instant, Valeria realized her glass was full again. But the wine was so good. "Well, no. David isn't really a 'sweep you off your feet' kind of guy. It was all very…planned."

Ava winced. Valeria had to admit even Camille looked disappointed. Valeria gulped down the rest of the wine, "David just…well you know…went in and undressed and then patted my side of the bed."

Ava's jaw dropped, "This guy has all the romance of a cow!"

Even Camille was aghast. "No!"

Both Camille and Ava held their thumbs down while they booed.

"Well, I'm certain I was no real prize for him. I mean, I had no idea what…was supposed to happen." Valeria said, feeling the need to defend David.

Camille finally burst out having clearly had too much wine, "Val! What are you doing with this man?"

Just then, there was a knock at the front door. Ava jumped up heading to the door, "Oh no! You don't get her back tonight!"

Valeria brightened seeing Alex step through the door, "Sorry, I wanted to get my shaving supplies and a change of clothes."

Alex's eyes narrowed at Valeria. "Ava, you know Valeria isn't much of a drinker. Don't plow her with too much wine, right?"

Ava shrugged sarcastically, "She's fine!"

"I'm fine." But Valeria realized that she had already drank too much.

From the bedroom Alex signaled to her. Valeria rose and realizing she was probably staggering just a bit, walked to where Alex was standing, noticing his eyes were again lit with amusement—and something else equally pleasant. "Are you alright with me leaving you with them tonight?"

Valeria looked at Alex as she stood a bit too close to him, occasionally weaving even closer and answered a little too flirtatiously, "I'm fine." She slurred. "But if you wanted to join us—I'm sure that would be okay…good…I mean fine." Suddenly, Valeria heard what she said and was horrified. Alex laughed his beautiful laugh and looked into her eyes again.

"We still have a lot of—," he looked up, "details…that must be resolved." Alex touched her nose as Valeria moved her face close enough to touch his, "Otherwise, I would probably have to run them both off and enjoy your company alone." Valeria let out a drunken little laugh—which she realized made her sound like a love-sick school girl. He laughed again and shook his head as he grabbed a sports bag and carried it out.

"Ava, leave us a few bottles of the good stuff, will you?" He smiled intently at Valeria, "I have plans for them of my own!"

Leaning on the arch to the bedroom, her face smiling drunkenly after Alex, Ava exclaimed with great emphasis, "Now, THAT's what I'm talking about!"

With a sudden pout coming to her face, Valeria wandered

back to sit on the floor again. "Yeah…too bad about that."

"What do you mean?" Camille asked.

"He is so very…sexy and romantic, isn't he?" Valeria giggled drunkenly.

Camille slurred knowingly, "You are totally into Alex, aren't you!"

"Well, of course she is! I mean look at her—she is practically swooning—hell, she IS swooning!" Ava added.

The words stopped Valeria in her tracks and she took a deep, unsteady breathe, "I don't want to think about that."

No, she really did not want to think about that. If she thought about Alex, she had to also think about the fact that he was taken. And she had spent a lifetime forcing herself to think about only those things that were possible. Thoughts about him completely overwhelmed her.

It was at that moment that Valeria realized she *most definitely had feelings for Alex*—and that it was simply too late to roll all of those fantastic, frightening, glorious emotions back under the carpet.

"Tell us!" Ava pressed.

"It doesn't matter." Valeria said sullenly.

Leaning her arm on the coffee table, Ava stared at Valeria, "Why is that?"

"I think that's obvious!" Ava and Camille just stared at Valeria, "Daphne!" Valeria looked back down, "I don't really blame her for being upset with me. I mean, he gave me their bed—".

Camille pulled her legs up onto the couch, "*What are you talking about?*" She said, easily two octaves above her normal voice.

"Alex and Daphne, of course." Valeria stared into the fire taking another sip of her wine, thinking how much she would have loved it if Alex was sitting here with her. "But men like that belong with women like Daphne." She furrowed her brows, "Well, not with her moodiness. But you know what I mean; women that *look* like Daphne. And frankly, I would have expected Alex to be with someone more like…I mean what's wrong with him? Camille is *far* nicer than Daphne!"

The popcorn that Ava tossed in the air missed her mouth as her head yanked around and wine spewed from Camille's mouth as they both burst into hysterical laughter.

"*WHAT*? Alex is like a brother to me!" Camille said, wiping the wine from her face and a tear from her eyes, before passing the towel onto Ava. Seeing that Valeria was serious, Camille continued, more gently. "Val, even if I wasn't in love with Jonah, Alex isn't my type. And Daphne is DEFINITELY NOT Alex's type!"

"But I heard them talking my first night. Daphne was upset because I was sleeping in their bed." Valeria insisted.

"Sweetheart, I think you misunderstood the conversation." Ava said gently, barely avoiding a snicker.

"But what about all the things Daphne has been saying…and what about Tavish?" Valeria protested.

Camille leaned forward, "Val, Daphne thinks that Alex belongs to her because she found him years ago after Aegemon had tossed him in the sea. She nursed him back to health and prevented his first brush with his Prima Mortis. She's helped him deal with a…a very difficult situation. But trust us! Alex has no interest in Daphne—other than an almost sisterly affection."

Valeria couldn't wrap her thinking around it—she assumed her slowness was from all of the wine. She shouldn't have allowed Ava to refill her glass so many times. But it felt nice and relaxed and she was having such a good time with friends! She had friends! And Alex wasn't with Daphne! *Life was wonderful!*

"What were you asking about Tavish?" Ava pressed, taking another sip of her wine.

"I thought…well, weren't you all trying to set me up with Tavish?"

This time Ava spewed her wine as Camille and Ava erupted into hysterics again. Camille grabbed the towel off the coffee table and tossed it back to Ava. "Tavish! Where in god's earth did you get that?"

Valeria thought for a moment and couldn't really think of how she had made that conclusion. "Daphne and Alex aren't…?" Had she understood correctly?

"Oath time." Ava chuckled. Camille placed her hand over her heart, while Ava held up her three fingers in a Girl Scout pledge. "I do solemnly swear that Alex has no carnal knowledge of Daphne—that I have been made aware of." Both Camille and Ava finished in a heartfelt and drunken, "*AMEN!*"

"They aren't together!" Camille added with a hiccup and then removed her hand from her heart to take another sip of wine. "And trust me! Although Tavish is a friend," she snickered, "we most certainly wouldn't '*set you up*' with him!"

Ava added between rolls of continuing laughter, "Besides, it looks to me like you're taken!"

Leaning against the couch Valeria closed her eyes. Ava thought she was taken—by Alex Morgan! What a wonderful dream world that would be!

Valeria awoke with a kink in her neck as she turned her head, she felt fingers gently massaging her neck. The touch was magical and she thought she was in a dream—the dream. She opened her eyes to see that she was on the floor. Camille was stretched out sleeping on the couch and Ava was gone. Valeria's mouth was parched and her body and her head ached. She reached her hand back to her neck and felt the fingers and they interlocked with hers as she heard his soft snicker. It was the most delightful feeling, despite the headache! Valeria turned and was shocked to see that Alex was there, knelt beside her. Her breath caught and she saw the gleam in his eyes.

"Well, I can see that I can't trust Ava to take good care of you!" He said in a whisper as he shook his head. "Letting you sleep on the floor!" Alex raised a brow critically, "And it looks like a bit hungover."

Valeria wondered if that was what was causing the headache and dizziness. It was her first hangover! "I'm fine." Valeria defended.

"Let's get you off the floor." Alex whispered, amusement danced in his eyes as he picked her up. She was in his arms! Valeria liked the feeling. She put her arm around his neck and snuggled in against his chest—and what a marvelous chest it was—all the while she was thinking that she should be arguing that she could walk. Then he set her down on the bed. She breathed in deeply taking in his wonderful scent.

She wished she were more awake to appreciate the experience. Still, she did notice the sun was just starting to come up. Glancing at Alex as he pulled a blanket over her, Valeria noticed that Alex hadn't shaved or changed from the previous night. A few minutes later, he returned with a glass of water. He reached in the bedside table and grabbed a few aspirin. "Here, why don't you take a couple of aspirin and you'll feel better in a few hours."

"I'm fine." Valeria said again, sleepily.

Alex chuckled, "Yes you are!" He ran his hand over her hair affectionately and then sat the glass of water on the bedside table. "I'm going to try to catch an hour or so of sleep." He placed the bottle of aspirin back in the drawer. "Help yourself if you need more."

Valeria faded back off to sleep with the memory of her face against Alex's chest and his wonderful scent engraved on her mind.

Chapter 12

The song of the birds woke her from the dream. Valeria's head still hurt but it felt good to consider all of the revelations of the previous night. She climbed out of the bed seeing that she had slept in the only other dress she had packed.

Camille was in the kitchen looking like she needed some aspirin.

"You look unusually chipper—considering how much we drank last night! Ava is fired as the official wine pourer!" Camille pronounced.

Valeria laughed, feeling entirely too much joy to allow a touch of a headache to ruin her mood. "Do you want an aspirin?"

"Yes please. And then I'm going to go shower."

Valeria turned her head to the side, "Camille, I woke up and Alex was here this morning. He didn't look like he had slept at all. But I'm certain Ava had been gone for some time so Lars and Alex must have finished long before I saw him."

"Of course, you don't think Alex is going to leave you alone with only Ava and me?"

Flushing, Valeria asked, "What's that all about?"

"Don't worry about it. That's just Alex! It's almost noon so I'm going up to take a shower at the main house. I'll meet you up there." She started walking towards the door. "If you could bring that bottle of aspirin with you I'm probably going to need it throughout the day."

Valeria showered and put on her jeans and her black turtleneck with her silver necklace and earrings. She still hadn't had any coffee. She was entirely too anxious to see Alex. As she started out the front door, she remembered the aspirin.

Pulling open the bedside drawer, Valeria pulled out the bottle of aspirin and saw Alex's elegant script next to it. She marveled at the intricate lettering and then realized she was seeing a love letter:

My Beloved Cassandra,

There is no true measure of time: For me it is divided amongst those painful eternities when I await your presence which is magnified exponentially and torments me-and those rare and too, too brief respites when I am at last with you and whole.

Events may momentarily distract-but there is nothing and no one that can ever fill the hollowness in my heart-except you.

The purpose of my existence can only be expressed in terms of you-I sleep only to dream of you. I awaken only to search again for you, your eyes, your smile, your soul.

My heart belongs to you.

Eternally,

Alex

Valeria's heart fell! Alex was in love with someone else: Cassandra! Ava and Camille had been wrong—this was what the trip to Italy had been all about! Somehow Alex thought Valeria could help him find Cassandra. He would wait for his beloved Cassandra. Valeria closed the drawer.

She headed up to the main house feeling heart sick… again. Half way up the trail, Valeria saw Alex, who had showered, shaved and changed.

"You look stunning…especially considering!" The corners of his mouth danced in mild amusement. "How are you feeling?"

"I'm fine." Valeria attempted a smile but the wound was too fresh.

Alex grabbed her hand, "Well, I have just the thing that will put a smile back on your face!" She relished the feeling of his touch, while mourning it at the same time. She was quite aware of the electricity in his touch…but he was just a friendly sort of guy, she decided. He led her to the dining room and poured her a cup of coffee blended perfectly with cream.

"It's wonderful. Thank you!'

His eyes narrowed, "Are you alright?" He asked, assessing her mood.

Valeria shrugged, "Just…tired, I guess." She buried her pain behind the coffee cup. He was about to further the query when he was interrupted by the arrival of the rest of the family.

Lars took control, "Let's talk about Prima Mortis." He leaned forward, "Val, there are a confluence of events brewing which will culminate in an opportunity for us to remove the major threat to our existence—Aegemon.

"There was some thought that you should be left out of

this discussion. But most of us here believe that it is only right that you be invited to participate. You have become a part of our secret and by that a part of our family."

Hearing the words, Valeria was momentarily overwhelmed. She had never been a part of a family. And to be part of this family, this incredible group of people nearly erased a lifetime of what she now realized was loneliness. She glanced to Ava and Camille, whose eyes twinkled—and then to Alex.

Instantly, Valeria knew that it had been Alex who had not wanted her to be involved in this discussion. She also realized that he did care for her. But having seen the love letter—and knowing that Cassandra filled his heart—Valeria knew that she was the "momentary distraction" that he wrote about in his declaration of love.

Desperately needing to run and shed her tears alone, but knowing there was no way to do that without revealing her feelings to him, she again buried her face in her coffee cup. It was at that moment, Valeria decided that despite her feelings for Alex, she would not permit herself to be a second choice—dumped when he reconnected with his love. That would just be too painful, she thought. And she would not let him know how she felt. She knew him well enough to know that he would want to soothe her and it would be too easy for her to take refuge in his arms, only to be rejected later.

Somehow, she had sensed that all of this–this Aegemon, the visions—all of it had to do with Alex's precious Cassandra. Perhaps helping him get her back to her was the gift that Valeria could give to this extraordinary man.

Lars continued seeming unaware of Valeria's turmoil. She forced herself to focus on Lars' words. "We have been attempting to discover what Aegemon's Prima Mortis may have been. We have attempted drowning, burning, bleeding, compression injuries. He has been dismembered many times in different ways and still he comes back."

Attempting to shake herself out of her newfound depression, she asked, "How does someone come back from dismemberment?"

Lars clasped his hands, matter-of-factly, "We don't know exactly but within about 24 hours we are normal again. If it's a minor injury we can recover quicker—like Alex's broken ribs a few days ago."

She interrupted, "You broke your ribs?" She realized that Alex had seemed injured immediately after the incident and then moments later seemed fine. "I thought I heard bones breaking."

"No big deal." Alex smiled nonchalantly. "Good as new!" He noticed that she looked away a bit too quickly. Something was wrong. Alex glanced at Daphne, but she seemed well behaved. He wondered if it was the discussion that was causing the problem.

Lars continued, "What we have found is that we remain effect of the cause if it continues. For instance, if we were to be stabbed through the heart, we would remain effect of our heart not working, until the knife or sword was removed, then in about 24 hours we would somehow be healed.

"Camille's husband Jonah may be stuck at the bottom of the sea and suffering from hypothermia until we find him. Or he may have surfaced and be living somewhere not remembering us. Hypothermia causes amnesia, as does electric shock."

"I didn't hear you say disease." Valeria offered.

"She's right." Alex's eyes rose with hope and he began to

pace. "We didn't consider disease because frankly in those days there was very little of it." Alex's eyes narrowed. "But, there *were a few plagues!"*

Lars jumped in, "Tavish, Daph, let's get moving on this. Camille, can you get Mani updated?" She nodded. "Also, we'll need to know what plagues may have been around the possible time that Aegemon stopped aging." Lars looked to Alex, "Lexi, you know him best—well you remember him best, anyway. How old do you think he was?"

"I don't know. I was young." Alex smirked, "When you're young everyone over 40 seems old."

"Perhaps Shinsu or Jeremiah know." Ava suggested.

"I don't trust that Jeremiah!" Tavish shook his head.

Nodding, Lars added, "I agree about Jeremiah. Perhaps Shinsu can provide us with some valuable answers. Let's do our research and regroup tomorrow morning at 10."

Alex seemed suddenly tense, "Tomorrow?" He pressed. "It feels like we are pushing the time envelope just a bit too tight."

Patting Alex's back, Lars responded, "We need the time to research this. Don't worry, we'll figure it all out." Lars looked to Valeria and nodded soothingly.

She followed Alex to the door, feeling silly and wondering if she should be following him, or even if he wanted her to follow him. She felt Camille smiling sympathetically at her, but she couldn't make eye contact with anyone, feeling so rejected and humiliated.

As soon as they stepped outside, he asked, "Val is everything okay?"

She looked away and swallowed, "Yeah…I just need a

nap, I think."

Alex nodded, distracted, "Alright. Well, I'm sorry, I just can't leave this to them. Would you mind, terribly if I left you on your own again?" He touched her shoulder affectionately. "I hate doing that. But my guess is that you would appreciate the rest."

She was again mesmerized by his eyes and his smile. Yes, she most definitely cared a great deal for Alex Morgan. As her heart swelled with emotion, she quickly and looked away, "No problem."

Stepping down the foot trail through the beautiful woods, she wondered if she could afford to be here when he was again reunited with Cassandra. Tears obscured Valeria's vision. She wiped them away—refusing to acknowledge the loss. Alex wasn't hers and never would be. He loved a beautiful princess; an extraordinary woman who had saved his life and his heart. She should have known from the painting; she had seen the look in the children's eyes—that look, though she had not personally experienced it, was *clearly love*!

Of course, someone like Alex should be with a princess—not a foul-tempered woman, like Daphne—or someone incredibly average like herself. Immediately, Valeria realized that while it was difficult and painful to think of him with Daphne, somehow she had known that there was not a tremendous amount of depth of emotion between them. But finding the letter that he had written to Cassandra had changed everything. No, she would not be able to stay at Morgana with Alex and Cassandra.

The temperature had cooled but was still pleasant. Strolling past the giant Gingko tree with its brilliant and magical golden leaves, Valeria sighed. She would bury herself in a great book. Not Alex's *Walden*— that would be a connection with him and she didn't want to think of him anymore today. If she had to mourn, she decided she would mourn someone else.

Valeria grabbed *Wuthering Heights* from his bookshelf and a cotton blanket. She laid under that beautiful Gingko and melted into the tragic story of Catherine and Heathcliff.

CHAPTER 13

With all but one detail decided, the family had sent Alex back to the cottage. He was getting loopy from the rollercoaster of his emotions and lack of sleep. And Alex—typically the optimist—felt the weight of the decisions that they had faced. Frankly, the "solution" was unacceptable; there were too many unknowns. A lifetime of planning and working towards this very moment and the results left only a *possibility* of success. But that possibility was all he had now—that and an evening with her alone.

Tomorrow, he would face his greatest fear—next to losing her again to death. He would have to tell Valeria the whole truth about who she was and what was about to happen. That thought left him nauseous and dizzy. He wondered how he would be able to hide his emotions from Valeria.

How would she respond to the information, he wondered. Would she run from him—only to face her fates alone? That thought forced his stomach into his throat. Alex stopped and leaned against a tree. Breathe, he thought. Having her die alone would be more than he could bear! Or would he be able to convince her that their plan—no matter how wild—was worth the effort, only to lose her in that effort? That thought was equally as overwhelming. Alex tried to steady his head.

These might be his last hours with her for who knew how many eternities? Camille had said that he needed to find a way to be with Valeria and rejoice in this time. Right now she was alive and with him. Alex needed to distract himself from the rest of it. But there was only one thought that could distract him. Those were the thoughts that he worked constantly to keep at bay when she was with him. He had to remind himself that she may have a sense of familiarity—but *he had the memories*. He had to give her time…but there was none.

With his anxiety peaked, his only solace was in her. Looking into her eyes and showing her his heart the day before had been dangerous for him. Alex could see the passion in her eyes that matched his own and made him dream of her again. He imagined how it would be to feel those lips against his and taste her sweet mouth. He imagined the feel of her soft curls against his neck and her body wrapped in his—flesh against flesh, heart against heart. And he dreamed of what it would be like to have his desire for her finally fulfilled.

The hunger that had consumed Alex for thousands of years overtook him. To have a few nights refuge from a lifetime of fear and desire was an almost overwhelming proposition! And tonight she would sleep in the next room.

Taking a slow, deep breath, Alex worked to stave off his passion. He stared up at the stars; how had another day passed so quickly? They seemed to fly while she was here. Calming himself, Alex knew that he would not take the risk of pleasure now. He had a bigger dream than making love to her. It was that other vision that gave him purpose for everything else! Even, if it meant delaying indefinitely the pleasures that would lay only a few feet from him tonight. He was particularly vulnerable and would have to be on guard of his emotions. It would be too easy to go to her!

As he approached the cottage, he noticed that all the lights were out. So that he didn't wake her, he worked his way to the kitchen and flipped on the under-counter lighting. He looked around and didn't see her. Alex walked by the bedroom but the bed was made and empty. A bolt of panic went through him.

Why hadn't he had someone watching her? He turned on all the lights and now certain that she wasn't there, headed back up to the main house, nearly running, nearly heartsick. Had she left on her own? Or had Aegemon found her? Alex fought back the bile that rose in his throat. Why had he left her alone?

As he came around to the side of the house, the moon stepped between branches of the Gingko and he saw something under the tree. He approached and found her asleep on a blanket, a book still in her hand. Alex breathed a deep sigh of relief.

The moonlight caressed her face with gentle shadows. It was when she was sleeping that he could fully appreciate her beauty. He took a moment to take in every turn of the face that he adored.

"Hey, beautiful!" He said, gently nudging her. Valeria instantly shot up, startled and lost.

"It's Alex!" He said, softly.

Valeria reached for him and for a moment his arms went around her in the most marvelous way; pulling her into his chest as his hands seemed to be taking in the feel of her neck and back and down her arms. She felt his deep low breath of desire as his lips brushed the side of her face…and then she felt his back stiffen as his hands pulled back. *That's right—there was Cassandra*! Valeria pulled away from him, embarrassed.

He stroked her arms, "You're cold! Let's get you inside!" Alex wrapped the blanket around her as she struggled to wake up. He muttered to himself, "I should have checked on you sooner!" Then he realized that she hadn't eaten, "You must be starving. I'm afraid I forgot about food today."

Suddenly, she felt a pit in her stomach and wondered whether it was hunger or her heart. She gathered up the book and the blanket. Why did he have to be so damned wonderful? She sulked into the cottage and watched as Alex lit a fire. "Let me fix you something to eat. What would you like?" He went to the refrigerator but she could sense something in his mood that seemed dark and serious. He sighed deeply, "Eggs, chicken…pasta?"

Forcing the emotion back, Valeria shrugged, "I'm really not hungry." She wondered for a moment if he heard the strain in her voice.

As he stood in the light from the refrigerator, Alex turned and his eyes narrowed. "Is everything alright?"

Taking a deep breath to get control of her voice she did what she never did, she lied, "I ate a slice of pizza earlier." Well, it wasn't a complete lie—the last thing she had eaten was a slice of pizza. But she knew she couldn't face him without feeling a deep sadness for what she would never have.

"If you don't mind, I think the hangover has affected me. I think I will call it an early evening. Do you still want me to sleep here?"

Alex looked at her critically, "Of course." He closed the refrigerator and walked back to the fire. "That's probably just as well. I'm not good company tonight." He sat on the sofa in front of the fire. It was better that he avoided temptation.

From the bedroom window, the full moon peeked out from behind the Gingko tree. Valeria marveled, in her pain, at the beauty and romance of the evening. It was quite romantic—except that it was meant for someone else.

"Let me know if you need anything. I'll be here." Alex said woodenly.

Valeria felt jilted. Not that she wanted to jump in bed with him—well, not that she hadn't thought about that too. But somehow in the back of her mind she believed that this would be a new beginning for her; one where she realized her heart's desire. Well, she grimaced, she had realized her heart's desire—*but he was taken*! Still, life here with Alex and his family somehow felt fuller. It was as if always before she had been waiting for this level of...life and feeling. And now she knew that she could never be happy with the two-dimensional drawing that was *her real life*...the life without Alex.

Opening her suitcase, she searched for her oversized tee shirt that she slept in at home. How was it that she had fallen asleep in her clothes every night since she had left? She rolled her eyes. In her hurry to pack several days before, she had not brought a robe or pajamas—as a matter-of- fact; she had brought nothing that could be construed as comfortable nightwear except her sweats and tee shirt that were dirty from badminton.

Glancing at Alex, who was sitting on the couch staring at the fire, Valeria suddenly found herself getting angry. He had lured her here, pretending to care about her, when it all had to do with her helping him reunite with his true love. Why hadn't he just told her the truth from the start? She would have helped him—and then her heart wouldn't have been ripped to shreds! Now here she was, humiliated, with the man she had come to care about staring into the fire, imagining if only his lady love was with him.

Maybe Weege was right when she said that men were only capable of caring about themselves! Then Valeria realized it was just her pain talking. Obviously Alex cared about more than himself. She just wished it had been her that he cared about. She took a deep breath attempting to ease her pain—it didn't work. She should just ask him for a tee shirt. But Valeria couldn't bear to tell him that she hadn't brought nightwear to this obviously platonic weekend. She sighed and got her courage up.

"Uhm, Alex?"

"Yes." He stared at the fire.

He didn't even care enough to properly acknowledge her by turning around. Suddenly, she was afraid that her voice would crack. She pushed forward—courage! Deep breath—, "Alex, it's just that I didn't bring...I mean, I packed so quickly that I forgot to bring anything to sleep in."

Alex rubbed his head as if irritated. Valeria thought he at least could have been kind about it. Instead, she felt embarrassed and deflated for having gone away with him only to discover that he wasn't interested in her.

"Uh, well, what would you like? I have a number of..." His voice broke off, "You know there's tee shirts or ...well, whatever you like in the walk-in. Just help yourself."

The walk-in was huge. And just what she imagined his closet would look like. The dark wood had built-in lights and numerous drawers. Everything was perfectly folded, clean and organized. Half of the rack on one side was clear of any clothes, as if cleared for her—or awaiting Cassandra. Valeria saw Alex's maroon sweater from their meeting in New York lying in a pile to be dry-cleaned. Surprisingly, she found herself pull the sweater to her face. It smelled good, like him. She realized what she was doing and angrily dropped the sweater back into the bin.

Pulling a tee shirt from the hanger, she decided that would do. She changed in the closet and came out. Of course, she didn't need to worry about Alex looking; he was obviously distracted by thoughts of Cassandra. She crawled into the bed. It was the first time Valeria had a chance to evaluate it and the bed was incredibly comfortable. Yet with her heart rate rising from anger, she doubted she would sleep. She turned the lamp off. "Well, good night."

He grunted something.

She laid there for ten minutes and found herself getting more and more worked up. Finally she couldn't take it anymore. Did he really believe that she was so desperate that she would lay there in *his* bed, alone while he sat there and...*what*? She found herself sitting up in anger. She sensed Alex stiffen but not turn.

Trying to determine an outlet for her anger, Valeria got out of bed—she didn't know what else to do. But she knew she wasn't going to just go to sleep!

There was always David. At least David wanted her. He was probably in Prague by now. She could be there by morning—if she had a car. But here she was in the middle of nowhere. She went into the closet and came out fully dressed. She threw her clothes from the day before in the suitcase. That felt good. Alex turned sideways to peek over the couch.

"Val? Everything okay?" He asked. Valeria thought he almost sounded concerned. Well, it was just too late now.

She grabbed her cell phone. She only had a few bars but she dialed David's number. There was a long pause then his phone rang and went right to voicemail. Valeria left a message, "David, I'm at a private estate called Morgana about ten miles north of Trento, Italy. Will you come and get me?" By then Alex was standing, looking with concern towards the bedroom.

As he walked to the archway of the bedroom, Valeria began throwing the rest of her clothes into her suitcase with as much force as she could muster. "Val, what's wrong?"

Feeling herself hyperventilate, Valeria went to the bathroom and began throwing her bathroom products in the bag. "A little late for that!" She muttered to herself.

Alex came to the bath door with his hands in his pockets, feeling helpless. "Val? I'm not sure what happened. But would you prefer to sleep at the main house?"

She pushed past him and back into the bedroom to her suitcase. Alex returned to his stance at the archway attempting to stay out of her way, his eyes now wide with panic and pain. Valeria grabbed a pair of socks and her shoes and brushed past Alex to the stool at the kitchen bar and began putting them on.

By now she was shaking. She hoped he wouldn't notice. "No. I don't want to stay at the main house. I don't want to stay here at all. I've had enough of this Alex. Please call me a cab? I'll get a hotel in town."

Turning in the archway to face Valeria in the kitchen, he pleaded, "Please Val! Please tell me what I did wrong!"

She glowered, her face flushed in righteous fury, "Oh, you didn't do anything wrong! It's me! I made the mistake of going away with someone I didn't know." She put her hands to her head, "God! What was I thinking?" By now to Valeria's embarrassment, angry tears began to flow. She wiped them away with the back of her hand. "I know it's late but I'm sure you can call me a cab."

"Val, are you crying?"

She rose and walked back to the bedroom again brushing by Alex to get her suitcase. "No…" She lied again, "I'm leaving."

Closing her suitcase, she grabbed the handle and walked into the great room. Alex tried to take the suitcase from her but she pushed his hand off.

"Why?" Valeria turned to him defiantly. "Why did you bring me here Alex? I thought there was…well…something between us. Do you care *so little* about me? I came here because of you! But it seems like you've gone out of your way to avoid me since we arrived!"

Alex let out a small, nervous laugh. "Avoid you?" He pulled her around. His face was ashen, "Val, I have thought of *nothing but you*!"

She pulled away and turned from Alex. He sighed miserably. "Val, there isn't a cab that will come up the hill tonight. *Please*, just go up to the main house. Camille is waiting for you. She'll help you with whatever you want to do." He patted her shoulders. "We can talk later." Alex rested his hands on her arms as Valeria walked out the door.

Following the darkened trail towards the main house, she saw Camille walking rapidly towards her and the quivering waves of hurt became racking sobs. Camille hugged Valeria and then handed her a handkerchief.

"Let's go up to the main house. We can talk there." Camille said gently guiding Valeria. As they approached it, Valeria stopped and glanced warily at the house between sobs.

"Don't worry. It's just you and me. Everyone else has cleared out. There won't be other ears and we won't be interrupted." Camille soothed. "I'll put on some tea."

At the house, Valeria found herself beginning to relax as she stared out the window into the woods. "I can't believe I'm so angry over Alex." She choked. "I mean, really he has been quite admirable. He can't help it if I'm not his type."

Camille did a double-take, her voice lost its soothing nature and it again jumped up several octaves. "*Not his type!*" She regained her composure. "Valeria, I think you really care about Alex…probably more than care."

Gulping back a sob, Valeria thought for a moment, "I know I really shouldn't care this much, this soon. I mean, he could be an international criminal for all I know!"

Rolling her eyes in pretended irritation, Camille teased, "Now do you really have so little faith in your decision-making ability?"

"Alright, probably not a criminal." Valeria thought for a second. Tears welled up in her eyes again and she spoke in a whisper, afraid to hear herself, "Camille, I'm…I'm…"

"Val, are you alright?" Camille's eyes widened in alarm.

"Oh my god! Camille! *I'm…I'm in love with Alex!*" With the words out she suddenly felt a pain in her chest that made breathing near impossible.

Camille patted Valeria's back, "Breathe!" Valeria forced a breath. Once it was clear that Valeria was breathing again, Camille asked softly, "And the problem is?"

"He's in love with someone else." Valeria sobbed.

"I thought we straightened out all of that nonsense about Daphne."

Valeria wiped her soaked face, "It's not Daphne. I…well, I wasn't snooping…I was getting the aspirin for you and I found a love letter that Alex wrote. He said that anything other than *her* was a momentary distraction." Valeria sobbed, "He loves her. He will never love me."

"Hmmm…you found a letter to Cassandra."

"You knew!" Valeria's face flamed red with betrayal from her new friend.

"Look, this is really between you and Alex." Camille rubbed Valeria's back, "But Val, I can tell you with absolute certainty that Alex thinks of nothing but *you*."

"That's just not true! I mean, he seems to find almost any excuse to do other things with anyone else other than me! He's brought me here and has left me alone almost the entire time. And the other thing I really have to consider is…well, you know…the obvious."

"The obvious?"

Tears rolled down Valeria's face, "I mean…well…when Alex and I were together, I saw all these really extraordinary women—beautiful women—they were falling all over themselves to talk to him. I could see what they were thinking…what is a guy like *him* doing with a girl like me."

"To address what you call 'the obvious', first of all; anyone that would think that, simply doesn't *see* you! Secondly, I don't think you see yourself very clearly. And lastly, Alex didn't choose those other women. He chose you!"

Taking a deep breath, Camille continued, "And as far as Alex not spending time with you, well, there's a lot on Alex's plate right this minute. But also, I think he is forcing himself to try to give you space so that you can decide on your own if you like him. He doesn't want to scare you off. I think he's also probably scared."

"Alex? Scared?" Valeria's eyes narrowed in disbelief.

"He is going through a lot with you here. He's trying to manage it. Alex isn't perfect but I know that if you level with him, you will discover everything you want to know about him and exactly how he feels about you…and *anyone else* you want to ask him about."

"Camille, what are you suggesting?"

"Tell him that you love him!" Camille insisted.

"*Tell him that I love him*?" Valeria said, incredulously. "I couldn't possibly do that!"

"Why not?"

Reflecting for a moment, Valeria realized she had spent a lifetime learning how to avoid people knowing how she felt. "I...I can't...I don't want him to see me as some foolish girl...probably one of many that are...in love with him."

"Whatever you're thinking...tell him."

"Why? When all it will do is make him feel sorry for me. I can see that he likes me. I can see that I could be a…a substitute. But why would I set myself up for humiliation when he obviously loves someone else." Valeria sobbed.

"I know this sounds kind of harsh, but Val, you don't strike me as a coward." Camille put her arm around Valeria's shoulder. "And until you are willing to be straight with your feelings, why would you expect him to be straight with his?"

"I can't." Valeria murmured.

"I know that somewhere in you is the courage to put your heart on your sleeve and ask for what you want, instead of only taking what's offered." Camille's words sunk in like a knife.

"I know you have it in you. Find it!" Camille offered Valeria a wistful smile, "It will set you free!" She continued, "Give him a chance to respond before you decide that it will be rejection." Camille winked mischievously, "And then you can also satisfy your curiosity about Alex's possible criminal activities."

Valeria shrugged, desperately unhappy. "I don't know, Camille. Right now I'm so humiliated and the only thing I want to do is leave."

"I'll tell you what. You tell him what you feel—and listen to what he has to say. And then once all is said and done, if you still insist on leaving, I will drive you to town! Okay?" Valeria cringed, but nodded. "But just food for thought—not to guilt you into anything—but Alex has probably not slept since he met you in New York. If you leave, he most certainly will not sleep tonight either."

"Come with me." Camille led Valeria to the deck, "First of all, what do you want me to tell Alex? You know he's asking."

"Please, Camille! Please, don't tell him anything."

Camille nodded and then started down the stairs. "Go talk to him. But if you insist on being stubborn and leaving Alex in agony all night, you are welcome to sleep at the main house. We have a room for you here. I don't recommend it—not much privacy, especially for the next few days. Besides if you sleep here—so will Alex."

Glancing down the hill, Camille urged, "He's waiting for you. He's worried that he's upset you. *Tell him how you feel*!"

Lifting a finger, Camille added, "One last suggestion—ask Alex for the full tour of the cottage."

"The full tour? I don't understand." Valeria frowned.

"Alex is quite an artist. Ask him to show you his studio."

"I don't know." Suddenly, Valeria realized that Alex had

painted the picture of Cassandra and himself.

"Be the courageous woman I know you to be!" Camille hugged Valeria again and then lifted an eyebrow, "You know, last night after Lars and Alex finished up, Alex came down to the cottage and stayed on the porch until morning." Valeria looked at Camille doubtingly. "He wanted you to have some fun. But even then, he couldn't stay away from you."

Smiling, Camille pointed down the hill. Even through the darkness, Valeria could see Alex's frame lit by the lights on the trail, looking at her, waiting for her.

CHAPTER 14

Valeria tentatively walked down the path to Alex. His hands were nervously steadied in his pockets. He stepped towards Valeria and hesitantly reached out to hug her, "I'm sorry, beautiful! I never meant to make you feel anything but safe."

He broke from the hug quickly and took her hand. "Come with me." He guided her into the cottage and sat next to her on the sofa in front of the fire. "Camille says we have some things to discuss." Alex muttered to himself, "I'd say that was an understatement."

Sitting with him, holding his hand and seeing how hurt he was caused her to love him even more. She had hurt this extraordinary man whose only crime was to love someone else. But Camille had suggested there was more to the story. Valeria needed the truth to be out in the open.

"Can I ask you some questions?"

Alex nodded as he wiped the tear that flowed from her eye.

"Is Cassandra your Symbolon?"

Alex's eyes narrowed. "That's not an easy question."

"I have time." Valeria crossed her arms. Alex let out a small, nervous laugh.

"Let's just say 'yes'—for sake of argument."

"Are you still in love with her?" Valeria held her arms, knowing the answer. Why should she expect anything else?

Alex's eyes rimmed with emotion, "With all of my heart."

"I know I shouldn't ask…" Valeria already knew the answer and it really didn't change a thing. But she had to see his response. "She's beautiful, isn't she?"

"Extraordinarily so." He whispered.

She gulped and took a deep breath. "I saw your love letter…it's the Princess Cassandra…the one in the vision." Alex's nod was barely perceptible.

A cry escaped Valeria's throat, "Well…I've decided I'm going to help you find her." Valeria swallowed her pain. Alex was in love with someone else and always would be. She hesitated, "Alex…what if you never have the chance to be with her?"

Looking away for a moment, he responded, "I'll *never* give up…" Valeria's face dropped. He lifted her chin and spoke softly, "Before I say anymore, Camille tells me that I need to listen to everything you have to say."

Nervously, Valeria gulped. In all of her life, she had never asked anybody for anything. She had lived her life providing for herself what she needed. For the first time, she needed something from someone else—something from him. Valeria wondered if she had the courage to say it. She doubted it, but realizing that it was only her cowardice that kept her from stepping forward, she spoke, "Alex, I wondered if there was any possibility...I mean...let me start over..."

She breathed deeply, again gathering courage, "Do you think there would ever be any possibility that you could...care about someone as..." A tear escaped Valeria's eye and she rapidly pushed it away. *Coward! Say it!* "Do you think you could ever care about me?"

The tears gushed from her eyes. At least she had said it. Alex reached for her face and she forced his hand away—she didn't want or need pity.

Then, she realized that she hadn't actually told him. *Just tell him,* she told herself. With a breath of courage she began, "Because Alex...I am so sorry..." She choked again, "I am so embarrassed… but I promised Camille and myself that I would have the courage to say it...but… in the course of well...I guess really only a few days...as ridiculous as it may seem—". She looked into his beautiful blue eyes and saw a fire in them, "I fell in love with you."

Emotion swirled in his eyes. He swallowed and then took her hand. "Camille is right, you need to see my studio."

He guided Valeria to an attachment of the cottage. He opened the door and switched on the light. She gasped; there were paintings and sculptures of bronze, ceramic and marble.

Stepping towards to the rear of the L-shaped studio, Alex flipped on another light and said, "I don't usually share this." His eyes nervously flashed around the room.

Valeria stopped at the first painting. It was the young Cassandra. It was breathtaking and obviously painted in love.

The next work was a marble sculpture. Alex moved back to her side cautiously watching her expression. Valeria thought she was hallucinating. She wiped her eyes. It was a sculpture of herself—but she thought, far more beautiful.

She couldn't quite take in what she was seeing. Valeria looked at Alex and then back at the sculpture. "Alex, I don't understand…" They wandered to the next work.

It was a painting of Valeria's face with her hair pulled into braided wraps and a blue gown from the renaissance era. The work was titled "Isabella 1574". Valeria stepped by each piece of amazing work—all with her face and each with a different date and name. Another sculpture said "Jenni 1903".

At the back of the studio, there a bust of Valeria looking towards the heavens with a haunted look. She stared at it for some time.

"It's a bronze." Alex offered

She was mesmerized, "Uhm, bronze? But the color."

"I added a metallic patina." Alex continued feeling as if reality had left him and he was now on a new plane; one that he had never even dared dream of. "But on this one, I experimented with fast-drying acrylic paints. I think it looks more lifelike." He said in a hushed tone.

She couldn't take her eyes off the sculpture. "Is that really me?" Alex's nod was nearly imperceptible. Her brows pulled down, "Is that how you see me?"

He let out an uneasy laugh, "No." She turned to look at him. His eyes again welled with emotion. His hand brushed her face. "I could *never* capture your spirit. It's the most beautiful thing I've ever seen in my life."

She was electrified by his touch, by him, by the work…*by the truth*. She swallowed again allowing it all to sink in. She had to focus on the work—not him! "But the eyes…" Valeria blinked so she could speak, "My eyes aren't that color."

"They were that color." Alex whispered to contain the emotion.

"They were?"

He nodded.

"It's...it's like yours." Focus on the work, she reminded herself. "How did you make them that color?"

Alex moved his fingers to Valeria's jaw line, "Well, I...uh, well, I crushed and used Lapis, Tanzanite and Azurite to get the color." He sighed, lost in this new world. "It isn't an easy color to duplicate."

"Your...work is beautiful." She was finding it difficult to breathe.

"It's the subject." He murmured as his hand moved to her neck.

Valeria saw a tag at the bottom of the sculpture. It said, "Cassandra 1186 B.C."

"Come with me." He said taking her hand.

As they walked to the door of the studio, Valeria looked at the first painting and suddenly it all made sense. The painting was of the little girl in the vision.

"It was me?" She said incredulously.

His face lit as he took her hand and led her to the sofa in front of the fireplace. "I should have put you up at the main house. But I have spent so many years creating this cottage for you that I jumped too soon at the opportunity to share it with you. Instead you felt uncomfortable."

Was she dreaming? Her voice came out in a cry, "I love this place! It feels like...*everything* I love is here." She glanced shyly at him and then she looked around the room with new eyes that saw every detail with a new appreciation.

"The cottage was modeled after a number of homes you designed. I would go to them, after..." Alex gulped, "Well, after you were gone. I would wait, sometimes generations, to purchase what I could." He looked up and smiled but his eyes were melancholy.

"You loved blue hydrangea and bougainvillea."

"I still do." She smiled softly.

"I plant bougainvillea every year, as hard as I've worked to preserve the vines, it is just too cool to bring them out now." Alex pointed to a basket on the table. "That was a wine casket that I converted. Most of the furniture here came from your homes or I had it replicated. Some pieces, like your china, I had to wait almost a century to get. That pattern of Limoges was designed for you."

Valeria was stunned. "What else?"

"Do you want to know more?" He asked.

"I want to know everything."

"There's a lot to know. Not all of it is pleasant."

"Show me." She sat her hands out palm up.

He brushed the side of her face and turned it towards him so that she was looking into his eyes. Then he took both of her hands in his and the force she had felt with Mani began.

Valeria saw herself as a young girl—similar to Mani's memory, only from a different angle. She saw the little girl, herself, smiling at Alex, a special smile, like they were secret friends. Valeria saw her own drowned face from Alex's viewpoint and heard his sobs and felt her own lifeless body. She saw Alex in a castle. She saw him battling the robed man—Aegemon—many times over. She saw herself in Alex's arms and numerous scenes with Alex's triangular tattoo wrapped around her unconscious or dead body in different kinds of clothing, in very different locations.

Finally, the visions stopped. Valeria felt a rush of intense emotion for Alex and for the first time felt why he treated her with such fragility.

She wanted to move her mouth the short distance to his. She wanted to reach over and touch his face. Instead she clung to his hands, like a gift. His touch had a whole new level of emotional electricity to it, as if all his love had just been released. Suddenly all the years that she had suffered, without love, was filled, like a vacuum with the realization that he loved her!

Valeria offered a soft laugh as joyful tears rimmed her eyes. "That letter…it was to me." She whispered in astonishment.

His thumb played across the top of her hands. She could see that there was still a deep sadness in his eyes of something unsaid.

"Alex, was I a true oracle?"

"You are."

"Sibyl's or oracles have visions. I don't have visions. And I'm certainly not immortal like you."

"We don't really understand it." Alex took a breath. These were the questions he wasn't prepared to confront yet. She would have to know the rest. But tonight, he had almost lost her *again*. Because of his own fears she had been hurt and had wanted to leave him. Distracted, Alex moved his hand to her knee. He did it smoothly and naturally and then felt the heat move through him. He swallowed and pulled his hand back.

Alex needed to keep his head about him—especially over the next few days. Everything—her life, his life—rode on the precarious edge balanced on his wits. He was inches from her mouth. The mouth he had spent a millennium dreaming of, painting and carving—the mouth he had touched in stone and bronze and clay. He had dreamt of again feeling the warmth of that beautiful wide mouth responding to his. He could see the desire in her eyes. But he knew that if he started now, they wouldn't stop.

With extraordinary effort, he forced himself to reduce the temptation by moving his face further away from hers. "Beautiful, the next few days are going to be…important. It would be better if we kept things…just…" He let out a deep sigh and then looked into her eyes. Valeria could see the fire again. His voice filled with the passion that he felt. "I could get lost in this…so easily." He closed his eyes for a moment. "But I need to stay focused."

Giving into her absolute need to be nearer to him, she leaned her face against his chest and as she did she felt Alex shudder. She moved her body against his and heard him say something unintelligible under his breath. Then slowly his arms went around her, pulling her in closer. She saw his eyes close and could hear his heart wildly pounding—or was it her own?

She didn't want to be in control of her responses to him. But if she was going to keep herself from kissing him, she would need to think of something else. She drew in a jagged breath, "Do I…reincarnate?"

Gathering control, Alex took another deep breath and let it out slowly, "Well…it…uh seems so."

He opened his eyes and looked down at her and then smiled softly, "You come back with different names…" He stroked her face, "But *always* you."

She longed to move her mouth to his neck that was inches from her but she could see that it was important to Alex to not get carried away. And for now she would respect his wishes. She wasn't quite certain how it worked when you wanted someone so desperately—did you just wait? With David, she never had this problem. Valeria's mind reeled into reality—that's right, she was engaged to someone else! Perhaps that was what was holding Alex back from kissing her.

"Is that how it works for people that aren't oracles? Does everyone—other than immortals reincarnate?"

"I don't really know." He kissed the top of her head, "I only know about you."

Pulling her hand along his chest she was at once amazed by the wonderfully chiseled feel of him. All she could think was, *oh my*! Valeria felt Alex shudder again. "You have a very strong beingness that seems to completely...vivify a body. And you seem to come back time and time again—*thankfully*! I don't ever know where. Caleb believes he is your compass. He believes that he can find you. Sometimes he can get a general idea of your location and sometimes he can't."

"Caleb?" Valeria asked incredulously.

"When he found me, he told me he was going to help me find you. And when he isn't distracted—as I've discovered 12-year-old boys frequently are—he seems to be able to help."

Alex's hand started to move down her spine—causing her heart to pound even harder and the heat to rush through her. He seemed to sense this, stopping himself as he swallowed, "As an oracle we all have visions of the future. But for some reason most of my visions seem to be centered on you." Alex shook his head, "Our visions aren't as strong as they once were. But we still receive the guidance we need."

She smiled, "What was it like…with us?"

"Well…you don't make it easy for a guy." His eyes danced in the firelight, "And…I should tell you…" Alex's mouth curved in a playful smile, "You do have the most frustrating propensity for royal families that I will…" He closed his eyes and shook his head, heavily, "never understand." They both laughed softly.

"Well, not this time!"

"Evidently not." Alex's face got serious again. "I wish my visions had helped you more. But the problem is that they rarely tell me where you are. I have to concentrate and hope there are enough details to ascertain time and location."

Valeria sighed as the side of her mouth touched his chest and she felt his heart thunder. "You did save my life!"

Alex nodded as if upset with himself, "That one was easy; Central Park and the street signs and the time of year." He paused, "It's earlier that I was referring to."

Unable to restrain the flinch, she said, "Your visions of me…they were only when my life was threatened… or… how does that work?" She bit her lip nervously.

"It seems to be my lot in life to mostly see your challenges." Alex looked down at her, his eyes pained, "I'm sorry I wasn't there then."

"I don't know what you mean." Valeria lied again.

"I searched everywhere for you, trying to find the white house with the green trim." He said with tormented eyes.

She buried her face back in his chest. "Alex, please tell me you didn't see that!"

Recognizing his error immediately he pulled her tightly into him. "I'm sorry, Val…I shouldn't have said anything."

Feeling an old tear rising, she closed her eyes and inhaled slowly through her nose. "Really, it wasn't a big deal." She tried to bury it. "It isn't like they raped me…really it was nothing." She pushed off from his chest and looked away with sudden panic. "The rest of them—," Valeria glanced up towards the main house, "—they don't know, do they?"

Alex turned her face to look into his. "No one else knows." Then, he stroked her hair and pulled her face back into his chest, "Those kids…they did worse than harm you physically. They betrayed your sweetness and your trust."

"It was my own fault that things went as far as they did." Valeria admitted. "The girl told me all I had to do was cry and they would stop." She whispered, "A normal person would have cried. I don't know why, I just…"

He kissed her forehead, "Please! You were an innocent child!" his eyes lost in pain. "…and I couldn't find you. And your father…"

"Yeah, well, Dad was never one for noticing fine details."

His jaw clenched. "Like the fact that his 12-year-old daughter was wandering down a busy street lost and covered in mud?" Valeria gave a nervous laugh. She didn't want to be talking about this now…or ever.

"That's why my visions are both a gift and a curse." Alex swallowed, "I can't always protect you." He pulled her in even tighter, "But I swear, whatever I have to do this time, I will protect you! Whatever I have to do, I won't let anyone ever hurt you again."

Suddenly her pain was buried with another emotion that was so much stronger; so much more significant. She stroked his face. *God, she did love him!*

"You can't do that Alex. Sometimes I'm going to be hurt." Valeria smiled at him, "But the pain will always be less now…" She choked, "*because you love me.*"

He pulled her into him and brushed his face along the top of her head, repressing the urge to kiss her again. His voice a whisper of the emotion he felt, "That I do!"

Feeling his arms around her she could forget everything else. "Tell me about a good vision you had."

"Well, there was one particular vision." Alex answered softly, as a blissful expression replaced the anguish. "We were together."

"Like now?" Valeria snuggled into his arms.

"Kind of." She looked up to see Alex's eyes lit in recollection. And then seeing her looking at him, he tried to curtail the vision.

"When were we together?"

Alex flinched. "We… haven't been."

"I don't understand Alex?"

Stroking her hair, he stared into the fire. "I don't know…unless it hasn't happened yet or unless…unless it was just a fantasy."

She thought for a moment. "Well, we are together now and we can make it a reality." Valeria noticed Alex was still a bit tense. She wanted to hear him talk. "So, how did you happen to save me in New York? I get that it was not the first time you've spared me from death."

"New York? That was really nothing. I saw that vision…well," Alex looked up to calculate, "I guess almost three years ago. It was obviously Manhattan. I recognized Central Park. I knew it was fall. I knew it hadn't happened yet. So, I took a fall teaching schedule each year at Columbia to give me something to do. I knew you had to live in the area. I waited for you every day at that intersection for at least a few hours."

"You were there every day for three years?" Valeria asked.

"No. Not every day..." Alex offered a conceding smile, "Well, yes, I guess I was there every day. The rest of the time I walked the streets where I saw you coming from, hoping to see you."

Valeria found herself drifting off to the soothing sound of his voice. She didn't want to move. She didn't want to sleep and miss a moment of him. But she closed her eyes; listening to his heart beat and fell into a deep, restful slumber.

She dreamed of him—she dreamed of the feel of her face on his chest and his arms around her.

CHAPTER 15

For the first time in several days Alex slept...and dreamt of the past:

Florence, Italy 1898

He raised his arm to bid at the auction. He was there to purchase a few more pieces of the Limoges that had belonged to *her*. The bids had been raised beyond what he had hoped. But what was money if he could not allow himself this eccentricity.

Besides, doing so helped him bide his time until the next vision would steer him towards her, perhaps this time arriving in time to save her. No—he thought—not perhaps! This time he would save her! He had waited over a hundred years, since his last vision of her. He wondered how much longer it would be until hope again filled his heart.

Alex's absolute belief that someday *she* would be at Morgana was his overriding passion. He often recalled

Myrdd's words and believed them; that he would not have been given the visions if there was not an opportunity to change them.

He didn't know if the visions were from Apollo or Gai or another deity. But he knew that no one could be that cruel; and *that* would be the ultimate in cruelty. Alex *had* to believe that within the visions was a key and an opportunity. Otherwise, they were merely his personal hell; to see her suffer over and over again without ever having the opportunity to relieve that suffering.

Mani had reminded Alex of this the last time he had found her. He had arrived on time—but had been unable to change the fates. The French Revolution was not a safe place for royalty or the educated. For Alex, the guillotine had been only a short and even welcomed distraction from his pain. Knowing that his beloved, then only an innocent child, had suffered the same treatment, had been excruciating—and with her, the results had been more permanent.

Raising his hand to finalize the high bid, Alex knew no one could outbid him forever on an object he desired. He merely had to be patient. But patience was Alex's downfall as Daphne had so aptly pointed out. Although he was not known for extravagance in his lifestyle, his bids did tend to get ostentatious. Why play a game simply to satisfy the masses, Alex justified. The fact was that he had unlimited resources in terms of funds and the most important resource, the time to get what he needed or wanted. Still, he did feel a bit of pity for those that he bid against. They could never win against him!

Doubling the current bid, already bored, Alex sensed the flickering in his vision before it actually began. He thanked whatever source might have given him the gift of opportunity and hope. He stepped into the aisle before the winning bid had actually been announced and threw down his entire purse to the officials and his calling card with the address to ship the Limoges bowls.

He had minutes before he would no longer be able to see and he knew from experience that mortals tended to see his response to the visions as a madness—and they were right to a degree! It was best if he were alone.

Finding an unoccupied alley, he leaned against the wall as the kaleidoscope effect continued from the outer edges of his sight and then slowly obscured it all. He took a deep breath—ready to recall every detail of the vision—important facts could save her life!

He noticed a muddied street and a park. The leaves on the trees appeared to be early spring. The vision expanded—yes, he needed an expanded view—a park. He saw a riverfront. There were small twinkling lights and an orchestra playing a new kind of music. Alex memorized the tune. Then *she* stepped out from the crowd. Involuntarily, he let out a small cry.

She wore her beautiful brown hair, full and fastened in a bun, as was the newest style, with small tendrils escaping along her face and neck. She took the arm of a man and laughed a beautiful full laugh that lit Alex's soul. She wore a gown that was low on the breast with very large sleeves. He had seen that trend in Paris Haute Couture. Since the bustles had gotten smaller, the sleeves had gotten larger.

Fashion timeframes were easily traced; especially when they were changing so rapidly. He guessed she was young; probably nineteen or twenty. The man whose arm she held, was tall and straight and at least twenty years her senior. Something in the man's eyes made Alex wary.

The view expanded and he dropped to his knees in thanks;

there was the view of the white obelisk, the Washington Monument, which had been the tallest structure in the world, next to the newly constructed Eiffel Tower.

Following a location and approximate date, he needed details of how she would be harmed. The man led her off the curb and into the road, as he left to attend to their buggy. Alex had heard the man call her "Jenni".

Another buggy was loading with a couple and a horse reared. Jenni was distracted by a call from behind her and turned as the man in the buggy attempted to whip the horse into obedience. The horse lunged and reared in response. Jenni turned back in time to see the horse's hooves coming down towards her. The horse shied further due to Jenni's presence.

"Oh no! No! No!" Alex cried—wishing it was possible to avert his eyes. He watched in horror as she fought to move out from the horse's hooves. The horseman continued to whip the horse causing further trampling. At last, leaving Jenni's beautiful body bloodied and beaten beyond survival—her eyes frozen and staring off blankly.

The vision was ending and the retching had already begun. Kneeled and sobbing, he heaved the contents of his stomach. The visions were his gift and his curse. He had learned that it was best to walk the streets only when he had control of himself and his emotions. Almost thirty minutes later, with the trembling almost under control, Alex rose. He needed to get to Rome and then from there a ship to Washington D.C.

"Dear Lord, whom provides me these visions, *please let me save her this time*."

∞

The trip had been just shy of two weeks. Alex had already been perusing newspapers scanning for a "Jenni" or "Jennifer" looking for a last name for his love and for the gentleman. He had yet to come across either party. It was winter, so he had a few months, if the vision was from this year.

He knew that the event in his vision was of a special society outing. He would have to ensure that he was invited to every social outing that spring—especially those that would take place on what they called the mall, the greenway where the vision had occurred. This was always a trial to his patience; society's social games. He had mastered the game of mystery. One leaked out information but never directly answered a question; instead insinuating that there was far more to the story than one might guess.

Of course, there was *far more* to Alex than one might guess. The rest of the game was to appear to be absolutely fascinated and delighted in whatever frivolous and inconsequential babble and gossip he was offered. The women were important to this society—they did the inviting. So, Alex had learned to combine interest with mild flirtation. Oh, how he hated that ridiculous part of the game! Alex always expected that the women would realize his deception but their vanity rarely permitted it.

The fact was that he despised deception and so took great care that there was never any harm created by his exaggerations; preferring to think of it as kindness rather than flirtation. Alex justified it all as what was necessary to save *her*. And he would play whatever part was necessary for that opportunity.

It was a pity that society women had been barred from most intelligent conversation. Those women that took the time to become educated and had something intelligent to offer were rarely included in society.

∞

After two months, he had taken to spending his late afternoons on the National Mall between the Washington Monument and the Potomac, where Congress had just approved the building of a memorial to their assassinated president Lincoln and watching for signs of events. He had spent hundreds of hours ingratiating himself with multitudes of gossiping women or laughing over distasteful jokes with men who drank too much. As a result, Alex had secured invitations to virtually every major party.

Then in the newspaper he saw the man's face: Harelton Parker, of Georgetown was returning home from abroad. There was no mention of a wife or a daughter. Alex recalled that in the vision the man, Parker, had addressed the girl as "Jenni". That would only be appropriate in public if she were his daughter or wife…or fiancée.

Alex had to decide if he would play this round "up front" or "in the background". It all depended on the players. If he felt that he could glean more information by befriending the players, he would play it up front. Another consideration was the location of the threat to her survival. If it were behind royal walls, he would have to ensure that he had already crossed those walls by letters of introduction or employment in order to ensure free access to her.

If, on the other hand, he felt that the players were suspicious of most people, which was the case of Harleton Parker, then Alex typically played it in the background;

watching and waiting for the moment in the vision.

Days and weeks went by. Soon it would be too late in this year for the vision. Then, one afternoon as he dined near Harelton's home, Jenni stepped out of a carriage with Harelton.

Alex's heart soared! She looked extraordinarily beautiful! Harelton and Jenni were seated next to Alex. He overheard pieces of their conversation. She had recently arrived from Paris but was fluent in English. Evidently there was a relationship; Harelton had the look of a man in love.

That Sunday, Alex saw the mall set up with the lights and tables. Immediately, he contacted the hostess and was offered an invitation. At the luncheon, he watched as Harelton introduced Jenni around and she graciously smiled and easily charmed them all.

Harelton escorted her to the curb to retrieve their carriage. The horseman with the uncontrolled horse lurched forward as Alex's arm moved around Jenni's tiny waist, lifting her to safety as he also grabbed the reins of the horse. The horse responded by trying to rear—but Alex had an iron grip with his fine leather gloves.

Jenni's eyes were wide with shock. She glanced down at her waist where his hand had been moments before as if she expected to still see it there. Then shaking her head in confusion, she smiled. "Merci beaucop!"

Alex held the rearing horse with a solid grip as he gazed at her, with a look in his eyes that she couldn't quite identify; perhaps relief and *something else*. "I don't mean to be melodramatic—is that how you say it?" She smiled, "Yes, I believe that it the word...Monsieur; I believe you saved my life!"

The coachman lashed the whip against the horse. Alex

reached up with his gloved hand and tore the whip from the driver's clutches. Alex's eyes were still and serious, "You will kill someone. Find another occupation, my man."

Then, easing his expression, Alex turned back to Jenni, who was smiling with wide-eyed amazement. He tilted his head nonchalantly, "It was my pleasure! I'm Alex Morgan and you are?"

"Jennifer Jardin." She held out a gloved hand for him.

He took it, looking into her eyes and kissed her hand. "Enchante, Mademoiselle." He bowed as she offered a small curtsy and her face flushed.

She smiled, "Parlez-vous français?"

"Oui! Though, I'm afraid your English is much better than my French." Jenni's eyes sparkled. Oh to see her alive, he thought!

Just then Harelton returned, "Jenni, our carriage is waiting." Harelton ignored Alex.

"Harelton, this gentleman, Monsieur Morgan, just saved my life." Jenni said sweetly. "The horse went out of control and Monsieur Morgan's swift actions prevented the horse from trampling me."

Alex shrugged, oh how he had missed her sweet voice. But now was not the moment to permit himself to enjoy her company. Parker would most certainly notice any possible affection. Alex had to stay cool for this gent.

"Is this true?" Harelton's eyes narrowed at Alex, evaluating.

"It was nothing." Alex met his eyes cautiously, removing any possible challenge.

"Harelton, we must thank Monsieur Morgan. Perhaps he

could join us for tea tomorrow."

"Whatever you like, my dear!" Harelton again glared at Alex, "Here is my card, please join us for tea tomorrow at three."

Harelton helped Jenni onto their carriage and Alex smiled to himself. It appeared that she wasn't married. She was alive...and he would see her tomorrow.

The next day, Alex walked to Harelton's townhouse where he saw two small children at the door. A servant rushed them away to their rooms. Jenni entered, her face lit in a smile, "Monsieur Morgan!"

Alex removed his hat and bowed his head slightly. Jenni curtsied. "It is a pleasure to see you again, Mademoiselle."

Harelton walked through briskly, "Jenni, I have to go to the office." He glanced up, "Oh sorry old chap, it completely slipped my mind that you were coming by—business, you see." He was busy evaluating Alex. "I'm sure you understand!"

Jenni had a distressed look on her face, "Harelton, we invited Monsieur Morgan for tea."

"Well, we will simply have to reschedule. I'm certain...I'm sorry what was your name?"

"Alex Morgan."

Harelton shook his head as if the name meant nothing to him. Alex could see in his eyes that he intended to end any idea Alex had about joining them for tea.

"I'm sorry, what business did you say you were in?" Harleton asked, his eyes narrowing.

Alex wanted to tell Harleton that *he hadn't said.* He wanted to say that it was none of his business. But instead Alex smiled pleasantly "Oh, this and that—mostly investments."

Harelton nodded coldly, trying to pick up clues from Alex's fine Italian clothing. And finally, getting nowhere, he ended the meeting. "Well, business beckons!" Harelton shrugged coldly at Alex, "I'm sure Mr. Morgan understands!"

Alex smiled kindly, "Of course!" Alex understood *perfectly!*

"My dear, I will see you tonight. Again, sorry old chap!" Harelton shrugged nonchalantly and left.

Again, Jenni was embarrassed, "Please forgive me for this… Harelton is not usually so…busy." She took a deep breath.

Alex smiled pleasantly knowing Jenni was uncomfortable because now they would be unchaperoned for tea—which this society had deemed inappropriate. Harelton knew that good manners would require Alex to leave immediately.

"Actually, it is I that must apologize Mademoiselle; I only have a few moments." Alex could see some relief in Jenni's eyes.

He took a deep breath, "Perhaps another time?"

Again, he sensed her tension easing.

"Yes, please Monsieur, give us an opportunity to thank you properly!" She smiled. "I am certain that Mr. Parker would insist!"

"Thank you, Mademoiselle…or is it Madam?" Alex waited anxiously for the response.

"Mademoiselle." Jenni flushed. "Harelton is my second cousin. His wife passed away a year ago. He has made an agreement with my family to marry me before the year is out."

Alex could see that this was an arranged marriage. He could steal her away! He could see that there was no romantic interest on Jenni's part. Alex wondered for a moment if that would be the right thing to do.

The children ran down the stairs, "Jenni! Jenni!" They grabbed happily onto her skirt and Jenni shrugged, as if to say that they were why she was here.

Sighing, Alex took his cap, "Mademoiselle, let us not be such strangers. I am a tutor and occasionally take on students. Perhaps I can be of assistance."

Jenni smiled, with a look of gratitude in her eyes.

Walking back to his apartment, Alex continued to reel at the revelation that *he had at last changed the vision*! She was alive! Deep inside him, the knot in his gut told him that there was still a possible threat…that it wasn't over yet. But Alex forced himself to believe that because she had survived the attack in his vision that she was now immortal. She would outlive Harleton Parker in not so many years…and Alex would stay by her side. Then they would have their *eternity* together!

∞

Alex watched on as Jenni married Harelton. Soon afterwards, Harelton left for Europe and was gone for over a year, allowing Alex precious time with Jenni. She counted on Alex for help with the children and her affection blossomed into what he suspected was love.

The formalities of the times called for protocols, such as always addressing each other in formal terms; Mister Morgan and Madam Parker. Because Alex was employed as a tutor, he was permitted occasional brief moments alone with the mistress of the house on official business, often over tea, as was their habit. At any time, Alex could have asked Jenni to run away with him and he was certain she would. But the children would have been left without love. They had already lost their mother. And Jenni would have mourned the loss of the children's affections.

Six years later, Harelton continued his tradition of frequent and often long trips abroad. Alex suspected that Harelton had lovers in other countries. There had been rumors of a girl in Africa—and that there were children from this mating.

Jenni's heartbreak had been the hopes that she might, at least, bear children. She might have felt sad from the lack of affection from Harelton. But Alex's presence gave her hope of something more. *That*, she refused to think about. Jenni did love her stepchildren, who were now about to enter their teen years and would soon be off to boarding school, at Harelton's insistence. Alex was certain that Harelton's insistence had to do with ending the employment of their tutor!

Alex planned to wait until the children left for boarding school and then he would ask Jenni to run away with him. With his accumulation of wealth, they could disappear and never again worry about Harelton or curses. The last, was Alex's prayer that he clung to for sanity. He chose to believe that averting the tragedy with the horse had resolved the curse.

That summer, Harelton left for business in Africa and would continue on for a safari. It was the happiest time in Alex's existence, with the freedom to see Jenni daily without Harelton's watchful eye. Jenni seemed to blossom in her husband's absence. Harelton wasn't a bad man. Alex had watched his beloved married off to men of bad intentions. Harelton seemed to care for Jenni, as much as he might care for any other of his possessions; such as his children.

One day, Alex responded to a knock on the door to his

apartment to find his good friend Mani! Mani explained to Alex that in his search for answers to their existence he had found extraordinary research facilities at Johns Hopkins in Baltimore.

"Alex, I would like to run several tests on Jenni. Can you bring her to Johns Hopkins?"

The underlying message was clear. Alex knew that Mani was not confident that Jenni was safe—and that time was running out. He couldn't think about that.

"Doc, do you believe that is necessary? I've not had any visions. I believe we are past all of that business."

"I would like to take any and all precautions. Perhaps you could call it a visit for the children to tour a great university."

Alex brushed his hand through his hair, concerned. As soon as he accepted the possibility that Jenni was not yet immortal, it caused his hope to drop into the pit of his stomach. But he couldn't risk anything with his beloved.

"I'll find a way to bring her up to Baltimore. I'll need time to make the arrangements; perhaps next month?"

Mani shook his head, "Alex…"

The pit in his stomach became heavier. "Next week, then."

As part of their science studies, Alex invited the children to see the new medical discoveries, including a new kind of microscope! Of course, Jenni was confused, but excited by the invitation. Frankly, she was looking forward to time with Alex away from the watchful eyes of the Washington gossips. Harelton would not be pleased to hear of this trip. So, Jenni sent a letter, knowing Harelton would receive it after the trip was completed. At Alex's insistence the maid accompanied them as a chaperone.

Jenni and the children were shown to an extraordinary suite on the Old Bay Line steamliner that would take them overnight from Washington D.C. up the Chesapeake to Baltimore. As the children excitedly ran into their rooms, Jenni's eyes narrowed.

"Is there a problem, Madam Parker?" Alex asked as his eyes sparkled. He could actually envision the day when he would leave with her—perhaps by ship.

"Monsieur Morgan," she swallowed, "Perhaps this is not an appropriate question, however, propriety requires that I…" She bit her lip, "How does a tutor's salary afford such a luxurious suite?" Alex smiled and shrugged.

"As I suspected," she said hesitantly. "I knew you to be a scholar. But your demeanor…" Her finger went to her temple. "May I ask? If you did not require the income, then why did you take a position as a tutor?"

Knowing that if he were not cautious, Jenni might feel the trip was inappropriate, Alex responded, "Madam Parker, I took the position because it *pleased* me to do so."

Arriving the next day at John's Hopkins Hospital, the children were taken on a tour by one of Mani's associates. The maid accompanied the children. Alex smiled gently at Jenni, "Madam Parker, this is Mani—Doctor Castro and he is doing some specialized research. Would you be willing to submit yourself to some of his tests?"

Jenni looked nervously from Alex to Mani. "What type of tests?"

"Madam Parker," Mani began, "please excuse my friend, when it comes to you he tends to rush things. Let me explain, I have begun a particular field of research and I would like take your information for this study."

"Doctor, I am in perfect health! Is there a reason?" She looked to Alex.

"Dr. Castro requires a specific type of person for his tests: a fine woman of French decent in order to create a…a baseline for his study. You meet his specifications perfectly and I was hoping that you would agree. It won't harm you. But it could provide very valuable information for his specialized research. It could very well save a life!" Alex hadn't lied, he justified.

"I would not want my husband concerned with these tests." Jenni's eyes fluttered nervously to Alex. "He might mistake the intention."

Alex understood. Harelton, most certainly, would not approve!

"I understand perfectly Madam! Our records would be held completely confidential. There would be no mail or calls on your home. Further, the records would only be released to you…no one else."

Jenni relaxed, "Well then…I see no harm in these…tests."

Mani called his assistant who escorted Jenni to an examination room.

The results showed that Jenni was in exceptionally fine health. That pit in Alex's stomach began to relax. All his previous times with Cassandra had shown her to die on or before her twenty-seventh birthday. Jenni's birthday, which was on Christmas day, was rapidly approaching.

∞

To Alex's absolute delight, the snow had fallen hard enough to prevent him from leaving on Christmas Eve. Jenni seemed pleased to have him there to celebrate with the children and servants.

It was mid afternoon Christmas day when the children ran off to play with their gifts permitting Alex a private moment with Jenni. His eyes lit with desire for her.

"Madam…" He looked and saw the desire in her eyes as well. "Jenni," he said softly, "I hope I am not being too forward, however, I have a gift for you."

Clearly pleased to see that Alex had dropped the public formalities, she blushed. They had exchanged formal gifts, of course. But this was a personal gift…one with very special meaning, a declaration of his intentions. She took the small box that Alex held for her and opened the beautifully wrapped package. Then she saw the bracelet of Platinum grape vines with five, three carat stones of the most extraordinary blue. Jenni's blush deepened. This was not the gift of a friend or an employee—*this was the gift of a lover*. And he could see that the meaning of the gift meant even more to her than its extraordinary beauty.

The snow began to fall again outside the window. Jenni's eyes filled with emotion and she was unable to speak. Alex, overwhelmed by the moment took her in his arms. She seemed stunned and then looked at Alex with so much confliction that suddenly became intense desire. Her mouth went to his willingly and hungrily for only a moment and then pulled away—stunned by her own reaction to him.

"I know you cannot wear this gift now." He brushed his hand along her face. "I would like to keep it for such a day when that is possible; perhaps next year, when my services as a tutor are no longer required."

Jenni whispered, "I will dream of that day, Alex." She pulled herself away from him. "I must...go now...and see to the preparation of the Christmas meal."

Alex's heart soared! He would have to endure a dinner with the return of the overly polite conversation that was appropriate for a mistress of the house and an employee. But Alex now knew that Jenni loved him.

Christmas dinner was about to be served—but the lady of the house was missing. Alex asked the maid to check on Jenni. He was prepared to check on her himself, knowing that she had been upset by the kiss. But after considering it, he decided that his presence at her bedroom door might increase her discomfort.

A few minutes later, Alex heard the maid's scream. He bolted up the three flights of stairs to discover Jenni lying on the floor of her room, her body long cold.

∞

Despite his inconsolable grief, Alex forced himself to write the letter to Harelton and handled the funeral arrangements. Alex knew that Harelton would not take the time to attend the funeral. The cause of death was announced as a brain aneurysm. Mani asked Alex if he could perform an autopsy. As heartbreaking as it was for Alex to think of his beloved being violated by knives for the autopsy, Mani convinced Alex that the information might prevent this tragedy from occurring again.

Waiting in the corridor of Mani's lab, Alex regressed into self-loathing. If only he had not kissed her, then at least he might been with her when she needed him most.

"Alex," Mani said softly.

Unable to speak, Alex waited for the news.

"There were severe burns through her brain. I can find no medical cause for this. The assumption of a curse seems to be most logical. But Alex," Mani placed his hand on Alex's arm, "she could not have suffered long."

Alex knew that his good friend was trying to give him solace. But there could be none. He had seen Jenni's room; how her dressing table was over-turned. He had found her kerchief, damp with tears pulled to the floor with the rest of the contents from her dressing table as she attempted to drag herself to the door to alert him. She had known that she would not survive and she died with her arms outstretched towards the door.

A few days later, Alex watched the casket lowered into the ground. How many times had he seen this now? He didn't want to count. Alex had held off burying her, clinging to the dream that she was now immortal and her body would heal but he knew better this time than to await her rising. She would not.

CHAPTER 16

The morning birds began their melodic song of a new day outside the cottage when Alex awoke with a start. Although his neck had cramped—he had been sleeping sitting almost vertically—there was something that thrilled him that he couldn't quite realize at first. Immediately, the feeling of Valeria's body, gently sleeping against him, stirred his emotions. She was alive! He stroked her head as it lay cradled in his arms and pushed back the curls that stubbornly stuck to her cheeks and neck to reveal her face, so full of beauty.

Alex rejoiced with the feel of her warmth and breath on his chest. An overwhelming joy took him and he kissed the top of her head. He wanted to let her sleep a bit longer but, as if it were beyond his own volition, he pulled her into him and lovingly stroked her face—knowing without question that whatever he needed to do—she would survive this time!

Under his gentle hands, Valeria stirred. A smile lighting her face before her eyes opened.

"Good morning, beautiful!" Alex completely shed the dream of the night before and smiled with the gift of the new and glorious day. She looked up at him and had the overwhelming desire to kiss him.

Turning her face into his chest, she breathed in his wonderful scent and wrapped her arms around him. It was intoxicating! Valeria heard Alex chuckle nervously, before pulling her in closer. Then, waking enough, she realized that she must be a mess. She pushed herself away and sat up, providing her an opportunity to recover from his closeness.

At that moment Valeria desperately wished that her hair and teeth had been brushed and her face washed. She wondered if any make-up had survived the tears of the night before—and if so was she wearing it below her eyes.

Leaning back, Alex put his arms behind his head and stretched out a bit. "If you want to shower first, I'll get us breakfast." Then he popped up and kissed the top of her head again.

"Okay." She said, wondering if her eyelids were swollen in that perfectly awful way that they did when she cried.

Was it her imagination? The world looked brighter! Avoiding the mirror, she jumped into the shower. She dried her hair, put on mascara and a bit of lip gloss and threw on her blue jeans and a blue, v-neck sweater. When she stepped out of the bedroom, she saw that breakfast was set. He offered her a cup of coffee just the way she liked it. This time she noticed the Limoges china and was grateful for everything he had done.

"Thank you." She blushed.

"I wish we could have a leisure morning, but everyone's meeting in about thirty minutes."

They ate the fresh fruit and yogurt. Alex had toasted up a

brioche and brushed it with what he told her was a combination of honey, butter and a hint of orange juice. "I'd like you to have some protein." He said as he ladled scrambled eggs onto her plate. Valeria ate every bite!

After eating, Valeria offered to wash the dishes while Alex showered and changed. There was a great energy and joy to the morning that consumed them both.

"We need to go." Alex winked as he came out of the bedroom dressed. As they started to walk out the door Valeria pulled on Alex's hand to stop him. *How do you do this kind of thing*, she wondered.

"Alex?" She said hesitantly.

He turned to her, unable to remove the smile from his face. "Yes?" Sensing something sensual in her mood, he moved in closer.

"Uhm…I was wondering something?"

His eyes twinkled romantically. "Anything, beautiful." She bit her lip nervously. Alex became more intrigued. "Yes?" He asked, as Valeria smiled shyly.

"Well, in all those lifetimes, did we…I mean, you said we weren't 'together'…but did we ever…well, you know what I mean…" She blushed scarlet.

Pulling around, Alex framed her against the wall. His heart started to race as he brushed the side of her face with his hand. She looked up at him and so wanted to kiss him.

"Well," he said, flirtatiously, "I may have stolen a kiss here and there." The fact was that it had only been the one time. But Alex didn't want to talk; he wanted to pull her into his arms and cover her mouth with his. He could feel the trembling of desire beginning and there was no time for that now. Still he couldn't pull himself from her—the look in her eyes held him like a magnet.

"May have?" Valeria asked, her heart racing by his closeness as a luscious anxiety arose in her gut. She swore she could already feel his lips touching hers—though he was still almost a foot away. His blue eyes were so close that she could see every detail. Alex nodded as he held himself back from her with every piece of rational thought he had in him.

"Well…" She sighed as his hand moved to her neck and she brushed her lips against his arm instinctively and heard Alex's muffled response to her touch.

"Yes?" He knew that he should not continue this line of conversation. He knew that he should be sensible and tell her that they would have later—though a piece of him wasn't so certain. If Alex had been able to reason, he would have justified that Valeria wanted or needed something and that it was the least he could do to give her that chance. In fact, there was no reason in this conversation—only a lifetime of desire.

"Well, I was thinking that—," Valeria gulped, nervously. *Courage,* she thought! "I guess, I feel like you remember everything…and I don't." Alex nodded softly. She continued, "Anyway…" Her voice faded as his thumb brushed along her lower lip, sending an electrical charge all the way to her toes. Her mouth caressed his thumb. His eyes closed, lost in reverie. When he opened them a moment later, Valeria could see his eyes were luminous with desire. She continued softly, "…I mean, this is the…the 21st …century. Women…women kiss men…all the time." She sighed.

Alex cocked his head to the side, a crooked smile turning the corners of his mouth in the most amazing way. "Of course." He replied softly.

Leaning his face inches from hers, his arm moved around to the small of her back—willing his hand to stay as it was, while the other hand caressed her jaw line.

There was a deep trembling inside her. Before she had made the decision, she realized that she had kissed that beautiful turn of his mouth. Alex moved to close the distance, feeling the delightful warmth of her soft lips on his. His heart slammed, demandingly, against his chest and he longed for more of her. He moved his fingers across her spine, aching to pull her in closer.

After a moment, he regained his reason and pulled away, his voice hoarse. "You know," Alex sighed as he kissed her temple while his hand brushed the side of her face, "I wish we had the time for this." Valeria saw the ache in his eyes, as he took a deep, jagged breath. "But we need..." He corrected himself, "*I* need to stay focused. And right now isn't the time for us to...for me to..." Alex kissed her lightly and then forced himself away from her—recalling the dream.

Sensing the cloud in his happiness, Valeria stroked his face. "It's all right, Alex. Nothing bad is going to happen to me this time."

She would have to know the rest soon. But he wanted to give her a few more moments of innocence. He could so clearly see her trust in him. Alex pushed away the darkness that had been his nearly constant companion.

"I know." He said resolutely, as he stepped away from her still holding her hand. Alex looked at Valeria to ensure that she was all right with all that had transpired. She had recomposed herself and nodded calmly.

Pleased with his level of control and with his rationality returned, they stepped onto the deck. They were going to be sensible about this!

Then suddenly, overwhelmed with desire, they synchronously pulled together and his mouth came down on hers like that of a starving man. Her hands knotted in his hair, feeling his lips hot against hers. Her mouth parted and his tongue gently, hesitantly, moved into hers. She moaned into his mouth and he immediately lost all his tentativeness. His hands streaked down over her hips, and up her back, pulling her into him as his mouth worked over hers, his tongue and teeth moving in her mouth. She pressed into him—forgetting everything—except him. Alex moaned, deeply. She felt her head spin and her knees weaken. Then suddenly he felt her body go lax and concerned, he lifted his face inches from her, his brows raised in curiosity.

"What happened?" his voice husky.

Not ready for it to end, Valeria held him close, "I don't know…my knees just went…weak." She said softly, and leaned back to kiss him.

Amusement played on Alex's lips as he kissed her lightly. "I made you weak-kneed?"

She stroked her hand down his face, somewhat embarrassed by her response. "Yeah…it would seem so!"

"That was…" His eyes twinkled as his thumb moved across her lip again. Then, suddenly distracted, he looked up towards the main house and took another jagged breath. "Caleb's here!"

Caleb's voice came from the trail. "Daph says you need to get your ass—well she says you need to knock it off." Then, he laughed, "But me…I say go for it, Alex!"

Lowering her brow in amusement, Valeria asked, "How did they know?"

With effort Alex pulled his hands from her back and face, ending the embrace—his heart beat exploding in his ears. "I'm afraid that I responded to them while we were..." Alex shook his head, embarrassed, "Sorry!" He rolled his eyes while letting out a deep breath and then bit his lip in a smile that betrayed his desire.

"More company!" Alex stepped away from Valeria as Mani came off from a trail. She was surprised how pleased she was to see him and for Mani to see that she and Alex had become closer.

"Hello Valeria!"

"Mani! I'm sorry, you had asked us to stop by your lab in New York, but I'm afraid everything just happened so fast!" Valeria said as a deep flush moved over her face. "And well...here I am!"

"It's perfect! My lab is here." Mani offered Alex a knowing smile and then kissed Valeria on the cheek. "Love looks good on you!" Valeria beamed in response. He glanced to Alex with a wink. "I apologize for the interruption."

"Not a problem, doc. We were just..." Alex cleared his throat. "We were just walking up to the house." Valeria bit her lip as she smiled playfully at Alex.

With a subtle hint of amusement, Mani nodded, "Yes...I could see that." As he guided her back to the rocker, "Have a seat, Valeria. This won't take but a few minutes." Mani sat on the foot stool and placed a case on the table. "I want to test your blood so that we can develop some answers to your future. Can I have your arm please?"

Valeria looked quizzically to Alex. "Beautiful, Mani identified a difference in our DNA, as opposed to others. This will be the first time we are able to test your DNA to find out if you are like us. He also needs to test for any other potential issues."

"Well, thank God! I thought this was going to be another transference!" Valeria offered a mock wince.

Having tied the band to Valeria's arm, Mani removed several tubes from his bag and then began to tap on the inside of her elbow. He painlessly inserted the needle and drew the blood, changing tubes several times, before removing the needle. "That should do." Mani smiled. "It will be about a week for the results of the DNA. I'll have the other results within the hour."

Mani left to attend to the samples.

Alex took Valeria's hand and they walked joyfully along the trail. "Well, I think that should last me a while." He winked to her as they arrived at the main house. But Alex knew that now that their passion had been fueled, it would haunt him until she was alive and safe and his.

CHAPTER 17

As soon as Valeria stepped through the door, Camille's face lit up. "Everything better?"

Valeria beamed as Alex slid his arm around her waist. "Wonderful!" And unable to stop herself she kissed his cheek—even with Daphne watching. Valeria squeezed Camille's hand. "Thank you for the intervention!"

"Anything for a good cause!" Camille winked.

Knowing that this was going to be a difficult day, Alex was glad that they had taken the few sips of pleasure earlier. Lars stood by the fireplace with Ava on the edge of the sofa near Camille.

Kissing her forehead, Alex began. "I think it would be easiest if we do this the old fashioned way and discuss it. That way everyone can contribute."

Daphne shook her head, "If we are going to be talking about Aegemon—I have my own opinion about the whole situation." She looked at Alex and Valeria and her face revealed her anger. "I have no idea why we are tiptoeing around this. But let's be honest about this—it's her problem! She started it! Let her solve it…or not! Why are we even involved?"

Valeria didn't know what this was about. She thought that they had buried the hatchet. Although she was certain that her updated status with Alex would be a source of upset for Daphne.

Turning towards Daphne, Tavish said, "Face it! Aegemon would have eventually found you, even without the girl! And if it wasn't for the girl, you might have ended up a virgin priestess!" Then, Tavish mumbled to himself and laughed sarcastically, "That would have been something to see!" Tavish pointed an accusatory finger, "It was Alex that caused the problem. Aegemon wouldn't have even have known about us if *he* hadn't gone back for the girl."

Lifting his hand to silence the debate, Lars offered, "Alex…*and* our absent friend, did what they thought was right. Myrdd isn't here to defend his decision. But any of you might have done the same."

Alex snapped, abruptly exasperated, "You know we keep going over old ground. But Lars is right; *you would have done the same.*"

"What happened?" Valeria asked.

"Oh, for crying out loud!" Daphne declared. "You are the reason Aegemon even knows about us! He watches you. Do you think he doesn't know that you are with Alex? Do you think he doesn't know that we want to destroy him, before he destroys us?"

Alex's voice sharpened in almost anger, "That's enough, Daph!"

"That's right. It's not the girl's fault. As I said, it's Alex—," Tavish added.

By this time Ava had listened to enough of Daphne and Tavish's accusations. "Aww, put a sock in it, you two!"

Lars smiled, "That's my girl!" Ava winked at him. Lars continued, "Valeria, Alex told me about your discussion last night. There are a few critical pieces that we all felt were better to discuss after you both had some sleep."

"Alex?" Valeria asked, sensing his increased tension.

Although Alex knew that Valeria had a right to know; he desperately wanted her to be free of the fear that had occupied most of his existence. But with this plan, she would need to know. Lars was right—it had to be handled now. Alex was also anxious to hear the rest of the details.

Taking a deep breath, Alex said, "Val, before we get into the details, I want you to know that we believe we have a solution. Alright?"

The only thing that would cause her any alarm is if she wouldn't be with Alex. Valeria nodded, nervously. Everything else now was unimportant.

"Beautiful, last night we talked about your…well, your previous deaths." Valeria noticed that Alex's jaw tensed. "There is something I need to tell you about them." He pulled his arm down and took Valeria's hands in his.

"In all of those pictures of the…deaths, did you notice that you looked about the same age?"

"I don't know…I guess…" Suddenly the realization hit her.

Lars broke in, "Valeria, all of us here, including you, are the true oracles. We were given immortality. But for some reason, it hasn't seemed to…occur with you."

With her heart pounding nervously, Valeria spoke up. "Do you know when I'm going to die?" Tears formed in her eyes and she could see Alex was just as upset. Before last night, it hadn't mattered if she had a short life. Now, all she wanted to believe was that she could have *forever* with him!

Stroking the top of her hands with his thumb, Alex continued. "Val, the reason we are all here—the reason I didn't give you a chance to adapt to me in New York—is because I discovered long ago that if you live long enough… you die on your 27th birthday."

The blood drained from Valeria's face as shock moved in. She dropped Alex's hands and walked to the window. "That's tomorrow."

How could that be? She had finally found happiness and now it would be ripped from her in a day? What kind of god would permit that?

Alex rose and went to stand helplessly behind Valeria. He put his arms around her. "I won't let him take you this time."

Lars gave her a moment to let it sink in. "Hon, that's what this is about. The good news is that we have you with us before the…event—which is rare! We also have our collective brain power and finally have technology working for us with a plan to resolve it! We believe we have a chance to break this curse."

Staring out the window, Valeria spoke softly, "And to think, I usually just celebrate with champagne and strawberries. I guess this year I should add chocolate."

Alex pulled Valeria around and hugged her, then led her back to the couch. "I'm certain we've figured it out. And Tavish is right, it is my fault. Aegemon wouldn't have caused a problem, if he had never seen me. But he has seen me enough to know I will be here for you—it puts you in more danger. In other words, beyond the curse—we are going to probably have a personal battle with Aegemon as well."

"Is that all of the bad news? Or is there more?" Valeria asked. Everyone in the room looked at Alex. Valeria was still in shock. "So, something mysterious will kill me tomorrow and to top that off—if this mystery curse doesn't kill me, Aegemon will?"

The room was silent. Finally Lars spoke, "I would say that about sums it up. But remember *we also have solutions!*" Lars began to pace. "Here's our angle: one, see if Mani can give us some answers from your blood work to stop this medically. Two, locate the source of the curse continuing, probably Aegemon, and stop him. And three, find a way to break the curse."

Valeria leaned her body into Alex's as he pulled his arms around her tighter and kissed her neck. "Which one are we going to try?" She asked.

"All three." Lars answered.

The front door opened and Mani entered.

"How do you go about breaking a curse?" Valeria asked woodenly.

"Just in time." Lars nodded towards Mani.

Taking a few steps towards her, Mani began. "Valeria, when you analyze what we call a curse, we have to ask, is this psychosomatic? Is it physiological? In other words, perhaps your body is only designed to live so long. Or is there an unknown virus, bacteria or autoimmune response? I am analyzing the physiological aspects now. But if this is some kind of curse, I believe Alex and I have located a possible resolution in the laws of Statics and Motions."

Finally Alex spoke up, "The simplest way to explain it is that if the moment when something occurred is repeated precisely, it ceases to be."

Everyone else in the room still looked confused. Alex began pacing, "You, Valeria…well actually Cassandra, drowned. You go back to the place where it occurred, your Prima Mortis, and—".

Daphne interrupted sarcastically, "Absolutely brilliant, Alex! We are going to drown her again? Why wait for Aegemon?"

"Beautiful, I wouldn't hurt you. Okay?" Alex reassured Valeria. She tried her best at a smile. Alex continued, "Our plan is to get you in the water at the same location. I know it's changed some but I'm certain we've located it. By Mani's estimation you don't have to drown; you simply need to be in the same location."

Daphne spoke up, "Alex, you know the dangers in any of us being there! And despite our discussions of the past few days, I don't believe that it is fair for you to ask us to risk our lives in this absurd venture!" Daphne paused and for a moment anguish replaced her anger. "Alex—please don't do this! If the water doesn't kill you, Aegemon will."

"Is that true?" Valeria said, barely able to catch her breath.

Ignoring Valeria's question, Alex addressed the group, "I agree that this is too dangerous for all of us! And I wish I could in good conscience ask you all to take the gamble. But you have convinced me over the past few days that it would be better to limit the risk."

"Kill yourself. See if I care!" Daphne glared at Alex.

He went back to Valeria and looking deep into her eyes

assured her, "I'll be on the boat. Lots of people go boating that can't swim. But I can swim! And I'll be ready for Aegemon."

Stepping to the couch by Daphne, Mani sat down and patted her knee gently. He knew that Daphne was in love with Alex. "I believe that Valeria only needs to be in the same location. Of course, I'm not 100% confident that this will work. I believe we need a plan b and c as a back-up. I just received the package today that will help us with that. We do still need to resolve the technicalities."

Tavish snarled sarcastically, "*Some* technicality!"

The tension in the room was building when Lars walked to the kitchen counter and refilled his coffee. "Tavish, let's solve the problems not just find them. Camille, what did you discover about the temperature of the water?"

"I believe that Valeria will need a dry suit. How long does she need to be in the water?"

Valeria spoke up, "I should tell you that I'm not crazy about water."

"Most of us agree with your sentiments." Camille nodded.

Mani continued, "Valeria, we don't know exactly what time you drowned. Alex and I have worked it out to within a three-hour period."

Turning from the coffee pot, Lars spoke up, "Yes. She will definitely need a dry suit."

Mani shook his head. "No. There can be no rubber on her. That could kill her."

"What are you saying?" Lars sat his cup back down with concern.

Now Mani leaned forward. "Lars, she cannot be in anything that would be electrical insulation. The two examinations I conducted on Valeria's past bodies indicated death was from an electrical charge. She cannot be insulated with rubber."

"Mani, what are you talking about?" Valeria asked.

"All right." Alex took over and paused the discussion to answer Valeria's concerns. "Val, as you saw from the transference last night, I found you, well," Alex looked down, "I found you too late. Mani was able to examine you several times but only once with reasonable medical equipment." Alex looked to Mani, "Well buddy, how are we going to handle this one?" Valeria could see the tension in Alex's eyes.

"I've been investigating other insulators." Mani responded. "I don't believe that insulation will be as much of an issue as it currently appears to be. However, to answer your question on insulators, we believe that the best we can do is wool."

"Mani, how long can a person survive? The Adriatic this time of year will be about 50 degrees." Lars queried.

"Valeria appears to be in good health. I believe she would be conscious for perhaps thirty minutes or as long as an hour. And as long as we can keep her breathing, I believe she could live from one to three hours...perhaps longer."

Suddenly, Alex had backed out of the discussion; he was looking a bit pale. Lars jumped in, "We need three hours." Then Lars noticed Alex's expression, "Lexi?"

Alex's head was hung low and he was slowly shaking it, as if to ward off the nightmares, Valeria squeezed Alex's hand.

"Go on Lars." Valeria said. Lars evaluated them for a moment.

"Tell you what—let's table that item and go to the next.

Mani, any answers from Valeria's blood work yet?"

Mani shook his head, "At this point, I have found nothing in the blood work that would precipitate any kind of illness that we have witnessed from past deaths. That eliminates physiological. We are left with psychosomatic or some kind of curse." Mani looked to Alex, "I believe that the next discussion will help us handle the issue of the cold water."

"All right, for now let's move on to Aegemon. Ava?" Lars directed.

Everyone looked to Ava, who was busy sipping her coffee, "Oh, Aegemon will be there. I've seen it clearly in every vision."

Lars winked at her and Ava winked back seductively, then Lars spoke, "Valeria, we all have different gifts. For some reason Ava seems to see Aegemon. Aegemon watches you. So, you and Ava have a special kinship in that connection."

"If Aegemon watches me, I don't understand why we are we safe here?"

Ava responded. "I don't know. But you are. I've never seen Aegemon here."

Lars continued, "Valeria, Ava's visions are good. That's why she was never drowned. She saw his intentions. That's why we felt you were safe here at Morgana." Lars smiled, "Of course, Alex isn't going to rely on anyone else's visions. That's why he stays with you."

"Beautiful, I finally have you safe. I'm not risking a change of venues to lose you." Alex shifted nervously. "I haven't seen Aegemon's involvement. Then again, I haven't had a vision of this event, for some reason. Ava is our expert and she says Aegemon will be there. We need to figure out how we are going to handle *him*."

Although Alex couldn't admit it, the fact that he had not seen any visions of this threat to Valeria's life gave him both hope and concern. Hope that there was no more danger. But deep inside he knew that there were enough real threats to her life the next day that he couldn't quite accept that answer. The concern, beyond the obvious, was that he would be walking into the situation blind.

Pacing the room, Lars stopped near Valeria. "So, the challenge was and has been to discover Aegemon's Achilles' heel. Val, I believe that you gave us the answer last night—disease. Camille, Ava and Mani attempted to locate his Prima Mortis, and I believe they found the answer."

Lars smiled to Ava. "There were a few plagues in Ancient Greece; including one near Aegemon's location.

"My research shows it to be the pneumonic plague." Mani informed them. "That is the bubonic plague or black plague infected into the lungs. It also happens to be the most contagious."

Valeria asked, "Isn't the plague extinct?"

Daphne interrupted, "What? We are going to put an infected flea on a rat and place it on Aegemon's boat? What are you thinking? I thought you were supposed to be smart."

Ava rolled her eyes at Daphne, while Mani smiled kindly at her. "To answer Valeria's question, the plague still shows up from time to time. And Daphne, I appreciate your question. We considered the point of infection—and unfortunately it will be necessary to convey the germ to Aegemon directly."

"A hypodermic?" Alex asked.

Mani shook his head, "No, the only way the germ will survive the cool conditions of the sea is if it has a human carrier."

Finally, Alex spoke, "Do you mean for one of us to be infected? It wouldn't be our Achilles' heel, so we would survive. That makes sense. I'll do it."

"Aegemon would never permit you to get close enough..." Ava responded. "But Val could!"

Feeling his blood start to boil, Alex stood. His fists tightened in anger. "Whose idea was this?" He glared accusatorily at Daphne and then to Lars. "No! I won't permit it!"

Placing a gentle hand on Alex's shoulder, Camille attempted to calm him. "Alex, let's think about this rationally; this is our opportunity to do whatever we can to save Valeria! But if you were infected how would you help her? You need to have your wits about you—and your strength! Valeria needs that!"

Pacing the floor, Alex began to shake. "This is crazy! We are *not* going to sacrifice Valeria to get to Aegemon! I thought you all understood. We need to come up with another plan!"

With Alex approaching hysteria, Mani's voice came through calmly and rationally. "Alex, my friend, sit down. You are upsetting Valeria."

Hearing this, Alex looked at Valeria and saw that she was nearly in shock. He sat down next to her, feeling ashamed and pulled her into his arms. Nuzzling into her neck he said, "I'm sorry."

Speaking softly Lars said, "There's no time for another plan."

Mani continued, "I believe this is a good plan. Alex, this isn't the dark ages. We can cure pneumonic plague. Valeria would need an antibiotic injection within 24 hours of infection.

219

Further, she would not be contagious until she *has symptoms.* One of the primary symptoms is a high fever. Our thinking is that this is the perfect blend of solutions! The fever would reduce or eliminate the threat of hypothermia; while the cold water would reduce the fever from the illness."

Alex stroked Valeria's hair as Camille spoke up, "The critical piece to the plan is that Valeria will need to get within a few feet of Aegemon for the bacteria to carry."

"If it is Aegemon's Achilles' heel, it will take him out within a week." Ava added. "Alex, it would probably be best if you left before Aegemon arrives."

"I've survived many encounters with Aegemon and *I'm not* leaving her alone with him!"

Taking a deep breath, Lars nodded.

"Beautiful, tell me what you are thinking?" Alex asked.

Valeria looked exhausted, "Alex, if there is a chance that I can be with you, I am going to take it." He pulled her back into him in a tight embrace and clenched his eyes shut to block out the vision. "But I think that Ava's right. You can't be there when Aegemon arrives."

Keeping his eyes closed, Alex muttered in her ear, "That just isn't an option. I'm not leaving you alone with him."

Feeling her gut twist from the tension, Valeria realized it was one thing for her to be in danger; another altogether to think of losing the one person she knew she couldn't live without. The discussion wasn't over.

With a deep sigh Camille spoke gently, "Alex, I think we can save Valeria." He nodded without opening his eyes.

The room grew silent. Twisting her neck to relieve the tension, Ava walked to the fireplace to continue the discussion.

"I've arranged for a Catamaran with jute netting that is loose enough that Valeria can be submerged with the exception of her face. It's in the harbor in Venice. I tried to find something that would heat the water around her. But we couldn't get anything constructed in time. I'm sorry."

Mani rose and began walking to the door. "I am activating the plague bacteria. We will need to infect Valeria's lungs no later than seven pm tonight. She won't be contagious until at least five am. But at that point, Valeria cannot be around mortals. Alex, you must keep all others far away from her."

Camille looked at her watch, "Alright! Valeria and Alex, it's noon. Why don't you two spend some time together? Go to town, enjoy each other's company. Order champagne, strawberries and chocolate and just have fun. After all, tomorrow is Valeria's birthday. And she came to spend it with you." Alex nodded again without speaking.

Suddenly, all eyes looked out the window. Alex turned to Valeria, "Caleb is on watch, he says someone is here."

A black limo pulled up in front of the house. Lars looked down at the driveway, "Aegemon?"

"The car says 'Diplomat'." Ava said.

Valeria got up, "It's David." She walked to the window and watched as several muscle-bound men stepped from the car. Then she saw David glance cautiously up at the house and then move up the stairs with one of the security men. David smoothed his short brown hair before knocking on the front door.

"Hello, I'm looking for—". Suddenly he saw Valeria and went to her, "Oh, thank God!" He pulled her into his arms and she went willingly. "I thought you had been abducted. I didn't know if I would ever find you!"

Smiling graciously, Camille offered David her hand. "David, it's nice to meet you. I'm Camille. Valeria came here as our guest."

David snarled, "If she is your guest then why was she calling me last night telling me she needed a way to leave? That doesn't sound reasonable, does it?"

Pulling her into him protectively, Valeria allowed her face to be buried in the familiarity of David's arms. They seemed a long way from death, pneumonic plague, hypothermia and curses. She was surprised to find that there *was* a comfort there.

"David, I'm so sorry. I was just upset. These people have been very kind to me."

David calmed and spoke to Alex, "I'm sorry. It's not often that your fiancée phones and says…" Alex flinched at his words. "Well, in any case, thank you for being kind to her. Darling, I'm here now. I have a room in Trento. Let's get you back where you belong! Where are your bags?"

Taking a deep breath, Alex turned to keep David from seeing his face; wondering if he should speak up. But Alex decided this was for Valeria to handle—not him.

"Val, you intended to stay here a few more days, right?" Ava offered.

After a moment of silence, David retorted, "It doesn't appear that she's interested in staying any longer."

Camille tried another tactic. "All right…well, Val, why don't you and I go pack up your things while David gets to know everyone. David would you care for a coffee or tea?"

With desperation in her voice, Valeria looked up at David, "Please," her voice cracked, "I just want to go. David, can we just go?" She buried her face in David's chest.

She permitted herself a brief glance up, avoiding Alex. She saw the stunned expressions. And out of the corner of her eye she saw Alex turn to her—almost pleading. She looked away.

"What's wrong, Valeria." David asked, looking suspiciously at Alex.

As her tears began to fall, she whispered, "Please, I need to go." Looking at Lars, Valeria sobbed, "I'm sorry. Thank you—really! But I think you've mistaken me for someone…that I'm not." She wiped a tear, "This is who I am and where I belong."

David's face filled with that of the protector. He ushered Valeria to the door and opened it. She turned back. "I just want to spend my time like this. I hope you can respect that." Valeria tried to turn as far as Alex but she couldn't do it. Tears flowed from her eyes along with silent sobs.

The family watched as Valeria got into the black limo with David, never looking back.

∞

The limo disappeared behind a cloud of dirt as it pulled out of the drive along with Alex's dreams. Camille let out a little cry.

Daphne spoke hesitantly. "Alex, it just wasn't meant to be." She touched Alex's arm kindly and left.

The others took a moment to realize what had just happened.

Lars took a deep steadying breath, "Let's regroup—it's not over."

Alex interrupted, "It is over." Choking back his emotion, "It was all just too much for anyone to—." He shook his head.

"She isn't just anyone. She has lived it. She knows." Ava pointed out.

He sat on the loveseat where only moments before, his beloved had been with him. Alex buried his head in his hands.

"Alex, I've been thinking," Camille brushed his back. "I don't think she was overwhelmed." Shrugging, she continued, "I mean, yes, she was overwhelmed but I don't think that's why she left."

The devastated expression on Alex's face stunned the family that had known him for eons. He face was ashen and his eyes without hope. "She left because she would rather risk a curse than the only solutions I could find for her. But…it just doesn't matter now." And with that he walked out the door.

Ava approached Camille, "What were you about to say to Alex?"

"I was about to say that Valeria is in love with him. She didn't leave because she was afraid for herself. She left because she doesn't want Alex in danger." She said resolutely.

Ava took a deep breath and nodded. "Well then sister, you and I are going to go find her."

CHAPTER 18

Caleb insisted on going to town with Ava and Camille.

They all split up, heading to the major inns and hotels. Camille gave Caleb very explicit instructions that he was to look for David's limo and when he found it he should call them.

On Ava's third stop, she went into the Grand Hotel and offered the doorman $100 for information. The doorman immediately responded, "Yes. The gentleman just left."

Clarifying that the diplomat had taken his suitcases and left, she phoned Camille and Caleb. Then she slumped in a chair in the lobby awaiting their arrival. Knowing the search was over, Caleb decided to hang out at a local Marvel Comics store.

As elegant guests entered and exited the hotel, Camille rushed in, "What are you waiting for? Let's get a helicopter and chase it down!" Ava shook her head. Giving up was not something either woman did easily.

"If Val left Trento, she doesn't want to be found. We

can't make her come back if she doesn't want to." Tears formed around Camille's eyes and Ava patted her back in sympathy. "Next time." Ava promised.

They started for the door as a waiter carrying a tray ran behind the women towards the elevators, a bit too close. Camille's hand hit the tray shattering the contents on the marble floors.

The waiter began swearing at them in Italian. Camille apologized and bent to help pick up shards of glass—noticing the foaming champagne, a broken single glass, a box of chocolates and strawberries scattered across the floor.

In an instant both women realized the contents of the tray. Camille's eyes lit up.

∞

Valeria answered the knock at the door in the hotel robe, expecting room service. On seeing Camille and Ava, she hesitated and then signaled for them to come in.

"If you were planning on hiding from us, you'll have to do better than this!" Camille pointed to tray that the she had tipped the waiter well to recreate and to divulge the room that the tray was to go to.

Staring at the tray for a minute with a bittersweet expression Valeria said, "I guess it's kind of a last meal."

"It doesn't have to be." Ava interjected, as she popped a strawberry in her mouth. "What happened with the boyfriend?"

"I told him I needed some time alone and that I would see him in a few days." She looked at Ava, "I couldn't bear the idea that he would watch me keel over." Valeria's eyes rimmed with tears. The fact was that she couldn't bear to be with David when her heart ached to be with Alex. The agony in Alex's eyes when she left haunted her.

Entering the large room, Camille placed the tray down on the bedside table. Ava, avoiding Valeria and Camille walked around to the other side of the bed and tossed her entire body down so that she was in easy reach of the tray.

"Like Ava said; it doesn't have to be." Camille said, as she sat down on the bed next to Valeria, avoiding Ava's arm reaching for a strawberry. "Val, Alex is heartsick!"

"Heartsick is much better than dead." Valeria said flatly.

Camille smiled wistfully, "You know...sometimes I wonder about that myself." Then her face became sympathetic. "Val, this plan can work. Are you really willing to throw away any chance of what you two can have for—," She looked at the tray, "Really bad champagne, winter strawberries and well—*pretty good chocolates.*" Valeria had to laugh.

Ava grabbed another strawberry, "Strawberries aren't bad." Then looking at the TV, she got a disgusted look on her face, "What on Earth are you watching?"

"*I Love Lucy* with Italian dub-in. I couldn't find any English books." Valeria confessed.

"Well, we are going to celebrate your birthday so get dressed. Come on we are going shopping. My treat!" Camille commanded.

Valeria would have argued. But she knew by now that it wouldn't matter with Camille—eventually she would get her way. Besides, Valeria was looking forward to time with them. She changed back into her jeans and shirt as Ava broke into the chocolates, "Oh! We are taking these!"

They walked out the door and Valeria grabbed her Louis Vuitton bag. Ava looked at it, "Nice bag!" Ava said with her mouth full of chocolates.

Camille turned and examined the bag critically, "Valeria, you should know before we shop together that I don't do knock-offs!"

Ava got a disgusted look on her face and said to Valeria, "How did she know that? Did you know that?"

"I bought it with Weege in a windowless van in Chinatown. So, I kind of figured that it was a knock-off."

Heading out the door, Ava said, "All right, well, count me out on the shopping expedition. I'm a mail order girl. I am going to go spend some time with my very sexy husband!" As she strode towards the elevator.

Camille knew all the finest stores in Trento; first, she took Valeria to a luxury lingerie shop. Valeria blushed when Camille insisted that she get an off-white, silk camisole set with spaghetti straps and French lace. Then, they went to a dress shop where she selected a flowered cotton dress for Valeria. It had a scoop neck and buttoned down the front with a gathered waist, which Camille said enhanced Valeria's figure. Camille, of course, took her to a local jewelry store for accessories and then to a shoe store for heels.

After an hour, to Camille's disgust, Valeria had exhausted her shopping threshold. So, she steered Valeria into Elizabeth Arden to have her make-up and hair done. The receptionist obviously knew Camille well, but argued with her in Italian. Valeria assumed it had to do with the fact that she had no appointment. After several calls were made and a slip of substantial cash from Camille, the receptionist lightened up and kissed her on the cheek before she took Valeria back. Elizabeth

Arden was far more elaborate than Valeria would have ever done for herself.

Having been primped and pampered and with her new clothes on, Camille and Valeria walked down the cobblestone street. Valeria struggled in her new four-inch heels on the cobblestones. Camille explained that she should be walking with her toes, not her heels over the cobblestones, when they came to a small outdoor garden cafe with heaters and very romantic seating.

Camille stopped, grabbing Valeria's numerous shopping bags, "This is where I leave you." Valeria realized a very anxious Alex, was the only customer at the restaurant. He brushed his fingers through his hair nervously and then shoved them into his pockets for something to do with them.

Valeria's heart leapt and she ran to him, throwing her arms around his neck. "I'm so sorry, Alex!"

She felt Alex pull her in slowly and completely, as if he almost couldn't believe that she was back in his arms and was hesitating in case it was only a dream. He didn't move for a few moments and then she realized that Alex was trying to push back his overwhelming emotions. She felt him take a deep, jagged breath and then he nuzzled into her neck, "Please, never leave me again." It was in that instant that Valeria realized the degree of Alex's love for her.

She kissed his neck and moved her mouth up to his jaw at last facing his incredible face. She saw the pain that she had caused him and desperately wanted to erase it. "Not as long as I can help it!"

They held each other's gaze knowing that tomorrow would answer that question. Then, Alex's eyes seemed to release the pain and love replaced it. His hands moved along her neck, appreciating every turn of her face. His other hand moved against her spine, pulling her to him. Their mouths came together with such tenderness and such hunger that Valeria forgot about everything that was to come the next day and the world became a warm, wonderful glow that was just the two of them.

Minutes later, there was an, "Ahem!"

Refusing to acknowledge the outside world, except on their terms, they ended their kiss slowly and gazed back into each other's eyes. Alex became aware of their waiter standing next to them—and Camille standing in the street with tears streaming down her face. Valeria choked a soft sob of happiness.

"Val, don't you dare start crying! You'll ruin all that work!" Camille teased. "*And please*—enjoy some *good* champagne to go with your new look!" She added nodding to the waiter and then walking away.

"By the way," Alex cocked his head to the side, emotion still rimming his eyes. "You always look so beautiful to me—but I have to say..." Alex pulled back from her and appraised her dress, "You look stunning!" Valeria blushed. Alex crinkled his eyes in thought, "And I've been thinking that things have just been too dark and too serious." His eyes lit, "I would like *at least a bit of an opportunity* to court you!"

An evening with Alex and no more meetings about death and disaster sounded perfect to Valeria!

They did order food, although Valeria wouldn't be able to recall if they even ate. The sun started to sink behind the buildings, lending itself to an even more romantic mood. Alex refilled Valeria's champagne glass and then kissed her neck.

"I do love you with all of my heart. Do you know that?" It

was the first time that he had actually said it to her and it caused Valeria's heart to overflow with emotion for a second time that afternoon.

"Yes. I do know that." She smiled softly, holding back the tears. "Alex, I love you so very much!"

"I'm sorry all of this has been so…fast. I was worried that it would be too much for you."

"Despite the fact that I haven't had enough time with you, this has been the most extraordinary adventure of my life!" Valeria stroked his face. "And if this was all that there was…my only regret would be to not have had more time with you."

He looked up, tears in his eyes, "You know Val, this family, this group of us, we have our eccentricities and oddities but when we love, we love for life. And for me there is no choice—it is a sad and lonely world without you in it. You are my Symbolon."

Valeria kissed his face. Symbolon? She thought for a moment, "Alex, I know that we have something very special. But I've wondered something." He nodded. "Is it possible that you are in love with Cassandra and I just happen to look like her?"

"I've had 3500 years…and I do *know you*! Better than you know yourself, I might add." He winked. "I love *you*!"

"Well, I'm a pretty ordinary kind of person." Valeria saw Alex's objection. "Alex, it's just that…" She sighed, "what if you realize that I'm just not as exciting as she was, or not as clever? I don't want you being disappointed later." It was fun to talk as if they had a future—even if it was about confronting her inadequacies.

Alex's eyes narrowed. "Let's see," amusement danced in

his eyes, "I believe that you argued that you weren't ordinary just last night, remember?"

"I don't mean it like that—Cassandra was obviously extraordinary. But I'm not her...anymore."

"Beautiful, you are the very least ordinary person that I know!" Alex's eyes narrowed and he took her hands in his. "But if you prefer, let's handle this analytically—if that could possibly resolve your misconception about yourself...or maybe your lack of confidence in my analytical powers." Alex winked.

"By numerous writers of history, Cassandra was known as one of the most spectacularly, beautiful women in ancient Greece." Alex nodded, as if that argument was moot. "Do you require the list?" He cocked his head to the side in the way she loved.

"No, thank you." She shook her head, smiling. Placing her chin in her hands, she listened to him talk. She loved listening to his voice and watching his expressions change. "I can accept that there is a resemblance—okay more than a resemblance. But it's like those pictures of people that you see that you think are attractive and then they open their mouth and all of a sudden you realize that there is nothing terribly beautiful inside to support that. That's what I mean. I've seen Cassandra's confidence and wisdom. I don't have that."

"Well now, didn't you tell me that you educated yourself and, alone, grew the most successful floral franchise in Manhattan within ten years!" Alex raised an eyebrow. "And you know what they say?"

Valeria shrugged grudgingly.

"If you can make it there..." The corners of his mouth turned up playfully, "you can make it anywhere."

She broke into a wonderful, carefree laugh. He had her on the analytical end of the argument. But she wasn't prepared to abandon her battle. "Alex, don't you worry that you would spend time with me only to discover that...I'm not someone that you could—," Valeria struggled, "love?"

Without a moment's hesitation, Alex responded. "I'm afraid you are just stuck with me! I know you! I know your heart—your soul! I also know that if you truly saw yourself, you would understand how much I love you! I've spent 3500 years waiting for you."

Alex kissed her lightly and Valeria felt a lovely warmth run through her body.

"There's something I've wondered about; in all of those years you must have loved others."

Alex looked up considering whether to share that information with Valeria. Finally he nodded. "I did marry once."

The waiter cleared their plates and refilled their coffee. Valeria took a sip, hiding her hurt. "I understand. That's an awful long time to be alone!"

Shaking his head, Alex said flatly, "I would have waited forever for you!" He looked down and then square into Valeria's eyes. "I didn't give up on you! But we simply didn't know the rules of immortality then. Really, we are still learning them.

"When you drowned the first time, I pulled you into the boat with me and tried to revive you. We didn't know what we now know about Prima Mortis. The seas were rough that day and I was afraid I might lose you, so I bound us together with rope. When the boat capsized, we were washed up on the shore days later.

"I revived and prayed that the same would happen to you. I kept waiting for you to awaken. But…" Alex pushed back the memory. "I believed that you were gone from me forever. Daphne kept trying to convince me to bury you." He paused. "Finally, I brought you to Morgana. I grieved for 500 years. During that time, I had no visions of you.

"As the years went on, we discovered more immortals and through the purges decided that the oracles needed to stick together. I offered Morgana.

"Then I met a woman—a sculptress. She was kind to me, despite the fact that she knew that I could only love you. Still—I think she was happy for a time—and I wasn't as lonely. Until the day I had a vision of you in danger."

Valeria could still see the pain of the decision in his eyes, "What did you do?"

"There was…*no choice*!" Alex's eyes were resolute. "I could never stay away from you." Valeria could feel the pain of his decision. This was a man that kept his word.

Reaching out, Alex pulled Valeria into him. She loved the feel of his arms around her. He kissed her forehead and whispered, "So, you are it for me, Val."

She choked back a tear, "Alex," he looked at her. "Please don't risk it all tomorrow."

"Val, this is our chance. I am going to put everything I have into this, to make it right this time."

"Please be safe."

He shrugged, noncommittally, causing her eyes to narrow in concern. "Alex, you aren't giving up, are you?" She asked.

Tightening his grip on her hands for a moment, Alex looked up at the darkening sky with first stars appearing.

"There are so many things that can go wrong."

She whispered, "Alex, I *need* you to survive this." She choked this time. "I don't want you to risk your life for mine. I'll come back. But *what would my eternity be without you?* Please don't give up on us—even if it takes a thousand years. Promise me."

Trying to regain control of his emotions, Alex closed his eyes trying to decide if he could really make that promise. But he owed it to her. He nodded.

Leaving the restaurant, Alex took Valeria's hand as a Puccini aria escaped from a nearby window. They rounded a corner and Caleb's laugh arose from an arcade housed in an ancient building, "SWEET!"

Alex and Valeria laughed.

Shaking her head, she said, "Caleb is something!"

"*Most definitely* something!" Alex smiled and rolled his eyes. "But, you know, the rest of us, we've all had loves." He squeezed her hand. "Caleb can't even enjoy human touch. And even if he could, Caleb has spent centuries in a body that is neither child nor man. He'll probably never see his own children. He may never know the joy of mature love or make love to a woman. Still, Caleb knows it and he tolerates it quite well."

Caleb's joyful laughter again shot down the street.

Valeria furrowed her brow, "I don't understand, I mean, he's really...what, over 2300 years old. Surely, experience has aged him."

They stepped onto a curb in front of a flower shop. Alex pulled a gardenia from a bin and tossed some cash on the counter. The owner wrapped it in paper and handed it to

Valeria.

"Thank you! I love gardenias!" She breathed in its wonderful fragrance.

Alex kissed her cheek. "We don't know a lot about Caleb but as far as immortals go, we all stay the same as we were at our Prima Mortis. Even Jeremiah is subject to the laws of his 147 years."

"Who is Jeremiah?" Valeria asked.

"He's an immortal; the oldest surviving, in terms of physical age."

"There are more like you?" She asked. "I don't think I would want to be that old forever, I mean what can you do at 147?"

The air was cooling and Valeria shivered. Alex, ever the gentleman, took off his jacket and wrapped it around her. She took in the feel of his warmth and his wonderful scent. Then his eyes narrowed in thought as another shot of laughter rose from the arcade, followed by Caleb's voice, "NOW!?"

Speaking in a voice that was too low to transmit the distance to Caleb, but loud enough for Valeria to be included, Alex said, "Yes buddy—now!"

"Don't worry. Caleb isn't riding back with us. He's catching a ride with someone else." Alex continued, "Let's see. We were talking about Jeremiah. That old guy has more spouses than any of us combined. He lives on an island where they think he is a god and collects young wives."

"Collects young wives? What for? I mean 147!"

Alex raised a brow, "Oh, Jeremiah's young wives always have the biggest smiles every morning." Alex winked.

Laughing, Valeria remembered how much she enjoyed

just being with Alex. "Well, poor Caleb! Stuck at 12, with 12-year-old hormones!"

"Yes, and obsessively intrigued with breasts—as all 12-year-old boys are!" Alex's eyes twinkled, "At least that's what I seem to recall." Alex glanced at Valeria with a smirk. "I guess you wouldn't know about 12-year-old boys."

Shaking her head shyly, Valeria went to her side of the car and Alex opened her door. As she turned to sit down, Alex grabbed her around the waist and kissed her with a burning intensity that left her wanting more. "Don't leave me again." He murmured.

Valeria pulled Alex's face to hers and kissed it sweetly, "I love you, Alex."

As they drove through the streets of Trento, Alex looked up in memory, trying to lighten the mood. "There's a funny story." He shrugged conservatively, "In the day of the Venetian courtesans, Caleb decided that it was time that he became a man—I'm not even quite certain he knew the details of what was involved…at the time."

Alex narrowed his eyes to ensure that this subject wasn't beyond Valeria's sensitivities before continuing, "The family discussed it and determined that Caleb had a right to make his own decisions about his life—knowing that he would not be able to touch her anyway. So, Caleb saved his money and found a courtesan. They went to her room. Caleb tried to touch her in the darkened room and his electrical impulse lifted her blouse and the static around Caleb lit the room. At first, the girl was frightened. But then Caleb laughed and somehow she decided it was fun.

"Down the street Lars and I listened to Caleb and the courtesan; we could hear the electrical shocks and then long laughs from both of them." Alex tilted his head to the side, "I guess he got a peep show out of it. But, Caleb could say that he had spent time with a courtesan."

Valeria and Alex laughed—she loved laughing with Alex. She loved the way he talked, the way he looked. The way he looked at her. *She loved him!*

CHAPTER 19

They pulled into the driveway but veered off to the right, instead of going to the cottage. Valeria saw a simple building located at the end of the road. Alex explained that this was Mani's lab and had been Alex's family home before they all died. It was where he'd lived for many years until building the cottage.

"I guess I never asked, are you okay with all of this?" Alex pulled up in front of the home.

"I know that if you think it's our only option, it is."

Alex jumped out and opened Valeria's door. She stepped out of the car and could see past his smile, a great sadness. She touched his face. "It'll be all right."

They walked down one of the lit trails to the back of the house. The lights were off at Mani's lab. Alex sighed, "Mani must be at Melitta's grave."

Valeria held Alex's hand, "Should we wait for him?"

"No. Let's go get him."

They walked behind the house to a beautiful garden. Mani didn't hear them; he was sitting on a stone bench speaking in another language to a gravestone.

"Hey buddy!" Alex said softly.

Mani turned, "How is it that it turns dark and I don't seem to notice."

Valeria saw several sculptures with names and dates. The one over Melitta's gravestone bore a beautiful winged angel with large eyes that seemed to see forever.

"Alex sculpted it for me out of Italian marble. It looks just like my Melitta."

"She's beautiful, Mani."

"It is so sad when we outlive the gravestones of those we love." Mani replied. Valeria noticed the name and dates had faded from the stone. She touched his shoulder.

As she turned, she saw a gravestone that said "Cassandra". It made her shudder and she averted her eyes, not wanting to see the dates, as if seeing her own death again.

They walked back to the house. It was a long narrow home built for simplicity. As they entered Valeria saw a single bedroom to the left, with a full-sized bed, neatly made. They walked through the main living area. Books occupied every free space with no sense of aesthetic. A couch sat in front of a fireplace midway through the length of the home, with a small dining table behind it. The kitchen—if you could call it that—was a single counter with a double burner stove, miniature refrigerator /freezer and a sink. Mani flipped on the lights in the lab and shrugged on his lab coat as the fluorescent bulbs slowly flickered on and yellowed the walls. The lab filled with test tubes and medical supplies seemed inappropriate for the setting in the ancient home.

Valeria tried to imagine Alex as a boy running through the house. She tried to picture his mother cooking and telling him to play outside. It must have been awful for her to lose him to Aegemon's troops. Valeria pushed that thought away, while the reality of the moment began to sink in.

Mani gestured towards the examination table and Alex lifted her onto it. She could see the tension in his eyes. Mani pulled the stethoscope from the counter and began taking Valeria's vitals and logging them on a folder that read, "Cassandra". Then he left the room and returned with a vial.

The room seemed to get darker with the knowledge of what was about to occur. Mani's eyes narrowed as he looked at Valeria, "Are you ready?" She took a deep breath and then nodded.

Mani took a long swab and dipped it in the vial and then very cautiously placed the swab in the back of Valeria's throat. Mani told her to take several deep breaths through her mouth. Then, he took the vial and the swab, tossed them into a metal bowl, poured a liquid on them and lit it on fire. Mani turned back to Valeria and put a hand on her back, while patting Alex's shoulder.

"Valeria, I've infected you with pneumonic plague. So that you understand, pneumonic means affecting the lungs. It is far more virulent—that means rapid and destructive—than the bubonic plague, due to the location of the plague in the lungs.

"The bacteria are now multiplying. As soon as you develop any symptoms you are contagious. I would guess, you have at least 10 to 12 hours until you see any symptoms, though it will not affect any of the family, except perhaps Caleb, and we will treat him, along with the staff here, with the antibiotics as a precautionary measure.

"The symptoms to watch for are fever, weakness, headache, rapidly developing pneumonia with shortness of breath, chest pain and coughing.

"Alex this is vital—Valeria MUST receive the antibiotics within 24 hours from the time of infection, in order to survive." Mani pulled out several vials and placed them in individual cases. "Alex, I am giving you two vials of antibiotics, one is a back-up. Valeria will only need one injection. What I would suggest is to give her the antibiotic when you see Aegemon approaching. But if the time is nearing the 24 hour mark, you must not wait!

"Valeria will only be contagious for three hours after the antibiotics."

Alex nodded nervously, "Got it." He placed the cases in his pocket.

"Now, let's discuss hypothermia." Mani continued, "Valeria will probably be too ill to have any symptoms from hypothermia. But you may notice that she acts as if she were intoxicated. Alex, I'm going to give you a hypo of morphine to give Valeria. It should reduce her discomfort with the disease and hypothermia. No reason for her to suffer through this without it.

"Tomorrow morning, you will need to take Valeria's temperature regularly—at least three times an hour. The plague should keep her temperature up. Her fever must not go over 105°. Use ice if you need to. As far as the hypothermia is concerned, her temperature must not drop below 96°. I would prefer to see her temperature near 100° so that we know her body is fighting the plague. Alex, if she gets too cool, your body heat will work best. But watch your own temperature. If you get too cold, you must warm yourself up, in order to care for her."

"It will be a balancing act to keep her alive. But she must remain in the water for the three hours to be completely safe. She will probably be unconscious most of the time. As long as her face is out of the water and her temperature stays between 96° and 105°, she should survive the three hours."

Mani sighed. "Ava and Lars constructed a wool wrap that should provide some relief from the water temperature. When she comes out of water, if she is conscious, which is unlikely, she will not have any body control. Place her in the bed, in the cabin, and warm her with your body heat immediately. And I want you both to understand that Valeria may suffer from amnesia."

Despite the fact that Alex knew that there was not much likelihood of either of them surviving long enough to concern themselves, he asked, "Doc, if she does lose her memory, is there some way to treat that?"

"None that I am aware of." Mani said.

Valeria looked to Alex, "It's not permanent, is it?"

"I'm sorry, I can't answer that, Valeria. Right now the focus is to get you through this alive. The rest we will worry about later."

Alex wrapped his arms around Valeria's waist, "It won't be the first time I've had to remind you. As long as you are alive, we can make anything work."

Shrugging off his lab coat, Mani continued, "Alex, in order that Valeria can contaminate Aegemon, you must permit her to get close enough for a transfer of the bacteria."

Alex lowered his brows in concern, "How close?"

"To be sure he is infected, I would say six inches, no less.

Once that is done—then the challenge will be to get both of you out of there alive."

"Anything else?" Alex asked.

Mani hugged and kissed them on both cheeks. "Kalo Taksiti! Enjoy this evening." He continued. "You are both alive tonight. So live, tonight!"

∞

Back in the car, Alex and Valeria's mood was somber. She noticed that as they pulled up in front of the cottage, it was dark, with no fire in the fireplace.

Stepping from the car, Valeria realized that the sky was now deep blue, lit with a million stars. It was a beautiful...no, she decided. She wouldn't let herself think that this could be her last night. This was a new beginning for her and Alex—one where they would discover the immense pleasure of being together...forever.

She noticed that Alex's mood had suddenly lightened and that his eyes danced with mischief. "I hope you don't mind." He took Valeria's hand and led her to the lighted path towards the main house.

"As I said before, it occurred to me...when you left...that things have been too intense."

"Alright." Valeria said, wondering what was up.

"This was Camille's idea. But I think it's a good one." Alex bypassed the main house continuing around to the backyard.

Small twinkling lights clung to the edge of the woods,

where the large, stone fireplace blazed its warmth onto the smiling faces of the family. The long, wood table was elegantly sat and adorned with a three-layer cake. A crystal chandelier hung above the table lit with candles. Valeria's eyes wandered to another table set for gifts. *Gifts*!

Overwhelmed, a tear of joy escaped the corners of Valeria's eyes as the family suddenly trumpeted, "Happy Birthday—Chronia Polla—Many years!"

Alex whispered in her ear, "Yes, love! Please live *many* years!"

Valeria shivered with the beauty of it all, the love that they freely offered to her, along with the love of this extraordinary man. It was a life she had never dared imagine and it was hers now.

The new glow in her eyes did not escape Alex. No words were necessary. He could see that she felt the full sensation of his all-consuming love of her.

Alex whispered in her ear, "Camille thought it would be fun for you to experience a Greek birthday party—most of our roots are Greek." Alex winked, "Especially yours!"

Camille and Ava approached with a glass of wine for Valeria and Alex. "Join the party!" They clinked glasses and yelled, "Opa!"

"I wanted to serve Ouzo—but I was outvoted by Alex and Camille." Ava pretended disappointment.

There was something about the evening that changed Valeria's perception of life. She thought for a moment; certainly, she had occasionally received gifts and had celebrations before—though not like this! Still, Valeria looked over the faces of the family; there was something different about tonight—something that took her a moment to synthesize.

She could sense that the revelation was monumental in its life-altering significance. Then it struck her and cocooned her in a delightful warmth with its far-reaching ramifications; she was loved! She loved them! *And she belonged!*

Raising her hands to silence the crowd, Camille explained to Valeria, "Okay…'Opa' is a Greek statement for a celebration of life! It is an affirmation that all that really matters is health, family and friends, right Alex?" He nodded.

Camille continued, "It means that you are where you are supposed to be." A tear escaped Valeria's eye. "Ahh!" Camille sighed, "And, that you need to take time to celebrate!" She turned to Alex, "Did I forget anything?"

Trays of food and drink started arriving by uniformed waiters coming from the main house. Another round of "Opa!" passed through the family as Camille and Ava hugged their new sister.

"You did great, Camille!" Alex said with joy in his eyes. "My father used to say that the meaning of 'opa' is that, having been fed and quenched our thirst, and having enjoyed friendship and love that we are filled with hope and confidence; that life abounds with all that we need." Alex raised his glass to Valeria and everyone yelled, "Opa!"

"That's beautiful!" Valeria smiled. "I would have liked to have met your father."

"He would have been…" Alex swallowed back the emotion. "…so pleased to know that I found someone like you!"

His eyes lit as he picked up a plate from a passing waiter. "My father said that we break plates as a declaration of the hope that tomorrow there will be more." Alex squeezed Valeria's hand and kissed her hair, "That seems to be particularly significant tonight!"

Alex smiled with joy and threw the plate to the edge of the fireplace where it shattered to another round of, "OPA!"

"I don't know what to say! I'm overwhelmed!" She choked.

Ava smiled, "That's the great thing about Greeks! When you don't know what to say—eat, drink, dance or say 'Opa!'" as the cheer rang through the crowd.

The music started, Lars played a mandolin, Tavish on the guitar. Different band members trailed in and added to the music, eventually replacing Tavish and Lars.

A team of waiters brought out trays of flaming cheese as appetizers, with another round of, "OPA!'"

As they ate dinner, one waiter occasionally breathed out fire, causing the familiar shout. Then the dancing began. Tavish danced, while balancing one leg of a chair on his forehead. Ava jumped in and tried to get Tavish to teach her how to do it. It became a bit of a comedy show with the chair continually crashing nearly on the cake, then nearly on Lars with Tavish somehow always catching it before anything or anyone was harmed. His expressions of attempted patience, followed by tried patience and exasperation added tremendously to the comedy. Valeria realized that she liked Tavish—but was grateful for his friendship *only*.

"Tell Alex what you thought about Tavish." Camille whispered with a gleam in her eye.

Valeria thought for a moment and then turned to Alex, "Well..." She bit her lip, embarrassed, "I thought you were setting me up with Tavish."

Alex's head rolled back in a beautiful, rollicking laugh.

He shook his head and kissed Valeria's hair. "Don't tell Tav! I don't want him getting any ideas!"

When Valeria looked back down, Camille had placed a wrapped gift in front of her.

"A gift? What was this afternoon?" Valeria objected. Camille shrugged as Valeria opened it and saw a framed picture of her and Alex at the restaurant, earlier that day. "How did you get a picture of us without me even knowing?"

"You didn't even notice me—once you saw Alex!" She hugged Valeria, "Imagine! After all of my *work* on you this afternoon!" Camille teased.

Valeria had always tried to avoid anyone taking pictures of her. She felt that she always looked like a cut-out stuck in the middle of a crowd of people. But not in this picture—Valeria was struck by the expression on her own face—*she was happy*! And both Alex and Valeria looked head over heels in love.

The old, Italian woman who had carried the flower baskets up to the cottage only a few days before approached Valeria and handed her something wrapped in tissue paper. Ava gave Valeria a look of amused caution, "Brace yourself."

It was a blue marble charm with an eyeball painted on it. Valeria was taken back. The old woman said, "Matiasma!" Then she pointed to her own eye with a wicked look and then to Daphne, who was busy flirting with one of the young waiters.

Ava smiled, "Knew that one was coming! It's to protect you from the evil eye of jealousy."

The music started slowly with Mandolin and guitar. Alex rolled up his sleeves as he looked seductively at Valeria, "Come on, we're dancing."

She pulled back, "No. Alex I can't dance."

The whole group surrounded them and pulled Valeria into 'Zorba the Greeks' Sirtaki Dance. The musical energy built and Valeria found herself dancing and laughing and hanging onto Alex. The Sirtaki finished and the music became softer as Alex spun her around to face him and wrapped his arms around her waist.

The waiters began throwing the plates down on the ground yelling "Opa!"

Through her laughter, Valeria whispered to Alex, "Please don't let them find the Limoges!" This was what 'happy' felt like, she thought.

As Alex and Valeria danced, first Ava and Lars came by to say good night. They hugged and kissed Valeria. One by one the others came by and then went back to dancing. Valeria thanked them but her attention was on Alex.

Drunk with love, celebration and the full moon, Alex kissed Valeria and she responded with much more than she might have intended in front of others. Their eyes met as they started down the path towards the cottage, playfully dancing and kissing.

Valeria stumbled trying to walk backwards in Alex's arms and he lifted her, as if she weighed nothing, and carried her the rest of the way to the cottage. Alex closed the door with his foot and placed Valeria square on her feet in front of him. The fire had mysteriously reappeared in the fireplace.

They stood for a moment, their heartbeats pounding at a marvelously fast pace. Alex forgot all of his carefully constructed rules, the love in his eyes was replaced with so much longing that the nightmares that they had faced, and would face, disappeared and it was only them.

Reaching for her hands, Alex stepped towards her, staring down into her eyes, his voice soft and husky, and his eyes intense with emotion as he whispered in wonder, "Do you have any idea how beautiful you are?"

His hand touched the edge of her face and then back to the nape of her neck, his fingers moving into her hair and gently tugged to pull her face up towards his. His other hand moved along her spine, to her waist. She reveled in the feel of his touch as each movement of his fingers released an electrical charge all its own. Valeria heard a cross between a sigh and a moan and realized that it came from her. In response, Alex pulled her into him.

The firelight danced gently upon them as his mouth brushed over hers with a teasing taste that became a hunger and soft kisses grew longer and deeper. Her body became alive with the taste of him as her breath strangled in her throat. Alex's hand brushed along her neck and then down to the front of her dress, as his mouth caressed her jaw line. Without permitting himself the time to evaluate, he unbuttoned the top button of her dress. Suddenly concerned with her response to his actions, he glanced down and seeing her desire, he quickly unbuttoned the rest. She pulled Alex's shirt off and felt that luxurious ache in her belly.

Staring at his well-muscled chest with the smattering of hair, Valeria ran both her hands down his neck and over his chest, feeling him shudder as she did so. And then she placed her mouth over his heart. She heard Alex murmur her name softly, almost as a cry.

"Oh…Val!"

She could feel his heart slamming against his chest and it

thrilled her and caused her to spiral deliciously out of control as she pressed herself against him.

Alex's mouth trailed along the curve of her shoulder causing an intense flash of heat that moved through her entire body. Her arms hungrily reached around his back pulling him even closer. Then his mouth moved back to hers as his hands pushed the dress back, revealing the new silk lingerie. Valeria's breath hitched, relishing in the extraordinary feel of his skin against hers with only the silk as a barrier.

While caressing her neck with his mouth, his hands ran down the side of the lingerie. His eyes gloriously intense, his voice smoldering, "Ohhh...my beautiful...love."

A moment later, Valeria sensed his hesitancy. She opened her eyes as Alex sighed and pulled back from her.

"What am I doing?" He let out another heavy sigh.

Valeria clung to him. Alex smiled and brushed her face with his fingers and then without moving his eyes from hers, he forced himself to pull Valeria's dress back together, covering her. He rolled his eyes and whispered, "Oh boy!" Then his mouth leaned against hers in a chaste kiss before forcing himself to step away from her. Alex turned, moving towards the refrigerator and pulled out a bottle of cold water, his voice still soft and husky. "Do you want some water?"

When he turned back towards her, he was stunned to see her standing only a few feet from him in the kitchen. Shyly, she pulled her dress back off her shoulders, but left it hanging from her arms and her waist. Her eyes glistened with desire, "Alex?"

Stunned into inaction, he just stared for a beat. Then suddenly overtaken, he dropped the bottles on the counter and with a single step pulled her back into his arms and kissed her with an intensity of mouths and tongue and teeth that melted her. As her dress dropped to the floor, she wrapped herself in his arms. He looked at her, with eons of love denied, lifted her and carried her into their bed.

They entangled, breathlessly as Valeria wrapped her arms and legs around him, needing to feel closer...and then she again felt his hesitancy as she breathlessly fought a losing battle. Finally, Alex found the strength and pushed away and sat up. She laid on the bed for a moment, crushed. He pulled the sheet around her and sat her up leaning against him.

"Val, I want you to understand something." He said breathlessly.

She looked down trying to hide her disappointment. Alex continued, "Tomorrow's a big day. I think we both need to get some rest."

A tear escaped Valeria's eye. "Alex, I know what may happen tomorrow. I don't regret anything." She leaned towards him and closed her eyes, "—except if I was never with you."

He kissed the top of her head and lifted her tear with his hand gently. He turned her to face him. "Val—" he smiled with such love that it overwhelmed her.

She interrupted him, "Alex, I've waited almost 30 years to feel like this about someone. And I want to spend whatever I have left with you." Her eyes intensified. "I mean...*with you.*"

He stroked her face, "Do you know how very long I have waited to be with you?"

"Then...please?" Gulping back her nerve, she crawled out from the sheet and crawled onto his lap, kissing his neck, "Please..."

With every ounce of discipline he possessed, Alex moved her next to him again and covered her with the sheet.

"Beautiful, it has to do with…with a vision." Alex said breathing and concentrating on discipline—pushing back the desire that engulfed him.

"It's bad?" Valeria grasped Alex's hands, while still feeling defeated. "I don't want to know."

Chuckling softly, he said, "No, it's…" He whispered as tears rimmed his eyes and he swallowed back the emotion, "it's…beautiful!"

"Then tell me."

Alex crinkled his nose and shook his head.

Valeria started to protest, "Then why—".

Placing his fingers over her mouth, he said softly, "That vision is…very personal." He looked into Valeria's eyes filled with a mix of hurt and desire. She needed an explanation of his reluctance. "How do I explain this?"

His eyes narrowed in thought, "When I was young I had a vision of you and I. We were together as husband and wife…" Alex looked into her eyes. "It was…well, it was our wedding night." He looked down, a touch embarrassed, and then back into her eyes. His voice softer, "While that vision has and does add passion to my time with you—it isn't something I can share with you. It feels very…private."

Stroking her face, Alex continued, "Besides, the fact is that it wouldn't feel…gentlemanly to share—".

Noticing that Valeria's imagination had taken over, Alex's face reddened as he quickly added, "Oh no, no! Beautiful, let me assure you that there is nothing that…violates your modesty! But to share the vision would feel like I was…I don't know…in some ways choreographing…*things*." Alex stroked her face. "I hope you understand. I hope you know how

253

much I want you." His face glistened with love. "But I want you alive more! And…I just can't *sacrifice* that possibility." Valeria hid her face in his chest.

Raising her face so that he could see her, Alex continued, "And there's something else; as long as that vision hasn't occurred, it's still possible! It is the dream that has carried me through thousands of years." Alex looked down, "Val, if I make love to you tonight, it will be like I've given up hope that we can ever have…more." He took her face in his hands, tears rimming his eyes. "And I want more than just tonight! I want you as my wife…I want you for eternity."

Tears rolled down Valeria's face. She kissed him lightly. She understood that this wasn't just about her. Alex had far more invested than she did. Overcome with love, she asked in a whisper, "Uhm, Alex?" She had a deep question in her eyes. "I guess I wondering…"

Alex nodded.

"Alex…*was that a proposal?*"

His mouth turned up slowly in that marvelous smile that she loved. He patted her leg, rose from the bed and left the room, returning a moment later with a small ring box. Valeria stared in disbelief. Could this really be happening?

He crawled back into bed with her, "This isn't exactly how I pictured this. But what could be better than here and now?"

He sat facing her, "Valeria, you asked me about the Italian phrase that I said the other day when we were discussing…" He smiled softly, "us." Alex repeated the phrase in Italian.

The moon lit up the room in a romantic glow. Valeria nodded sweetly as Alex continued, "Though, I am an avid reader, I am not much of a writer." He cleared his throat. "I borrowed this from Gretchen Kemp." He swallowed nervously. "There's this place in me where your fingerprints still rest, your kisses still linger, and your whispers softly echo. It's the place where a part of you will forever be a part of me."

Tears rimmed Valeria's eyes as she said softly, "It's…beautiful, Alex!"

He pulled up on his knee in front of her. "My…*oh so* beautiful Valeria," his eyes deepened with emotion. "Loving you has been the greatest joy in all of my existence! Will you do me the honor of becoming my wife?"

Alex opened the box. It was the most exquisite ring she had ever seen in her life. It was a three carat brilliant blue stone, wrapped with an intricate platinum grape vine.

"Oh my God, Alex!" Valeria exclaimed. He took the ring out and slid it onto her finger. She tried to find something to say. But no words could express what she thought or felt.

The stone seemed to capture the bit of light from the moon. "I found this stone 1800 years ago in Southern Africa and it reminded me of you; breathtaking and one of a kind. I call it the Cassandra Crystal."

Valeria went between staring at the ring and Alex in wonder. Her voice sounded raw from the mesh of emotions. "Alex, the color— it's…extraordinary…it's the color of your eyes."

"We call it 'oracle blue'." Alex pulled up Valeria's face, "So, you haven't answered my question."

Through her tears, Valeria smiled, "Well…is there anyone up at the house tonight that might be a pastor?"

"I'm afraid not." Alex responded. "But you say yes—and I

will find a pastor as soon as you're ready!"

She laughed and hugged Alex, "I am…" she caught her breath, "so very much in love with you! I thought this kind of love was…a fairy tale. There is nothing I have ever wanted more in my life than I want to be married to you!"

Alex jumped onto the floor and grabbed Valeria around the waist, swinging her around. They kissed and hugged and then curled up together in bed, wrapped soul to soul and drifted into a blissful slumber.

CHAPTER 20

A shaft of early light broke through the branches of the tall pines outside and made its way through the bedroom window. Alex thought he was dreaming; Valeria was wrapped around him. It felt so natural...so right. Then he shifted and realized that something wasn't quite right. He brushed her hair back and felt the heat. The fever! He kissed her face and was shocked how high the fever was already.

"Val?" He whispered.

His heart skipped a beat as he heard her breathing; it was rough and labored. Alex gently tried to wake her again. "Val?" Panic reaching his voice.

Moaning softly, her head rolled to the side and then suddenly she convulsed and coughed, before finally opening her eyes.

"Hello, handsome." She attempted a smile but instead turned and coughed again. She thought of telling him of the aching in her back and joints, but realized there was no reason to worry him further.

Wearing only his slacks from the night before, Alex went to the kitchen and brought her an orange juice. Valeria tried to take a drink but started coughing again. She leaned back in the bed and started to shiver, moving her legs as if they were in pain.

Alex watched helplessly. "Do you want the morphine now?"

"Uhmm, no, I don't want to…uhmm, sleep too much." This might be her last hours with him. She wasn't going to sleep through the precious time they had left if she could help it!

There was a knock at the door. Alex threw on a tee shirt before opening the door for Ava, Camille and Daphne. "She's sick." He choked.

"We're here to help Val get ready." Camille brushed Alex's face as she came in.

"She's going to be fine, honey." Ava gave Alex a sympathetic hug. "You go get your shower and we'll take care of Val."

Seeing that Alex was distraught, Daphne hugged him lightly, uncomfortable with the emotion. "Alex, I know I haven't been very kind to her… I'm sorry. I brought her my wool hat and gloves." He nodded, unable to speak through his grief.

All three women went into the bedroom. Daphne brushed Valeria's hair while Ava brought her a bowl so she could wash her face and brush her teeth. Camille helped her dress.

"Alex," Camille added as they were leaving. "I have a good feeling about this."

Dressed in jeans and a tee shirt, he went to the bed and pulled Valeria into his arms. "Well beautiful, are you ready?" She reached up and put her arms around his neck. He lifted her easily and carried her outside. It was a drab morning. The sky was gray and mist formed through the forest. Alex noted that the temperature was cooler than it had been. The family was waiting out by the car. Lars opened the passenger seat for Valeria and Alex sat her down.

Mani went through the checklist with Alex to ensure that they had all the necessary supplies and make sure that Alex understood the instructions. He hugged each of them as if to say good-bye.

Pulling Alex aside, Ava said, "The cat is loaded with wool blankets, sweaters and the medical equipment you'll need. There are also bags of ice in case you need it. Make sure she wears the wool. Also, remember to keep some of the blankets dry for when she comes out of the water."

Ava glanced at Valeria. "Don't worry about the sails...you'll do fine."

She went on, "You have plenty of time so take her nice and easy, especially getting out of the marina. I wish I could loan you my crew, but with the plague and...." Glancing at Lars, Ava said, "I wish I could be there for you."

"I know. It's just too dangerous with Aegemon."

She hugged him, "Love you honey." She patted Alex's face again. "Be safe."

Daphne brought out another blanket and handed it to Alex. Valeria was dozing in the car as he leaned her seat back and wrapped the blanket around her lovingly. She opened her eyes. "Do you want anything to eat or drink?" He asked.

She smiled weakly and signaled for him to come close,

she whispered in his ear, "Coffee." He kissed her and returned with a carrying cup of coffee that he had made earlier. She took a few sips and sighed before closing her eyes again.

Alex pulled out onto the highway, "I want to put some music on to soothe you." It was a challenge as his mood had a narrow tolerance particularly today. He had seen that she was a Puccini fan. And although his music was breathtaking, it was too tragic and was too close to his reality. "Instrumental alright?" He asked trying to sound off-hand.

Keeping her eyes closed, Valeria nodded. She didn't really care what was playing. He would hear the coughs—there was no hiding that. But she did want to hide her pain-filled moans, which seemed uncontrollable, and her breathing, which was getting raspy.

They winded down the highway with the sun rising above the Adriatic Sea. The weather looked early winter instead of fall. Alex followed the directions to the marina with the magnificent St. Marks to the west. He hoped that someday he would have the chance to share Venice with Valeria. For now she was sleeping. Her fever was at 103°.

"We're here, beautiful." He said touching her shoulder. "I'm going to load some supplies before I bring you out to the boat. Alright?" He asked. Valeria nodded weakly. "I'll be back in no more than five minutes."

Alex hated leaving her alone. He forced himself to close her door and walked into the marina where the Mariah would be docked. The temperature on the water was even cooler. The catamaran was just where Ava had said it would be. Alex went below into the cabin and cranked on the heat. He pulled down the wool covers on the bed and noticed that there was an electric blanket for use afterwards—he hoped there would be an opportunity to use it—but he doubted it. He walked quickly back to the car.

Forcing a smile on his face, Alex said, "Are you ready for our next adventure?"

Valeria opened her eyes, "Anywhere, as long as I'm with you." Then she slipped back into her restless sleep. He wrapped her from head to toe with the blanket and lifted her from the car. Stepping onto the boat, Alex brought her down to the cabin, laying her gently on the bed.

She saw that it was an electric blanket. "Can you turn it on?" She asked as she shivered violently. "I can't get warm."

Doubting that he could do anything to soothe her chills, he said, "Let me check your temperature. If we can get it down a bit…" He stopped talking so that she didn't hear the ache in his voice.

The thermometer read 102°. Not good.

Stroking her forehead, Alex said, "I'm sorry beautiful, I can't turn on the electric blanket. Your fever is too high." Valeria shivered helplessly. "Morphine yet?" He asked.

She shook her head no.

"How about Tylenol?" Alex brought Valeria some water and pills. She took a small drink of water. "Val, can you drink a little more water?" As she turned her head away, he pleaded, "Beautiful, it's important that we keep you hydrated." She forced herself to drink the cold water. Soon she was back asleep. Alex unhooked the ropes and pushed off as he raised the sail. He had not sailed anything other than a small, single sail dinghy in thousands of years. He remembered Ava's joke that it would be like riding a bike. It wasn't.

Navigating through the slips, Alex followed the waterway that would eventually grant him access to the sea—if he didn't put the Mariah on the rocks! A large boat passed them and the Mariah suddenly made a sharp turn out of his control, just missing another boat.

Alex had to take the boat back around and try it again. It was all he could do just trying to safely get out of the marina. Then he faced a mass of waterways where ships moved. It was intimidating. But finally he was out to open water with the view of Venice behind him.

Following about a mile off from the shoreline, Alex watched for the familiar inlet and looked at his GPS that identified it as the precise location. He looked at his watch. Valeria didn't need to be in the water for another twenty minutes. With the Tylenol, her temperature was still 102°. He gave her room temperature broth. She drank it, but Alex was certain that it only to appease him. Then he held her close and tried to settle her shivers—and to feel her in his arms before he had to leave her alone in the sea—wondering if he would ever again feel the life in her. He had to block that thought!

As the time drew near, Valeria coughed and saw blood all over her with spots on Alex. She shook her head in horror. He took a cloth and wiped up the blood from both of them. And then Valeria looked down and saw a large splattering of blood on the blanket. "I've ruined this." Alex assured her it was all right.

"It's time. I'd like to go ahead and give you a shot of morphine now." Alex said grimly. Valeria didn't seem aware. He took out the syringe and injected her hip. Then he placed the wool cap on her head and pushed her curls into it. He put the wool mittens and socks on her. Val relaxed and was unconscious or sleeping. At least she didn't seem uncomfortable. He prayed that she didn't feel the pain of the cold water as he wrapped her in the heavy wool blankets and lifted her body.

Alex could hardly see through his tears as he carried her onto the deck. Stepping cautiously onto the netting, he laid her in the harness that Lars and Ava had designed and tied all four of the straps that would keep the blankets around her and reduce the water flow. It would have been easier with Velcro. But for some reason Ava and Mani thought this was better. Alex lifted Valeria into the harness and to the portion of the netting that was in the water. As he stepped to seat her in the cradle of the net, a wave came up and the boat lunged, he momentarily lost his footing and dropped her. Valeria hit the water hard and gave a loud cry. He raced down the netting into the cold water, his foot went through and he fell on her. Fortunately, Valeria was wrapped so heavily in blankets that the fall didn't affect her.

Taking a moment, Alex sat and sobbed with her in his arms before moving her into position. She moaned but didn't wake—the morphine had helped! He hooked the harness to the netting and forced himself to leave her there. And then Alex sat next to her, free of the ice cold water with his hand on her only exposed part…her face.

Minutes later Valeria's shivers intensified. It was more than Alex thought he could bear. He imagined what it would be like to have the three hours over. He imagined her alive and smiling. Alex glanced at his watch for the third time since Valeria had been in the water. It had only been 10 minutes.

He wondered how he could survive this for three hours. Then he noticed that her skin no longer felt hot but actually cool. Another wave hit her face and she choked on it. Alex was helpless to watch it all. He was supposed to take her temperature every 20 minutes. But he took it every 10 minutes to give him something to do. The cold water had reduced her fever to 99°.

She opened her eyes slightly, shivering furiously, "Uhmm," she gulped and coughed.

Alex leaned down so he could hear her, "Yes beautiful. What do you want? A drink?"

"Morphine."

It would be another hour before he could give her more. But he couldn't tell her "no". He choked before answering, "I'm going to check with Mani. Okay?" She nodded.

He hated to leave her but he needed to hear Mani's assurance that she would be alright. Alex thought that perhaps he could give her more now and it would ease her suffering. He called on the radio and heard a response.

"How is everything going?" Ava asked through the static.

Alex choked back a sob. "Oh. It's…" He didn't know what to say but the truth. "It's not good."

Mani came on, "Alex, what's her temperature?"

"Down from 103° to 99° on the last check. Mani she's shaking really bad." His voice quivered.

"Alex, listen to me. The shaking is good. It means her body is fighting. And her temperature is good. Can you add more blankets? We don't want it dropping much more."

"I've used all the blankets; except the ones I'll need when this is done."

"Alright." There was a long pause. "Well, alright."

Noticing Mani's withheld communication, Alex responded. "She wants more morphine."

There was a silence. "Alex, more morphine right now

could kill her." There was another silence. "But the cold will give her some pain relief."

Alex's body wracked with sobs for a moment. He tried to get control of himself. Finally he said, "I have to get back out there with her. I'll let you know when we're safe."

As he stepped onto the deck, he watched as a large wave crashed over Valeria. He ran to move her face and adjust the netting. She coughed up more blood.

"I'm sorry, Val! I'm so sorry!"

Her temperature had dropped to 97°. She still had an hour and a half to go. Alex crawled in the water with her. It shocked his body feeling the cold and despite his intention he found himself almost jumping back out. He forced himself to stay in the water and unwrapped the blankets around Valeria. She moaned and coughed but was unconscious. Then he held her close to him and wrapped the blankets around them together. He shouldn't have given her the Tylenol, he thought, angry with himself. The cold water caused him to immediately start shivering and he could feel his hands begin to go numb. Within a short time he realized that although it made him feel better to be near her, in the end it just risked that he would have no body strength when or if Aegemon showed up. Alex pulled them both out of the water—surely a few minutes would be all right.

Valeria responded to his closeness by moving her head against his neck. He knew he couldn't keep her out of the water but her temperature was dangerously low. Pushing her legs back into the cold water, he held her body next to his, feeling the warmth flooding into her chest and limbs for five minutes and her temperature went back up to 99°. Then, with a shudder, he moved her back to the harness and lowered her. It was an action like cutting off his own arm.

Suddenly, Valeria's shivering stopped and her eyes opened wide in horror, "Dad, no! Don't go in there. There's spiders—the spiders!"

Mani had warned Alex that Valeria might hallucinate. But it was a shock to hear her like this. Still, the time was finally coming to an end. Maybe Ava was wrong and Aegemon wouldn't show up. Maybe he had finally died. Maybe there was no curse. Maybe they could survive this...

Alex went below and nuked some broth. He took it back knowing she was most likely still unconscious.

Looking at his watch, relief ran through him as he saw that there was only fifteen minutes left and then he could pull her out of the water. He could treat her as soon as Aegemon showed. Alex took her temperature one last time, 96°. Her temperature couldn't drop anymore or she wouldn't survive. There was only fourteen minutes left.

Unhooking her from the harness Alex again crawled into the cold water with her. Valeria let out a loud moan. She felt so cold.

"Boat approaching!" came Lars' frantic call over the radio.

There was no time to hook Valeria back into the harness. He had to get the antibiotic. As he worked to at least get one of the hooks tied, Alex shook his head, angry with himself; why had he unhooked her when they were so close to the end of the time? The boat was approaching and Valeria had to have the shot. Leaving only the tie around her waist, Alex ran to get the antibiotic.

When he returned, he sensed that something didn't look right about her position in the harness. To his horror, he saw that her head had turned and was underwater! He climbed into the water and turned her head. She wasn't breathing and her lips were blue. A cry escaped from him as he began to breathe into her mouth. Nothing happened. Pulling the blanket back he placed his ear on her chest; her heart was still beating but weakly. He breathed into her again. He had to be sure it was Aegemon before giving her the shot. How could he take the time to do that, he wondered.

As the boat got closer, Alex glanced up, he was certain the boat was approaching them and he thought he saw Aegemon. Alex removed the lid from the hypo and untied the harness, raising her leg out of the water. He needed to give her another breath. He breathed into her and in that moment the boat rocked again throwing him face first onto the netting. He scrambled to right himself and in the process dropped the injection. Alex saw it floating away and reached off the end of the netting. With his movement in the water the hypo was pushed further away. Alex leaned off from the edge of the boat as the hypo dipped below the surface.

If he had the opportunity to look up, Alex could have seen the occupants on the approaching boat. Alex tried one last lurch to grab the injection and lost his balance, crashing into the sea. He desperately grabbed for the netting, but the current from the approaching boat pushed him away. The hypo was long gone. He would drown and she would die! The realization nearly made him vomit. He had to get back on the cat and get the other hypo. One desperate grasp and he caught the rope! He pulled himself back onto the boat. Valeria was still blue. There was not enough time to go to her *and* get the other hypo!

With his clothes weighed down with sea water, Alex moved as quickly as possible to the cabin. He had placed the extra hypodermic needle in the drawer by the stove. Pulling it open he searched for it. It wasn't there! A new ripple of terror ran through Alex; she would die without the injection! He pulled open every drawer and searched with his heart moving into his throat. Maybe he had dropped it. Alex got on his knees and looked across the floor; *nothing*. He could hear the engine from the boat. They would be boarding in minutes! Alex forced himself to take a breath. Where could it be? He focused. It had to be in the drawer where he had placed it. With one last look he finally saw it. Holding it with an iron grip, he moved cautiously back to her as the approaching boat positioned itself alongside the Mariah. Alex prayed he could get the injection in and get her breathing before Aegemon stopped him.

When he returned, Valeria still wasn't breathing. He unwrapped the blanket from her waist and rolled her to the side as he plunged the hypo into her hip. His hands shaking so badly that he was grateful it just needed to go into her hip and not a vein.

Immediately he dropped the hypo, hoping that it would sink quickly. The three hours were still not up. He breathed into her lungs over and over again. The 40 foot yacht pulled up by them. Alex ignored their calls and continued to attempt to revive Valeria.

It had been over 500 years since he had seen Aegemon. But he appeared on the deck, looking like a wealthy yachtsman. His boat was named "The Oracle VI".

"Alexander! Let us help you with Cassandra!" Aegemon said in a soothing voice. Alex couldn't attack Aegemon with six men there to harm Valeria. A group of men came down a ladder and loaded onto the Mariah. Alex continued attempting to revive her. Her body felt so cold and limp. It reminded him of so many years ago.

There was a tap on Alex's shoulder. She needed 30 more seconds! She had to stay in that icy water until the last minute. Then, Alex had the morose thought that perhaps she had already been affected by the curse. Perhaps all of this had been for nothing and the curse had prevailed. Valeria's lips were still blue. Alex forced himself to abandon that thought. Then, he remembered that her heart had been beating! Was it still? There was no time to check. He continued breathing into her mouth.

Finally, Alex was thrown aside. He fought the men to get her the last few seconds. The time was up! Alex threw himself onto the netting next to her and pulled her from the water as he laid his head on her chest—he heard nothing at first, they tried to pull him off from her and he held on with everything in him. At last he heard it! It was weak but her heart was still beating. She was still alive! She had lived past the curse! It had worked!

Aegemon looked at Alex off-handedly, like a pest. "Throw him in."

It didn't require much effort and Alex was treading water. He tried to pull up on the ropes of the catamaran. One of the men stepped on his hand. When the man released it, Alex's hand was left without strength. He had to keep his body and especially his limbs moving. But he just couldn't get a grip on the netting.

Alex watched as Valeria was carried over the shoulder of one of the crew onto Aegemon's deck and tossed down without care. She didn't appear to be breathing. She had lived past the curse—but would she die now? Aegemon's man slapped Valeria a few times and the sound made him shudder. Then he saw her begin to move. Alex watched as she vomited seawater and took a deep gulping breath.

"Aegemon, please—let her live. She's done nothing to you." He said between hard shivers.

Aegemon waved off Alex's request. "What she is to me is *none* of your affair!"

Alex's feet went numb.

"But why? Aegemon, why can't you let us…" A wave splashed Alex and he choked. Aegemon ignored it, "Why can't you leave us alone? We are nothing to you. And you…" The shivering was overtaking him. Alex wondered if Aegemon, or any of his men, would get close enough to be infected or if all of this had been a waste.

As his arms started to go numb, Alex fought to keep his legs moving rapidly—keep the blood running through them. He knew that he didn't have long until he would sink. But perhaps at least she would survive.

The cold begged him to accept death. With everything in him, Alex determined that no matter what happened here, his future was with her! He worked harder and fought the overwhelming influence of the cold. Alex wondered how long it might be until he held her in his arms again. He wondered if he ever would. That thought forced the adrenalin into his body, forcing it despite the conditions.

Aegemon's men tied the Mariah to the yacht.

A comforting darkness enveloped Valeria. She felt it and wondered if it was death calling. A kaleidoscope effect began around the edges of her range of light through her eyelids.

She wanted to tell Alex. She wanted to see him and for him to know that she was alright. The effect increased and then she saw the vision:

The man was beautiful with light brown hair and soft blue eyes. His hand stroked her face gently. "Child, I must leave you."

Valeria could feel the stroke of his warm hand on her face. But it wasn't Alex. Maybe she was hallucinating. She heard her voice but it sounded more confident.

"Lord, the world will be darker without you." She bowed.

Apollo glanced to the horizon, "Cassandra, I must warn you that history will not be kind to either of us."

She covered her mouth, "Lord, you are the god of poetry and music! How could otherwise be written?"

"Do not trouble yourself with history! Reason does not always play well with history or politics." He looked up, wearily. *"There will be books written that are said to be prophesies of my precious oracles. They will call them The Sibylline Oracle."* His eyes narrowed. *"Child, there is only one book that is The Sibylline Oracle. Do you recall?"*

"The visions that Myrdd recorded?"

Smiling, he brushed her shoulder. "Yes. It is close to your heart. Our dear friend Myrdd holds your secrets."

His light blue eyes showed a tremendous sadness, "There will be a great war in Troy. I see hardships for you. I wish I could eliminate them. I cannot." Apollo sighed, "I have come to tell you that you must leave Troy if you are to survive. Remember that the walls of Troy will be your key."

"Lord, my family will not believe even my words that Troy would be unsafe."

Glancing towards the heavens, Apollo said, "You must convince them, as that alone, will lead you to your destiny."

Apollo smiled as he stroked her head. "Child, know that you will always be in my heart!"

"And you in mine, Lord!"

With a furrowed brow, he added, "Until you forget..." Then he smiled wistfully. "My oracle, Alexander, will seek you out. He must take you to your destiny. Your destiny is not an easy path, but it is worthy of my most favorite of all oracles!"

271

He smiled kindly.

Then Valeria saw a cold muddy land with many tents of animal hides and a community fire blazing in the center with large pots hanging over it. She saw a reflection in a pot and to Valeria's surprise realized that it was her own.

She warmed her hands by the fire as she glanced at her surroundings. The warmth felt good. There was a woman romantically teasing a man and then kissing him delicately. Cassandra sighed.

A beautiful, older woman stood next to her. "You look at other girls and their lovers with longing. But Cassandra, you would not do well as an ordinary girl. Ordinary girls are not princesses or priestesses." The woman admonished.

"Ordinary girls can fall in love."

"There would not be a man so unwise as to love you?"

"There is a man. But he cannot approach me." Cassandra added softly to herself, "But if I do not find him soon it will be too late."

"It is just as well! You are Troy's oracle and your visions are required! That is more important than a silly boy."

"I must find him." She insisted.

Cassandra saw the vision of Aegemon on the horse before he arrived.

"Lord Aegemon wishes to speak to me in private." She said to her mother.

The woman shook her head. "He may not meet with you in private! I will witness the meeting."

"This must be done alone." Cassandra exited, hearing her mother's trailing desperate cries of impropriety. But

Cassandra knew that her mother would never intrude on the meeting, fearing Aegemon's wrath.

Walking into her dark tent, Cassandra awaited his arrival. She knew what must happen and it would serve her plan. Aegemon stepped in, his brown robe wrapped loosely around him. In his late forties, he still was an attractive man. It would not be as bad as it could be, Cassandra thought.

Aegemon wasted no time throwing his arms around Cassandra, as he unwrapped his robe revealing his desire. He gave her a knowing smile. "You do not fight me. Could it be this is what you are hungry for?"

"Yes lord." Cassandra responded as his mouth and body enveloped her. She knew his intention; Apollo was no longer there to protect her. Once she was no longer a virgin priestess, she would have no value and she could find the one that had been promised to her.

∞

Cassandra would not require much; she took her bed roll. The walk through the village would be the worst of it and then she would be free to find him. She tossed the flap aside and forced her way through the angry mob as they spat on her and called her a whore. She held her head up and made eye contact with those that had picked up stones. If a stoning began she would not be able to stop it. So with a strong, confident glare she reminded them that she was Apollo's most favored!

This was all to be expected and the reward was well worth the price. Cassandra had known that Aegemon would betray her. But now she was free. She would walk across the northern section of the Adriatic. That was where she had seen

Alexander in her visions. Troy would fall. Even if she had stayed, she had seen that she would not be able to prevent it.

∞

Awakening from the beautiful dreams of her life to come, Cassandra stretched and smiled. It had been two days since she had left. Sleeping under the brilliant stars that held her future, she was at last free from the titles that had burdened her. Freedom and hope now filled her heart.

Then she saw that Aegemon was again approaching. He would not find her so accommodating this time! He had what he wanted. And she would tell him what he needed; about the wooden horse. She would not be believed. She knew that history would write her as insane and damned by Apollo. That meant nothing to her.

Walking directly to Aegemon, Cassandra offered him a cold smile. "I have what you want." She continued, "Sparta will invade Troy."

"Impossible! The Trojan Walls are impenetrable. Myrdd assured us of that!" Aegemon laughed.

"Troy will accept a gift from Sparta...a horse. That will be the fall of our great city."

Aegemon shook his head in disgust, "A horse?! Preposterous!" He looked at Cassandra and his eyes narrowed. "I could...take care of you. You would not starve." He hesitated, "I could, if I wanted to..."

Cassandra's face filled with loathing, "You have nothing I want."

Turning her back on Aegemon, she gathered her bed roll

and began walking down the road. He followed her, "What you seek, you cannot have!" He yelled angrily. Cassandra ignored him. "I tell you the truth!" Aegemon pulled her around to him and held out his hands for a transference.

Looking at him with disgust, "I don't require contact!" She snapped, the not so subtle invalidation.

"He is not there!" Aegemon said arrogantly. She glared at him, realizing that he knew about Alexander.

"What do you know?" She challenged.

Aegemon stood as if to tempt her desire for him. As if she would have ever wanted him! She spit on him.

The slap came hard from the corner of her eye and when she became aware of it she was already on the ground 10 feet from her previous position; not that she hadn't expected it.

One thing Cassandra knew was that although Apollo was no longer there to protect her physically, Aegemon would be wary of suffering Apollo's wrath, should she be harmed. If the other oracles were harmed, as many had been, Apollo would not be pleased. But harming Cassandra would be a completely different matter.

She crawled to her feet. Though it would leave a mark, it didn't hurt. There was nothing he could do that would hurt her. The side of her face was numb but she could feel the moisture of blood.

Aegemon realizing that he had crossed the line, scrambled after Cassandra. "He isn't there!" She knew his tricks. She pushed past him. He wouldn't hit her again. "I can help you."

"You have nothing that I want!"

"You will want to forget." She stopped. There was a

memory...there was something about needing to forget...it was Myrdd...and Apollo! Myrdd had said she would want to forget. But her journey and its goal were far more important.

Aegemon held out the drink. Cassandra glared at him and waited. "He is gone. The boy is gone." No. She would know if something had happened to Alexander!

"I did it myself. I bound his limbs and tossed him into the sea."

There was no trusting Aegemon. She turned, her eyes narrowed. "Tell me again what you did to Alexander." She had to see Aegemon's eyes when he spoke.

"I killed him!"

The transference showed her the many years that Alexander had been a prisoner of Aegemon; hard labor for fourteen years. It made her heart ache for him. That explained why he had not come for her.

She saw the oracles, stored like animals in the hole of a ship. Aegemon gave the order and they were taken up onto the deck. There were over 30 faces with the brilliant blue eyes of a true oracle. Aegemon looked down the line of oracles until he came to her Alexander, his defiant look matching that of her own. She watched in horror as his arms and legs were bound and he was thrown overboard.

The cry came from her before she had mentally even accepted it. Cassandra fell to her knees in pain; why didn't she know? How could Alex be gone and she didn't know? Long hard sobs wracked her body.

Dropping the bottle by her, pleased with his effect, Aegemon climbed on his horse. There was nothing else he wanted from her. There was nothing else she would give. Troy would need her information, although they would not believe it.

276

They would blame the insane Cassandra if it was not true. If it was true, he would be the hero. It was over.

The bitterness of the bottle and the nebulous mist moved insidiously through her mind and over her memories as a welcome relief. She wandered...to the sea.

The kaleidoscope effect ended abruptly, leaving Valeria confused momentarily. Then she sensed that she was not with Alex. *Where was he?* She heard a voice and realized that it was Aegemon. She glanced around and could see that Alex was not on the Mariah. She saw Aegemon speaking towards the water. *Alex was in the sea!* He would not have much time. She had to find her voice. There was no body to move.

"Aegemon?" Valeria called with all of her strength. She would need to use her voice to save them.

With confusion breaking his calm demeanor, he said with disgust, "Girl, you don't remember me."

"I do." She fought to get her body to respond with no luck.

Leaning his head back in the water, Alex frantically struggled to keep the limbs that worked moving—keep blood flowing.

He must be hallucinating...did he hear Valeria's voice? She had been unconscious for hours. He wondered for a moment if he was losing his mind. But then he saw Aegemon's expression—Valeria was alive and had spoken!

Knowing there was only moments left to get Aegemon's attention, Valeria cried, "The drink...it wasn't enough. I wish..." Her eyes softened and her voice became a whisper. She suppressed the need to cough.

"What did she say?" Aegemon asked.

A crew member knelt beside her. "I can't hear her, sir!"

"Bring her to me!" Aegemon barked. They picked her up by the shoulders and dragged her like a rag doll to him. Could she withhold the cough? She held her breath as her lungs convulsed. Aegemon leaned his ear near her. "You have something to say?"

Valeria smiled softly. Her hand had some feeling and she moved it towards his face. He slapped her hand away from him. "Aegemon…"

Narrowing his eyes at her, he decided that it was better to trust his instincts. Aegemon turned to leave. It was better that she died. She had haunted his dreams since he had first met her as a child. Maybe that was Apollo's wrath!

"Aegemon." Her voice was louder and more confident. This time he turned back to her, hearing the voice of Cassandra. He moved closer, she couldn't cause him any harm now, he thought. And this time Alex would be dead for good. Aegemon moved inches from her and she touched his face as he pulled in closer to her. The cough erupted from her in violent convulsions that racked her body. She looked up to see the blood splattered across Aegemon's shocked face and she closed her eyes and smiled.

Alex's left arm lost feeling. Waves crashed into his face and he swallowed the seawater.

Rage and disgust overtook Aegemon as he saw the blood and wiped it from his face. He said in repulsion, "You are…diseased!" And then pausing, he added, "Throw her in. Let them both be out of my life."

Valeria smiled, then coughed again as blood ran down the side of her mouth. The crew moved her to the edge of the boat and threw her into the sea.

Her body crashed through the water at least 20 feet from Alex. He tried to get his limbs working to move towards her. Her face came up for a moment and she looked at him with so much love. And then she went underwater. The yachts engines turned as Alex realized that he was between the boats! The exhaust hit him in the face and he momentarily lost his bearing. Then the Mariah began to lurch forward with the yacht. Alex dove to avoid being hit by the catamaran—under the churning water he found the strength to dive deeper. Although he missed most of the Mariah, a piece of the rudder hit his head and disoriented him slightly. He came up for a breath and looked for her. She was gone.

The realization sunk into the pit of his stomach. He had failed her again! They would drown alone in the cold sea. No, not alone—they would die together.

Alex forced his limbs to move, discovering the blanket that had been wrapped around her. He fought, pulling everything in him and dove down for her. Immediately he rose—he needed three deep breaths. And then he dove again and followed the bubbles until he saw the white flesh of her hand reaching for the surface, her hair delicately curling around it. He touched her fingers, giving him a new sense of hope. Her face stared into his in love and she grasped at him and he pulled her body into his. She kissed him and then she was overwhelmed as her lungs convulsed and she choked in the seawater. Alex held her close to him fighting for the last precious minutes that he would see her face, fighting the coldness, fighting to hold onto the last of the light that was them.

CHAPTER 21

There was a calmness in the inevitability of their future. Suddenly, the cold blackness soothed his anguish. Alex could still see her eyes looking towards him with so much life—so much love—despite the fact that she was no longer conscious. For Alex, at that moment, she would never die, she would never suffer—and his heart and hers were one. He pulled her closer to him, feeling the last of their lives and the last of eons of hope.

In the blackness, Alex saw a light. The light was a trick. The light drew nearer and there were shadows. Something hit his face but in the cold he couldn't fight it. Out of breath, Alex tried to kiss Valeria—but something barred his access to her. He turned his head believing it must be confusion from hypothermia. Alex drew the breath that would end it all.

It didn't hurt. If fact, he was still conscious. In his shock, she slipped from his arms. Alex fought to get her back—something stopped him. There was the light again. Through the darkness Alex heard the joyful laugh that was so familiar to him—Caleb!

Caleb loaded a tank on Alex's back. Alex used every bit

of his strength to reach Valeria. He watched for air bubbles in the blackness. Then saw the flashlight moving through the vegetation, where her face appeared, as he had seen it all those years before. Something rose through the water…Alex realized it looked like a rubber dinghy. Caleb produced a knife and Valeria was freed. Caleb and Valeria rose with Alex following.

Rolling Valeria's body into the dinghy, Caleb boarded and then helped Alex. Valeria was blue. Alex worked to pull his body up to a sitting position.

"Lean her neck back!" Caleb did so and Alex listened and found no heart beat. He pounded on her chest, hearing a crack as he did so. Unable to control his strength he had broken her sternum. He wouldn't let himself think about that now. Alex pounded on her chest repeatedly and breathed into her mouth. He watched her chest rise and fall. But she remained blue.

Caleb removed his mask, which had left bright red lines around his face. "Ava had an idea…" He said as he pulled the gloves off his hands. Alex nodded and ripped open Valeria's shirt as Caleb placed his hand over her heart. There was a spark and a jolt. Caleb removed his hands and looked hopefully. Valeria had a burn on her chest. Alex listened and heard no heart beat.

"Again!"

Caleb concentrated for a moment and then brought his hands down on Valeria's heart. There was the jolt.

Valeria now had a bad burn on her chest—but Alex sensed that something had changed. He listened and heard her glorious heartbeat!

At last, Valeria coughed and Alex turned her head to the side as the seawater and blood came out.

Caleb started paddling.

CHAPTER 22

There was a fog and darkness and his face—his beautiful face.

The nurses had learned that visiting hours didn't apply to Alex as he stood watch, day in and day out by the small plastic window looking in on the isolation ward. He watched as nurses and doctors—dressed in full protective gear—entered her room to adjust equipment and change out containers of various liquids. Alex longed to touch her—to feel the life in her. But he *could* wait now—she was alive!

Alex and Mani had hoped that having survived the three hours in the water, Valeria would now heal within 24 hours, like an immortal. Alex hadn't given up hope.

Valeria had suffered from many complications; the hypothermia had actually saved her life. It had shut down all of her organs long enough that there didn't appear to be any brain damage from lack of oxygen. Still, Valeria suffered from kidney failure and would require dialysis for at least a few weeks, or until her kidneys returned to full function. Valeria's sternum was cracked and would be painful until it healed. The plague was being managed with antibiotics. And Alex's love was alive and beyond her 27th birthday!

Sitting on the stool outside of Valeria's small window, near the nurse's station, Alex found that several times a day he would again realize that she was alive and would become overwhelmed with emotion. The sobs of joy frequently overtook him so that he had to leave to gather his wits about him. There didn't seem to be any end to it. Though, Alex realized that few could understand all of the years of yearning and loneliness that had absorbed his existence. And all of that was coming to an end, it appeared. He would have her with him for eternity. Alex felt the emotion overtaking him again and he took a deep breath and closed his eyes. A nurse passing by touched his back and again told him that she was doing fine.

That comment didn't ever help—he just had too much emotion in him to handle this casually. And he couldn't seem to leave her. Although he had purchased a motorhome and parked it in the hospital lot, thinking that he could sleep and shower there and then bring her home in it when the time came. He found that he ached when he left her. So, a few times a day he would lay down on the couch in the waiting room and try to shut his eyes. He forced himself to shower a few times a day and he went to the cafeteria or Mani would bring him something to eat. Then, thanks to Mani's influence, he was permitted to return to his seat by her window off from the ICU.

Mani assured Alex that Valeria was doing extremely well considering all that her body had been through. Still, it had been almost two weeks and she remained mostly unconscious. Occasionally, her arms would go into attack against an unseen villain. The pneumonic plague had created a severe infection in her lungs and the bacteria in the saltwater had not helped things! Valeria had suffered from pneumonia and Mani had warned Alex that he expected that she might have a few more rounds of it due to the weakened state of her lungs. Alex had watched it all and seen her body deteriorate as she lost 15 pounds on her already small frame.

It had taken three hours of Alex doing CPR and Caleb paddling the rubber dinghy without much progress until Ava located them floundering against the waves and currents of the Adriatic. A Coast Guard helicopter had flown Valeria and Alex to the hospital in Venice, while Caleb loaded onto Ava's boat.

Alex was held in isolation for a few days until it was determined that he carried no sign of the plague. During that time, he occupied himself by reading every book by and about Jane Austen. It would probably never be his favorite but he enjoyed it because she had read them!

And he waited...

At last, Valeria was removed from isolation. Knowing he wouldn't want to leave once he was with her, Alex had showered and taken a brief nap. When he returned, Mani relayed to him that one of the nurses had actually spoken to Valeria and that she had responded! Although Alex was ecstatic, he knew that if it had been any of the nurses that knew him, they would have sent for him immediately so that he could see her.

Entering her room for the first time in ten days, Alex was again overwhelmed by emotion. He had to get a grip on himself! He didn't want her to see him like that. He sat on the bed next to her taking in the feel of her hands and face. He desperately wanted to take her in his arms but there was too much damage to her body and too many tubes running into her. He kissed her forehead and she began to move slowly, pulling against the tubes and wires. At last she was breaking through the fog.

"Hey, beautiful!"

With great effort, Valeria forced her eyes open. She could see him. She looked around the room. It was a huge room with her bed in the center surrounded by pieces of equipment that could be moved in easily, should the need arise, with as much equipment attached to her. There was a glass wall in front that led to the nurse's station. She couldn't recall how she had gotten there. She did remember a moment when a nurse had asked her if there was anyone that should be contacted. Valeria had done the right thing, she thought.

Alex gave her a moment to take in her surroundings, while he was filled with such sudden wonder that it took his breath away! Her eyes were now that extraordinary color he had painted—the color that was *her* color, oracle blue.

Just then Mani entered. "How is my favorite patient?" Valeria smiled and her eyes went back to Alex. She took a deep breath and coughed, then winced, "Sore." She whispered weakly.

As Valeria looked around at the wires and tubes that came from her she became distracted by someone who was throwing their weight around in the nurse's station. It wasn't the first time Alex had heard it.

"It is very good to see you alert!" Mani said. "The last few days you have been in and out of consciousness. How much do you remember?" Valeria shrugged.

Mani continued, "We've kept you here in the ICU because of the plague isolation. But really the fever has broken and I think you are doing well. I'd like to see you out of here in a few days."

"I want to go home." Valeria said, her voice hoarse but stronger.

"Yes. I imagine you would! And there's someone else that has been especially anxious for you to leave here."

Valeria smiled sweetly at Alex. Both Alex and Mani held their breath to see if there was recognition.

Just then a chalky, smooth tenor voice dominated the room. David rushed to Valeria. "Darling! How are you?"

Easily dismissing Alex and Mani, David smiled at Valeria and then narrowed his eyes at Alex, who was still sitting by Valeria, holding her hand.

"Do you mind?" David said impatiently. "I understand from the nurses that you saved her life," his eyes became suspicious, "but frankly, it seems like you might have phoned me—afterall, *I am* Valeria's fiancé!" He glowered and then snapped at Alex, "How about some privacy!"

Valeria squeezed Alex's hand slightly. He looked at her but she was smiling her sweet smile at David. Alex, uncertain of his role in her heart, rose. David immediately moved in.

"Valeria, I'm taking you home!" He kissed her head. "*The plague*?! See what happens when you run off on your own!"

Replaced, Alex watched painfully as David sat where he had sat, and now held Valeria's hand as he had only moments before. Alex thought something about David's affection looked unnatural. Looking up from Valeria, David glanced coolly at Alex. "I believe I asked you for some privacy!"

Immediately David, ensuring that Alex was watching, embraced Valeria. She winced. David laughed, "I guess that isn't such a good idea yet!"

"No. Not a good idea." Valeria rasped.

"Don't worry, dear! I'm taking you to Prague this afternoon. I've arranged for an air ambulance to transport you and cleared it with customs. My staff will gather the remainder of your things."

Alex started to protest but Mani stopped him with a pat on the shoulder and slight shake of his head. David turned towards Alex, "Oh! You're still here?" He said with a smile that stopped short of his eyes. "I trust my staff won't have any problems arranging to pick-up Valeria's possessions?"

Biting his lip, Alex stared into Valeria's eyes for anything that said that she objected to David's plans. She took a deep breath and closed her eyes.

Finally, Mani spoke up. "Of course not." Alex's heart felt as if it had dropped through the floor. Valeria seemed all right with David's plans. Mani paused a moment, "Mr. Wiley, I was wondering, how did you learn Valeria was here?"

David looked surprised at the question. "Why, Valeria asked the nurse to phone me—as her next of kin—when she regained consciousness." Then David looked at Valeria, "But you caused me quite a scare in the meanwhile!"

Completely disregarding Alex, David continued, "Doctor, she can leave with my medical team, can't she? I've already cleared all the documentation for her medically."

Mani nodded slowly. "Yes. However, she has been quite ill. I recommend that she stay here a few more days so that I can keep an eye on her."

"Thank you, doctor. I've researched you and it does seem that you know what you are doing. But I'll be bringing in my own team of experts—I'll bring them *here*, if necessary!"

Again, Alex started to speak up and Mani took Alex's arm guiding him out of the room. "We'll give you some privacy." Stopping at the nurse's station, Mani gave instructions for Valeria's release.

Then, Alex and Mani walked outside of the double doors into the corridor with a glassed hallway looking out over the parking lot and the hills to the north of Venice. Alex began pacing, "What's going on Mani? How can she leave with him? He didn't even notice her eyes! He doesn't know her! He doesn't love her—and *she doesn't love him!*" His face became distraught, "Please! You've got to stop this!"

Mani patted Alex's back, "My friend, I don't know what to tell you. She hasn't said anything to me that indicates that she recalls any of the past few weeks. After all, it was quite a physical trauma with the disease and the hypothermia—to say nothing of the drowning! We spoke of amnesia." Mani shrugged, "Sometimes after a trauma the person loses their recall at the point of the incident, sometimes from months prior to the incident. And very occasionally, they don't recall their life at all. Like it or not, it is a good thing that she remembers David."

Alex started hyperventilating, "I could have sworn I saw familiarity in her eyes when she looked at me!" He searched for Mani's agreement.

"I don't know."

Continuing to pace, Alex's speed picked up as he grew more frantic, "Well is she...one of us now? I mean she is past her 27th birthday. That means something! And her eyes!"

"I've looked at her blood from before the drowning and after and—".

He interrupted Mani, "And?"

"They are identical."

Alex shook his head in disbelief, "Do you mean all that was a waste? It can't be! She's alive!"

Mani continued, "Both tests indicate that her DNA is the same as ours—immortal. So, I'm not certain what changes have taken place in her. I'm not certain about her memory. I don't know if she is now immortal. I just…don't know."

Finally, it was sinking in. She had lived past her 27th birthday. But she didn't seem to remember him. It appeared she was immortal but there was no way of knowing if the curse had been lifted, unless she aged, or died. Would she still reincarnate if she had? These were all unknowns. And now she was leaving to marry David. Alex's head dropped in despair.

Just then David stepped out of the ICU. "Excuse me doctor, but we really do need to be going now. Can you release her? Or should I bring my people in to handle this? Also, I've brought her some clothes. Please have a nurse dress her."

Mani nodded and again patted Alex on the back before disappearing into the ICU. Alex sat down on the bench, weak from the new reality. Less than 30 minutes later, David was pushing Valeria past him. She wore her hair in a ponytail. The slacks were dressier than she would like. She would have preferred jeans and a tee shirt. If David knew her, he would know that! Despite that, she looked beautiful! But she also looked terribly fragile. Valeria seemed to give Alex a sympathetic look as she went past him and towards the elevator.

Before he could stop himself, Alex was standing by Valeria at the elevator, "Val, I want you to know that…" He gulped back his emotion as he squeezed his eyes shut and drew a deep breath. "I want whatever is best for you. *Even if it's David.*"

"That's very kind of you." David said coldly, as the elevator door opened and he started to push Valeria's wheelchair forward.

Without looking at David, Alex kneeled down to Valeria's eye level and placed his hand on her chair, blocking its forward movement.

"I'm not done yet!" Alex said to David with a hint of uncharacteristic antagonism. Then, Alex's voice and attention returned to Valeria.

"Beautiful, things may change for you as you heal. Just *please do this for me*...it's the only thing I'll ask of you...don't make any major decisions on your life until you've had a chance to heal."

Alex saw a flicker of pain as she stared into his eyes, quickly replaced with compassion, he thought. "I'm afraid it's too late for that." She brushed her hand through Alex's hair. Just then David pulled the wheelchair back and went around Alex and onto the elevator. He watched minutes later from the second floor window as the black limo pulled up to the entrance of the hospital.

Wandering and uncertain what to do with himself, Alex returned to Valeria's room. Pulling the small box out of his pocket, he flipped it open and stared at Valeria's engagement ring for several minutes. Camille had brought it down with his change of clothes—and hers—the ones she would have wanted to wear. Alex sunk into the chair holding the ring. He wondered if there would be a time when this ring would be back on her hand. Mani entered from the nurse's station and sat on the bed, looking at Alex sympathetically.

"At least she's alive. I couldn't take existence if she wasn't." Alex choked.

"It isn't over." Mani said, "She will remember you if you stay near her. Some part of her always does remember you."

"Yes. Yes, you are right." Alex swallowed. "But do you

believe for an instant that he isn't going to take advantage of her weakness right now? I saw the look in his eyes. He just wants to win! He's going to run off and marry her as quickly as possible." Alex sunk further into his misery. Rubbing his hand over the beard stubble on his face. "I've seen it before…she's going to be a Diplomat's wife and have his children." Then, despite his heartbreak, Alex began to console himself with a new and very significant realization and he choked, "But, *she's alive!*"

"Let's go home." Mani said.

As they walked back into the hallway by the elevators, Alex watched the limo pull away. It drove up the road and turned and she was out of his life. Mani's phone buzzed and he looked at the message.

"The family is downstairs." Mani reported.

As they walked into the lobby, Alex felt the sudden accumulation of weeks of anguish and exhaustion. He noticed a haze seemed to fill the room as he followed Mani towards reception. Leaning on the counter, while Mani took care of some paperwork, Alex was afraid that if he sat down he would fall asleep.

"Alex?" The voice that he knew from all others came from behind him although it was softer than usual. Alex raised his head and turned—half afraid that he would find that he was hallucinating. Her fragile body sat in the wheelchair next to him. She hadn't left yet! Alex wondered for a moment, was their recognition in the way that she had said his name? Then he wondered, why was she still here?

Alex looked around for David. Then, sudden anger crossed him; David had left her alone! What was wrong with him? "Val, what are you doing here? Where's David?"

Valeria grabbed Alex's hand, staring at him with a smile enhanced by her extraordinarily beautiful, blue eyes. She pulled him down towards her. "Can you sit down? I'm sorry I can't..." She held her hand on her throat. Alex pushed her to a nearby chair, where he could sit next to her. Now, they would have to get *him* a wheelchair to get him out of here.

Taking his hand and pulling it towards her, Valeria said, "I'm sorry about David. I wanted to explain to you before he arrived. But I didn't get the chance." She took a deep breath and gave a weak cough, followed by a slight wince.

Alex stared into her eyes—*God how he loved her!* "Whatever is right for you. But whatever you do—you need to know that I am *always* here for you." Alex felt the emotion overtake him and he closed his eyes tightly trying to hold on to some degree of control. David would see him like this and that wouldn't be good.

"Alex, I needed to do things the right way." Valeria said hoarsely just above a whisper.

"Yes, I understand." Alex thought for a moment. "I know it was all a bit fast."

Confusion clouded Valeria's brilliant blue eyes and then she laughed softly, followed by a repressed cough, "Alex?" He looked at her, the pain so evident in his eyes. "Please, don't be upset. It's just that...well, I guess it was just vanity that wouldn't permit me to break off an engagement in a hospital gown." She smiled a devastatingly beautiful smile. "*I hope you understand.*"

Alex took a husky breath. He had to keep control of himself. "I understand. It was wrong of me to propose to you when you belonged to someone else."

He wanted to challenge it. He wanted to suggest that they

take things slower. He wanted to plead with her to give them a chance. Instead he said, "I know you don't remember but what we have *is* real."

Her face lit in sudden realization and she shook her head as she squeezed his hand. "Alex, can you do something for me?"

"Anything." Emotion rimmed Alex's eyes.

"Can you lift me out of this wheelchair?" She whispered.

Alex wondered what she wanted. Was she in pain? Despite his exhaustion, he lifted her up effortlessly. She swung her arm around his neck and leaned her head against him.

"Now, can you just sit down for a moment?" She rasped.

Alex sat back in his seat with her in his arms. What would David say when he came back, Alex wondered. He wouldn't permit himself to dwell on the feel of her in his arms—that would overwhelm him.

She looked into his eyes and her face filled with love, leaning her face near his. "Alex—I was talking about David...*I ended my engagement to David.*"

Unable to comprehend his sudden turn of fate, Alex choked back a sob of gratitude and buried his face in her hair. He kept his eyes clamped shut, not trusting his emotions. "You ended your engagement to David..."

"Of course!" Valeria kissed his neck. "There is nothing I want more in life than to be with you..." Tears flowed down Valeria's face as she finished in a whisper, "*forever.*"

After the eternities that Alex had waited to hear that; to have her with him, alive and loving him, he couldn't quite accept that the struggle was over. "I..." He breathed out heavily, "I thought..." He felt the overwhelm taking him in and embracing him.

Valeria gave Alex a moment and then said softly, "Will you take me home?"

Still unable to grasp his beautiful fate, Alex asked, "Where's home? New York? Morgana?"

Valeria's eyes brightened, "I don't care." She said dreamily. *"It's wherever you are!"* She laughed and coughed, "Just preferably not *here*!"

Holding her tightly in his arms, Alex brushed his lips over her forehead and down her nose, finally pulling her face to his and kissing her mouth. The bandages on her arms, neck and chest a reminder of all they had been through.

Alex took a deep breath and said in a whisper—which was all the voice he could conjure, "I believe I have something that belongs to you." He reached in his pocket and pulled out the box. Seeing her smile, he slid the ring back to its rightful place on her finger.

This time it was her eyes that welled with tears. "I love you, Alex!" She said as she brushed her hands over his face and kissed him deeply as his arms, moved around her, pulling her in closer.

From the other side of the room the family stood watching joyfully. Ava pulled a tissue out and wiped her tears and blew her nose.

Tavish looked at her, "Hah…women and their bloody emotions."

"Awww, put a sock in it…" Ava responded with a smile. Then, she looked at him. "Wait…Tav, what is that?" She pointed, seeing a hint of a tear on his face.

"That! That was nothing! Not a bloody tear!" Tavish said,

outraged. Finally, Tavish said, "Awww—shhhhh…," and took a tissue.

They all burst out laughing, as the box of tissue was passed down, each family member taking a tissue and wiping a tear or two.

Caleb piped up, "I saved her…and I got to touch a girl's chest!"

Patting his back, Camille laughed, "You saved her life! Yes…you did."

As he stood taller than usual, Caleb added, "Pretty cool, huh! Kind of like a super hero!"

The whole family was so proud of Caleb that they were bursting at the seams.

"And…she is pretty hot…*for an older woman.*" Caleb said with his famous laugh.

"You did well, Caleb." Mani patted the boy on the back, then noted, "Tavish's suit works well. I hardly felt any current!" Tavish had created a suit that resisted and channeled Caleb's current. It wasn't a cure but it definitely helped!

Watching Alex and Valeria kissing from across the room, Ava asked, "How do you think Daphne is going to handle this?"

"Oh, I'd say about the same as always." Caleb answered.

"Let's take her home!" Lars said as they walked towards Valeria and Alex.

EPILOGUE

The fall ended quickly at their cottage in the woods. Recovering from the infections weakened Valeria and it was many months of care until she began to feel strong again. But recovery was a blessing while cuddled against Alex by the fire, reading their classics—combined with occasional visits from the rest of the family—who were attempting to give them time alone.

As the snow fell, Valeria felt the joy of seeing her beloved cottage in winter; knowing that now she would have an opportunity to see it in spring and summer.

As Christmas approached, Alex and Valeria sat at the main house sipping wine. Camille rushed in, "I have it all arranged! Steamboat Springs for our family Christmas!"

Alex laughed, "We're in the Alps and you want to fly to the states for skiing?"

"I found a great lodge there that can house all of us, along with an executive chef!"

Valeria smiled, "Skiing? I've never tried it! But I would like to!"

Alex's eyes got wide with worry, "I hate to be one of those overprotective fiancé's—however, beautiful, you're just healing! I don't think you're up to it."

With all that he had been through, there was no way that Valeria would do anything to cause him a moment's concern! Christmas with Alex would be a dream come true! Still, somewhere in her, Valeria had hoped for these holidays to be filled with new traditions with her new family. But she hated to think that she would hold them back from their plans.

"You should go Camille!"

Camille shook her head. "I want all of us to spend our first Christmas together!" Her face lit in a playful smile, "And do I get to plan a winter wedding?"

When Alex had brought her home from the hospital he had said that it was important to him that they waited until she was healthy to get married. He wanted her to have the strength to enjoy their wedding and, he added with a seductive wink, their wedding night. Valeria knew it would be some time before her body was back in shape.

Lars and Ava intended to return to the Caribbean after Christmas to continue the search for Jonah. They had a new lead that they were researching, now that Valeria appeared to be safe.

Ava entered with a large glass of green liquid and handed it to Valeria. "Here you go!"

Taking the glass of green sludge, Valeria grimaced. "Uh…thanks?"

"It's Kale!" Ava said proudly as Camille and Alex made faces.

"Okay." Valeria said as she looked to Alex for support.

But he shook his head. He wasn't going to fight this one. Ava had made it her business to nurse Valeria back to health with all kinds of nutritional supplements. But the green sludge crossed the line!

"You know: nature's superfood!" Ava continued.

"So sorry, Ava...I don't think I can do it."

"Have it your way!" Ava took the glass and downed it. "Yum! You don't know what you're missing out on!"

They all laughed.

Caleb entered swinging himself onto the couch next to Valeria and putting his arm around her. Although his suit made it possible for momentary exchanges, it also made him sweat profusely, so he rarely wore it at the house.

However, since the incident at sea, Valeria now seemed to be immune to Caleb's electrical charge. It also appeared that Caleb had a bit of a crush on Valeria. Alex thought that was a very reasonable thing for any blue-blooded 12-year-old boy to have a crush on what he was certain was the most beautiful woman in the world.

"Caleb, just remember...she's my fiancée."

"For now." Caleb teased. Valeria messed up his hair affectionately.

Getting impatient, Camille said, "Focus people! We're talking about a wedding! When is the wedding?"

Valeria looked to Alex as he took a deep, pleasure-filled sigh, "Beautiful, I would marry you anywhere and anytime. But I think you would like to have an outdoor wedding."

"I wouldn't mind a justice of the peace...this afternoon!" She said softly, knowing this would ruffle Camille's feathers—though it was the truth.

"No, no, no, no!" Camille interrupted, "We need a big wedding! And Val, you don't need to worry about a thing! I'm taking care of all of the plans."

Even if they cared to, Alex and Valeria knew there was no sense arguing with Camille.

Raising his hand, Alex said, "Beautiful, I want this to be the wedding of your dreams! I know you really would like to have a garden wedding."

Valeria curled into Alex, "Actually, I would just like to have it at home!"

Camille's eyes narrowed, knowing that Alex was about to throw a hitch into her planning. "It'll be months before we can have an outdoor wedding here!" She said. "But we could have a candlelight ceremony in the main house."

Shrugging, Valeria said, "The only people I need or want here are the family and Weege."

Alex continued, "I had another thought." Camille just didn't want to hear "Justice of the Peace" again. "With all of the evidence we have of Val surviving the curse, including the change of your eye color—,"

Interrupting, Camille announced, "Of course! That's brilliant! I love it!"

Lars and Ava didn't look as excited.

"I would like to have an immortal marriage." Alex said. "Is that alright with you?"

"Anything, as long as we're married!" Valeria said with her eyes narrowing. "But what does that mean?"

Becoming suddenly animated, Camille jumped up. "It means a wedding in Greece! We can do an outdoor wedding in February! It'll be beautiful! I'll start planning now!" Camille turned, "Oh…and Christmas here!"

$$\infty$$

Back at the cottage, Alex turned on Sinatra's *All the Way* , as he pulled Valeria into his arms, gently rocking to the music. "Do you mind waiting until February?"

Valeria buried her face in Alex's shoulder, "What is an immortal marriage?"

"It means that we'll be together forever." He murmured into her ear, creating that delightful heat that ran through her body.

"Then I'm in!"

Titles by Delia J. Colvin

THE SIBYLLINE TRILOGY
The Sibylline Oracle
The Symbolon
The Last Oracle
For a free previews go to www.TheSibyllineOracle.com

Firefly Nights

Acknowledgements

Although I have been writing almost all of my life, I have been informed that this is the first thing that I've written that I've allowed anyone to read...and it took a tremendous amount of encouragement to do that! The love, support and enthusiasm of my extraordinary support team has made all the difference for me! Thank you!

I am ever so grateful to my beautiful, husband, Randy Colvin for his love, friendship and absolute faith in my writing ability and this story-and most importantly—keeping my coffee cup full! Randy's love served as a template for Alex's absolute devotion to Valeria. Also I want to thank him for his EXTRAORDINARY marketing efforts!

While nine months pregnant, Jen began reading my story...then demanding more. Jen's efforts in editing, and in her creative additions to the story, as well as spreading the word and creating my website and help with the covers and surveys has been SO Appreciated!

Joyce Wallace—I am so grateful for your love, support and patience! Sandy Rudiger, who calls herself "My number 3 fan" (after my husband and daughter)—for all your extraordinary support and belief in this book! Your enthusiasm and work to spread the word, carried me through the early terror that accompanied the release! Carrie Gardiner thanks for weathering the early draft!

The wonderful people that volunteered their time and opinion on the cover. Thanks for your time, guidance and enthusiasm: Jackie Blockus, Carol "CJ" Carter, Nicole Daniels, Leanna Davis, Mindy Detloff, Carrie Gardiner, Heidi Gilia, Kimberly Krum, Vee Lopez, Jessica Lowe, Katie Ludwig, Jennifer Mansfield, Angelina O'Connor, Kim Perry, Hugh Ramsey, Sandy Rudiger, Marisa St. Louis, Jennifer Slabik, Jackie Sulton, Diana Tahamata, Teri Van Dusen, Krissy Wright, Valli Youngs, Jessica Zumwalde. You are all awesome!

Friends & family that have made the journey more fun and always encouraged!

Weege Anderson-thank you for allowing me borrow your wonderfully unique name for one of my favorite characters who bears NO RESEMBLANCE to your exemplary character! Matt Townsend, Richard Reeves, Hans Hillestad, Camille Baker — the inspiration for the character, and my parents who made childhood a joy: Jerry & Doris DesJarlais,Don & Christina Alexander, Ed Barlow, Fran Bartlett, Bob Bermudez, Lisa Chinn, Tom & Liz Clapp, Jordan Colvin (extraordinary stepson), Travis Colvin (extraordinary stepson), Leah DeVeau, Suzannah Devereaux, Marilyn Dockx, Steve Drew, Rosanne Agoado Eskenazi, Jay & Timmy Evans, Dottie & Dick Fazio, Paula Fellers, Gordon & Kathy Flowers, Gail Galbraith, Lindsey Gildersleeve, Marv Halbakken, Sherri & Jack Hayden, Steve Hillier, Sam & Rosie Holland, Jim & Shelly Jones, Kamron & Danielle Jones, Homer & Julie Keefer, Fred & Cheryll Kent, Dave Khanoyan, Ali, Zohreh & Ava Khosravian, Leslie Lee, Craig Leth, Marilyn Lowe, Chris & Danae Mattis, Rich & Linda McChesney, Gary Meek, Dr. Manuel Moraes (the inspiration for Mani), Brian Morriss, Dr. Timothy Mountcastle-I wouldn't be here if not for your intervention! Nancee Niemec, Earle Noel, Curtis Norman, Mark & Michelle Oglesby, Carol & Lloyd Ostrander, Dr. Mary Jo Palmer (sister of my heart), Angela Poe, Mandy & Will Rohde, Monique Roop, Justin & Samantha Saroyan, Kirby & Linda Schwenk, Laura & Roger Sitcler, Betty Sorenson, Steve Spafford, Dennis & Linda Sperry, Dennis & Diane Stephan, John & Barb Warner, Linda Trombley, James (JJ) & Rose Upton, Adolfo Valero, Venkat & Lynda Varada, Laura Young,

Dan Youngs-son-in-law extraordinaire and
Aubrey Youngs (for being so darned cute!)

About the Author

DELIA J. COLVIN

Delia has lived all over the country from Fairbanks, AK, to Huntington Beach, CA to Knoxville, TN. but considers Danville, CA home. She currently resides in a suburb of Washington D.C. with her husband, Randy and their two Cavalier King Charles dogs.

She has worked as an Entrepreneur, Sales, Advertising, Air Traffic Control and as a Russian Interpreter.

For more information including frequently asked questions visit:
www.TheSibyllineOracle.Com